Even in the dim light, she could see that his eyes were searching hers. . . .

With great effort, she managed, "You . . . you may let me go now, Lord Tenbury."

"Must I? I had much rather not."

The hands at her waist moved around to the back and pulled her against him. Now her hands had no choice but to come again to his chest.

She thought he said her name once—so quietly she couldn't be certain. As he bent his head, she focused on his lips, then closed her eyes as his mouth met hers. She could never remember clearly afterward whether she had returned his kiss. She couldn't remember how long the kiss lasted—she only knew that it didn't seem long enough. . . .

Also by Lois Menzel
Published by Fawcett Crest Books:

A RECKLESS WAGER
AT DAGGERS DRAWN

RULED
BY
PASSION

Lois Menzel

FAWCETT CREST • NEW YORK

"The ruling passion, be it what it will.
The ruling passion conquers reason still."

—Alexander Pope
Moral Essays, Epistle III,
To Lord Bathurst (1732)

1

Anne Waverly sat alone in the library of Wildrose Cottage. It was not actually a library, but a small morning room her father had converted years ago, having the village carpenter fill the walls with shelves. On these he had stored his precious books. In this room he had spent nearly all his waking hours for the past thirty years. If he wasn't in his comfortable leather chair before the windows, his spectacles balancing on the tip of his nose while the daylight lit his page from behind, then he would be behind a heap of papers on his desk, endlessly poring over the Greek and Latin histories he had spent his life translating. It was appropriate, Anne thought, that he had died in this room as well, in his favorite chair, a volume of his beloved classics before him.

Anne rose from the sunny window seat and walked to the black leather chair, resting her hands on its high back. She would take one last look at everything, hold the pictures in her mind forever. All her memories were of this cottage, for she'd had no other home.

She remembered how, when she was young, she would slip away from her governess and creep into this room—her father's domain. She would hide behind the dark brown velvet window draperies, certain he had not detected her. Holding her breath, she would shiver deliciously until she heard his voice, just inches away.

"How now? A rat? Dead for a ducat, dead!" He would grab her through the drapery and tickle her, making it difficult for her to deliver her reply, "Oh, I am slain!"

She never tired of the game, and he was never too busy to play it with her. As she grew older, she gave up acting the part of Polonius and recited Juliet's lines instead. Her first history lessons were from *Richard II* and *Henry IV*.

Anne dragged an empty trunk across the floor and began filling it. Three-quarters of the shelves were already empty, but the task of sorting the books was taking longer than she expected. Since so many of the volumes brought back vivid pictures of the past, she found herself pausing often to reminisce. Anne was donating the books to the university, but when she came to one that held a special place in her memory, she set it aside. Those she would keep, for she found she could not bring herself to give them away.

As she pulled a thin volume of Pope from the shelf, tears filled her eyes. She and her father had read and reread it together . . . it seemed like yesterday.

A gray-haired lady in a neat black stuff dress stuck her head through the open door. "Would you like me to help you, Miss Anne? Seems a big job for only two hands, and the carter will be here afore long."

Anne placed the Pope on her special pile as she pulled the next book from the shelf.

"I'm very slow, Mrs. Nesbitt, but there are so many memories."

"Lord, child, I know that. Why do you think I offered to do this for you?"

"He's been gone nearly a year, but I still miss him dreadfully."

"Maybe it's best you're leaving, Miss Anne. It's not good for a body to grieve overlong."

2

"I'm not grieving, precisely. But I was always happy here. I am uneasy about going away."

"If the truth be told, miss, your father was a hermit. And so are you, for you live as he did. Stands to reason you should be frightened of change. But think of this, Miss Anne: Thousands of people live in London, and they all manage. Why, with your quick mind, and all your father taught you, you should be able to hold your own anywhere."

"What about you, dear friend?" Anne asked. "After twenty-two years of service here, the change will be strange for you as well."

"My sister's ague is worsening, and the doctor feels she may soon be bedridden. I will be busy, and that's as much as I've ever asked, Miss Anne."

"Perhaps I shall be busy, too," Anne responded. "My aunt and uncle have five children, the eldest not yet fifteen."

"Will you like that, do you think?"

"I believe I may. I enjoy children." She reached for another book, forcing herself back to her melancholy task.

When Mrs. Nesbitt returned with tea more than an hour later, she found the library empty, the shelves bare. Through the window, she could see her mistress sitting alone on a bench in the rose garden. Anne was gazing over the picket fence at the busy village street. Fixing it in her memory, Mrs. Nesbitt thought.

That afternoon the local carter loaded the late Mr. Waverly's library into his wagon and set off through the village, destined for the larger university town of Cambridge to the west. Anne rode along as far as the vicarage where they unloaded the trunk containing those volumes she had kept for herself. The vicar had promised to store them until she was settled.

"Natty Carson will bring my gelding by first thing in the morning," she told the vicar, Mr. Boone, her friend of many years. "You should have no problems with him; he's so gentle. Please remember he loves an occasional apple as a treat."

"I will keep him as long as need be, Anne," he replied. "And I don't want you to worry about the children becoming attached. I told them plainly that you would send for him as soon as you were able."

"I wish you would accept him as a gift," she persisted. "It's unlikely I will ever be in a position where I can afford to keep a horse, yet I can't bring myself to sell him. I know he'll be happy here."

"As happy as three doting children can make him, Anne. That you may depend upon."

As Anne walked slowly back to Wildrose Cottage, she wished that she, like her books and horse, could stay on in Ripley. But she could no longer afford the rent her father had paid Sir Hugo Scoville. Even when Sir Hugo became aware of her circumstances and offered her a greatly reduced rate, she refused to stay on. She would not begin accepting charity at twenty-eight. She was strong and healthy; she was well educated; she was determined to seek employment and earn her own way.

Anne rose early the following morning and dressed carefully in a dark brown traveling dress. The cut of the dress was no longer in style, but she had no other. It would have to do. She brushed her waist-length brown hair until it shone, then worked it tightly into a heavy plait. This she coiled with practiced hands at the nape of her neck, securing it with pins. She settled a plain straw bonnet over her head and tied the worn ribbons beneath her chin. Carefully folding her spectacles, she placed them in their case, then slipped the case into her reticule. She picked up her gloves and a book from the night table, glanced about to be certain nothing had been left behind, and joined Mrs. Nesbitt in the front hall.

Standing near the door were the two small trunks containing her personal belongings. While a village man loaded her things into the back of his wagon, the two women said their good-byes.

"I know you will never eat before a journey, love," Mrs. Nesbitt said, "but I have packed a few apples and a bit of bread and cheese—just in case. There are times when the mail coach breaks down and the passengers must wait hours before they can go on."

Anne smiled and took the small, tightly wrapped package. This warm-hearted woman had been giving to her all her life; she could not refuse this last offering, even though she knew she would not eat it.

Anne had only a short time to wait after the wagon driver conveyed her to the posting inn and unloaded her things in the yard. The mail coach was on time, her fare already paid. In a few moments her trunks were strapped on, she was handed inside, and the horses leaned into their work.

Fortunately the coach had only two other occupants, so Anne was able to obtain a corner seat. She carefully extracted her spectacles from her reticule and put them on, but when she opened the book to her marker, she found she could not read, for the bouncing of the coach made it impossible to keep her place. She closed her eyes instead and, leaning her head against the side of the coach, began to recite in her mind every piece of poetry she knew. Since the motion of any carriage made her ill, she had no interest in the springtime Cambridgeshire countryside. She never traveled unless it was absolutely unavoidable. If she was forced to endure a carriage, she ate nothing, then occupied her mind with anything but the trip.

As the mail coach made its way south it stopped often, discharging and collecting passengers and baggage. If the stop was long enough, Anne stepped down and walked about, finding comfort for her churning stomach in setting her feet upon solid, unmoving ground.

When they passed through Hertford near noon, several passengers bought what food they could during a stop of only a few minutes. Anne bought nothing, nor did she avail herself of the food she had brought with her. The parcel lay untouched in her lap.

Discharged from the mail on the outskirts of London in the midafternoon, Anne hired a hackney carriage and informed the driver of her aunt's direction. By this time thoroughly ill and equally sick of the poetry she had recited time and again, she had no interest in her surroundings, even though London was a city she had never seen.

At the Hodders' establishment in Oxford Street, Anne stood on the top step and timidly plied the knocker. When the butler who pulled open the door surveyed her creased, old-fashioned gown, Anne had the impression he was about to direct her to the servants' entrance.

"I am Anne Waverly," she said. "I believe my aunt and uncle are expecting me."

The man raised his eyebrows, but nevertheless showed her to a sitting room while he dispatched a footman to collect her baggage from the hackney.

"Please wait here, Miss Waverly. I will inform Mrs. Hodder of your arrival."

The room in which he placed her was not expensively decorated, but was lavish by comparison with Wildrose Cottage. Heavy brocade draperies hung at the windows and a plush forest-green carpet covered the floor. To Anne the room seemed to have too many furnishings, for chairs and tables jostled one another for space. A small bookshelf to one side of the mantel caught her attention. She had never met her father's sister, but she believed that the books a person owned told a great deal about them. The first volume was a collection of sermons, the second *Miss Henrietta Archibald's Guide to Etiquette for Young Ladies of Distinction*, and the third a collection of poetry by an author Anne did not know. She put on her spectacles, then took the book down and opened it to read:

"The rose of spring found but a dusty grave,
  hard trampled, 'neath the hooves of time."

She smiled as she thought what her father would have said of such a line. She replaced the book and turned to pace back across the room. She was not looking forward to this interview, for this was the part of her plan that had been most difficult—asking her aunt and uncle to keep her until she should find a position. She turned when she heard the door open behind her, forcing a nervous smile to her face as she regarded the rotund fiftyish woman on the threshold.

Cressida Hodder stared at her niece in open amazement. Had she given one second's thought to what her niece's appearance might be, she would never have expected this. Her brother had been a handsome man; she saw nothing of him in the woman who stood before her. She was tall—too tall—and thin as a rail, with no bosom to speak of. Hair of a nondescript brown was drawn savagely back from a plain-featured face. The dress! The dress was shocking—dowdy, worn, a horrible color. And worst of all, she was wearing spectacles!

When Anne came forward with an outstretched hand and said, "Aunt Cressida?" all her aunt could manage in return was, "Merciful heavens!"

As her visitor's face puzzled over this unusual greeting, Mrs. Hodder struggled to control her initial reaction to her niece's appearance. She curled her lips into a smile and took the slender hand the

7

young woman offered. "So you are Maxwell's girl. You don't favor him."

"No ma'am. It is said I bear a likeness to my mother, though I can't say. I don't remember her well."

"I was distressed that I could not come to dear Max's funeral," Mrs. Hodder continued. "But as I wrote you, my three youngest were laid low by the influenza at the time. I could not consider leaving them."

"Certainly not. Indeed, I perfectly understood your dilemma."

"Dear girl, I knew you would. The few times your father visited in recent years he never failed to remark upon your excellent understanding."

Anne half smiled, uncertain how she should respond. Mrs. Hodder soon continued. "I will have a footman direct you to your room. You will wish to refresh yourself after your long journey. Then you must join me for tea, and we will further discuss your letter. You said, I believe, that you desired my assistance in finding a position." She pulled the bell rope. When a footman appeared, she ordered tea to be served in half an hour.

Anne was ravenous after her long fast but would never admit as much. She silently followed the footman to her room, wishing her aunt had ordered the meal in ten minutes instead of thirty. She used the time to wash her face and hands, then exchanged her creased and dusty brown gown for a dark blue muslin. It was old and considerably worn, but it was freshly laundered and she felt better as she descended the stairs, the prospect of food raising her spirits.

As Mrs. Hodder poured, Anne helped herself to a biscuit and two macaroons. "Since you are seeking a position, my dear, I assume things were not left well?"

"Father's income ceased when he died. There was enough money to allow me to stay on these past months, but now that is gone as well. I couldn't pay the rent on the cottage so had to let it go. I hope to find a position, but I have no references or experience, and I know one must have them to secure a place in a respectable family."

Even though Anne hoped to find a position, she was fearful of going among strangers. Mrs. Nesbitt was right; she *was* a hermit. She had lived all her life with her father and was accustomed to solitude and privacy. In the back of her mind, she had allowed herself to hope that her aunt would offer her a home. Not that she wanted to be a hanger-on. Not Anne Waverly! If her aunt offered to keep her, Anne would make certain Mrs. Hodder never regretted the decision.

"You hope to go for a governess, then?" her aunt asked.

"I think I would be better suited as a companion."

"With your education? What nonsense! You should teach."

"I could teach history, geography, and modern languages, but I never applied myself under my own governess, and I must admit I do not excel in the womanly arts."

"You do not excel?"

"Actually, I have none. Well, perhaps one. I sew, but I cannot play, either pianoforte or harp, and I cannot sing. My painting is atrocious, and my dancing indifferent."

"Heaven bless me! And Max always claiming you were the best educated woman in the country."

"I have a university education, Aunt Cressida."

"A man's education, you mean, girl! Which is no education for a woman to have. Music, art, etiquette, a knowledge of all housewifely duties—these are the things that make a lady!"

Anne could no longer look at her aunt, but stared down at her lap, her hands clenched tightly and her knuckles showing white. "Thus I feel I would be better suited as a companion, Aunt."

"The position of governess has never been an enviable one," her aunt continued, "but you may believe me when I say it is infinitely preferable to that of companion. A governess at least has some say in her own schoolroom. No companion I know ever has anything to say." Seeming to notice her niece's dejection for the first time, she deserted that vein and added more briskly, "Nevertheless, if it is a companion's position you seek, I will inquire immediately among my friends and acquaintances. There may be some opening available."

Anne responded to this offer from her aunt with an offer of her own. "Until I find a position, Aunt Cressida, perhaps I might help with your boys. I tutored several young boys in our neighborhood."

"The boys are at school, and the girls have a governess, Miss Marsh, an excellent creature in most respects, and the girls like her, though her French is abominable."

Anne brightened. "I could help with their French—take over the French classes if their governess doesn't mind."

Miss Marsh didn't mind at all. When introduced to Anne and offered relief from French lessons, she found it impossible to hide her pleasure. French had always been a bitter chore for her. When they were alone together, she confided to Anne that her own governess had not been proficient in the language.

"I should like to sit in on the lessons myself," she admitted. "I'm certain I could learn a great deal."

"You would be most welcome," Anne assured her. "My father started teaching me French when I was six, and I've always loved studying languages. How old are my cousins?"

"Miss Victoria is thirteen and Miss Emily eleven."

"Are they good students?"

"They're biddable, and they try. Miss Emily's best subject is history; Miss Victoria's only interest is fashion. She pores over magazines and fashion plates, and her greatest concern is the arrangement of her hair ribbons."

The following day, while Mrs. Hodder entertained morning visitors in her salon and politely inquired of her friends for a possible companion's position, Anne met her young relatives in the schoolroom. In French, she greeted them by name and introduced herself. When she asked simple questions in the same language, they tried to understand and offer answers in return.

Their governess smiled in appreciation of Anne's method. Without realizing it, the girls were having their French lesson. They were even enjoying it. She settled back comfortably to listen, contributing only when Anne addressed her directly.

2

On the morning that Anne Waverly offered her first French lesson to her young cousins, just a few blocks away at a gentleman's establishment in Grosvenor Square, an altercation was taking place between Mrs. Arelia Saunders and her son's tutor, Mr. Osgood.

"I repeat, madam! It is impossible for me to stay!"

"But you said you would try the position for six months. You agreed to that much, at least."

"In truth I did, but I cannot honor the agreement. It would be a waste of your money and my time. If you will take my advice, you will send your son to school. That, in my opinion, would be the best possible place for him. Good day, Mrs. Saunders."

As Mr. Osgood left the house, Arelia stormed down the hall to her brother-in-law's study and burst through the door.

"Tenbury! I must speak with you. He is your nephew. Surely there is something you can do?"

A fair head lifted politely, and a pair of blue eyes regarded her with interest. "I assume we are discussing our charming Thomas. What has he done now?"

"What he always does—driven away another tutor. The man insisted he couldn't stay and recommended I send the boy to school."

"The last time Tom was sent down from Harrow, the headmaster clearly stated that they would not consider readmitting him unless he underwent a drastic change in attitude. Has he done so?"

"Of course not. We don't dare send him back. I can't even leave him in the country, for I never know what mischief he will be into next." She took a swift turn about the room, her blond curls bouncing, and the flounces of her spring-green walking dress skimming over the floor. "This must stop! I'm a young widow with two children. I should be attending every gathering that's held if I hope to meet an eligible man— someone who can take the burden of my family from your shoulders. But am I doing that? No! Lately, it seems I spend most of my time fretting over that tiresome boy."

"Surely you exaggerate, Arelia."

"Do I? It took me two weeks to find the redoubtable Mr. Osgood. Two weeks of following up references and giving interviews. And how long did he last? Four days! Four short days! Well, let me tell you, I have run out of ideas. I have interviewed every tutor in this city, and I am at my wit's end. You must help me, Nate!"

The Earl of Tenbury regarded his sister-in-law sympathetically. She had certainly had her share of bad luck. First the loss of her husband, to whom she had been devoted. Then just as she was about to emerge from a full year of mourning, her father had died unexpectedly, plunging her into blacks again. Her newest headache, young Thomas, had begun his shenanigans about eighteen months earlier. He had been sent down from school for a long list of transgressions, which included repeatedly putting various undesirable creatures into the beds of his classmates, writing obscenities on the slate board, and kissing a daughter of one of the masters. When one added to this mischievousness the fact that he was failing his form, the school saw no reason to permit him to stay.

"Very well, Arelia. I will look into the matter. You must not despair. I know you will find this hard to believe, but Thomas is much like his father was at the same age—and as you know, Henry turned out well."

Arelia's pretty face brightened as she answered, "You are the best of all brothers, Nate. I feel sure you will succeed where I have failed, for I am convinced this matter demands a man's attention."

"Perhaps. We shall see. Send the boy to me tomorrow morning. Shall we say ten o'clock?"

"Certainly, Tenbury, anything you say."

"And Arelia—please impress upon him the importance of being prompt."

Twelve-year-old Thomas Saunders was inordinately pleased to have successfully routed six tutors in little more than ten months. His pleasure, however, did not survive the information that he was to present himself before his uncle the following morning.

Since the earl had never been one of Thomas's favorite people, he knocked timidly on the door and, when told to "Come," entered with considerable trepidation.

Tenbury had been seated reading the newspaper, but he rose at the boy's entry. He was a strongly built man of above average height; to Thomas he had always seemed a giant.

"You are prompt, Thomas. That's good." The earl moved to the chair behind his desk and seated himself, while Thomas approached the desk and stood before it, his hands clasped nervously behind his back.

"Your mother tells me that Mr. Osgood has left us," Tenbury began. "What, pray, was his complaint?"

"I believe he was displeased with my grasp of the Latin verbs, sir."

Tenbury raised a brow at this rejoinder. The boy had more in common with his dead father than physical appearance.

"Do you *know* any Latin verbs, Tom?"

"Very few, sir."

"Easy enough then to comprehend Mr. Osgood's displeasure, wouldn't you say?"

"Yes, sir."

"We both know you have no liking for your studies. But tell me this," the earl demanded. "If you could at this moment do anything you wished, what would that be?"

"Anything, sir?"

"Anything at all," the earl confirmed. "If I said, go where you will, do what you wish for the next two months—what would you do?"

"I would go to Tenton Castle, sir."

"And do what?" Tenbury asked.

The boy needed no time to consider. "Fish, swim, snare rabbits, hunt badgers at night. I have a great friend there, Will Carey, the squire's son."

"Yes, I know Will. Tell me this, Tom. If I were to permit you to do just as you wished for two months, and if I found you a new tutor meanwhile, would you be willing to settle down to your studies when your holiday ended?"

"Could I stay at the Castle, study there, and see Will in my free time?"

"Perhaps. Do you know what a gentleman's agreement is, Tom?" When the boy nodded, Tenbury continued, "I will grant you sixty days from tomorrow to do exactly as you wish at Tenton, if you will agree to apply your considerable intelligence to your studies at the end of that time. If you progress, and your tutor is satisfied with your efforts, you may continue to see Will, and you may remain in the country."

The smile that had grown on Tom's face faded slightly when his uncle said, "There are a few conditions attached to this agreement, which you must

15

clearly understand. You must pledge to me that you will engage in no activity that is either indecent, dishonest, or illegal. You will agree not to distress my people at the Castle in any way, nor cause them alarm or inconvenience. You will be certain that someone at the Castle or at the Grange knows where you are at all times. And above all, you will do nothing to disgrace my name or your own."

He paused for a moment, watching the boy closely. Tom seemed to be considering the terms carefully, and Tenbury was pleased. Too quick an acquiescence would have worried him. "Well, Thomas," he said at last, "Do we have an agreement?" He stood and reached a long arm across the desk to his nephew.

Tom stepped closer and took his uncle's large hand in his own smaller one. They shook solemnly. "Yes, sir, we do," he said.

Barely more than two weeks after Anne's arrival in London, Mrs. Hodder visited the schoolroom late one afternoon at tea time. She was amazed at the sounds that greeted her as she entered the room. Her niece, Miss Marsh, and the girls were partaking of their tea, all the while chattering away in an uninterrupted flow of French! She hesitated in the doorway and listened, greatly pleased with the excellent progress her daughters had made. Later that evening, when an acquaintance informed her of a possible position for her niece, she replied, "Thank you, Sally. I will be certain to tell her, though I believe she may decide to stay on with us after all. She gets on so well with my girls, and she is an absolute wizard with needle and thread."

Cressida Hodder had discovered Anne's proficiency in sewing only a few days after her arrival. Victoria had burst into the parlor in tears over a torn flounce, and Anne had offered to mend it. In a short time, with tiny, perfect stitches, the dress was repaired. The following day, when her aunt mentioned there were a dozen new dinner napkins that needed monogramming, Anne offered to do them. Almost every day thereafter, Anne found herself busy. Either her aunt would drop a rather broad hint regarding some needlework, or the housekeeper would bring it by her room saying, "Madam thought that if you had a free moment this afternoon you might like to hem these sheets, miss. No hurry though, miss."

After a few days, even this small courtesy vanished. Anne would simply find a pile of work on her bed. Even during her French lessons she would have sewing in her lap. Finally Ruth Marsh was moved to protest. "Surely there is a seamstress in the house who can hem sheets!"

Anne looked up in surprise. "I'm happy to have the work. It's the least I can do to repay my aunt and uncle for their hospitality."

"But you sew from sunrise to sunset. Beyond that, in fact. You were sitting up with the candles last night; I saw the light under you door. You were sewing, weren't you?"

"Yes," Anne admitted. "My aunt especially wanted Emily's yellow dress today, and I was a long way from finishing."

"I hesitate to criticize your aunt, Anne, but she is taking advantage of you. Can't you see it?"

"I need to pay my way here, Ruth. I won't live on charity."

"But you are more than paying your way. You are doing the work of two seamstresses and teaching French as well. In return you are receiving room and board. You should be receiving a wage besides. And another thing. Have you not wondered why it is that your aunt hasn't discovered any position for you?"

"I'm certain she is doing her best."

"I wouldn't be so sure. Why *should* she try when it works to her advantage to keep you here with her?"

Anne refused to believe her aunt was exploiting her, but Ruth had planted the seeds of doubt. When next an opportunity arose, Anne asked her aunt if she had heard of any companion positions.

"As a matter of fact, my dear, I have. My friend Sally Shelton told me of an acquaintance of hers who is seeking a companion. I have written a note to the lady and am waiting to hear from her. There is also old Mrs. Humbolt who lives just down the street. Her companion recently became engaged to be married, and will no doubt be leaving her soon. I thought I would speak with Mrs. Humbolt about you. I must admit, however, that I have been wondering if you would consider staying on here with us. Why, during these weeks we have come to regard you as one of the family. The girls are so fond of you, too."

This was the very invitation Anne had been hoping to hear since the day she arrived at the Hodders'. Now that it had finally been offered her, she hesitated to accept. She had nothing truly critical to say of her aunt and uncle, nor of the treatment she had received since coming to live with them. Yet somehow she knew she could not continue with them indefinitely. She could not envision herself as the inveterate poor relation. If she could secure a position, she would earn her own wage, and even though she knew it would not be much—it would be hers.

Back in the schoolroom, monogramming a handkerchief for her uncle George, she asked Ruth, "What is a seamstress paid, do you think?"

"I imagine very little. But I once knew a skilled language tutor who earned fifty pounds a year—and that was only for one student, one language. You also know German and Latin."

"But I am a woman," Anne replied. "I cannot seek a job as a tutor."

"If your aunt should arrange an interview for you," Ruth asked, "what will you wear?"

"My blue gown is the best I have."

Her friend frowned. "Do you think you could justify some new lace or ribbon? A bit of trim would improve it dramatically, I think." When Anne looked doubtful, Ruth hurried on. "I am taking Victoria to some of the shops this afternoon. Come with us and see what you can find. Who can say? You may discover something quite reasonable."

Several hours later the three strolled down Oxford Street to its junction with Bond Street. A walk of less than half a mile brought them to the shops south of Grafton. While Ruth and Victoria stopped at Asprey's, drawn in by a handsome dressing case in the window that Victoria admired, Anne went on a few doors to a milliner's that offered, among other goods, a large variety of dress trimming.

She had little money left and was loathe to part with it, knowing that when it was gone, she had no way to replace it. Yet somehow the thought of being forever dependent on her relatives outweighed her reticence, and she looked over the goods with interest. She would refurbish the blue gown as Ruth suggested and try to look her best as she sought a position.

She selected some wide ribbon, reasonably priced, she felt, for the quality. She decided to buy enough to put two full rows at the hem of her gown. Remembering that her bonnet ribbon was much worn, she chose a length for that as well, concluding her purchases with two straw flowers to tuck under the band to add a bit of color. A woman at the counter cut the ribbon lengths she requested, then wrapped Anne's goods in a small bundle. After paying for her purchases, Anne smiled pleasantly then turned to leave. Before she had taken even one step, the woman behind the counter spoke, loudly enough for all the customers in the shop to hear.

"D'you plan on payin' for them furbelows, ma'am?"

Anne looked about curiously, as did most of the people present, wondering to whom the woman was speaking so loudly. She was profoundly shocked to find the shopkeeper staring at her.

"Excuse me," she said doubtfully. "Were you speaking to me?"

"Indeed I was, ma'am. And what I asked was, do you mean to pay for them ribbons, or just take 'em without payin'?"

Thoroughly confused and more than a little embarrassed, Anne stepped back to the counter and laid her parcel down. She lowered her voice, hoping the shopkeeper would do the same. "I just paid you—two and fourpence—you gave me change."

With no diminution in volume the woman returned. "I wrapped you a parcel, madam, ribbons and flowers. If you're not willin' to pay, then I suppose I will put my stock back on the shelf."

She reached for the parcel while Anne stood unresponsive. She couldn't think of a thing to say—didn't know what she should do. . . .

At that moment a silver-tipped ebony cane descended on the counter between the two women, nearly landing on the shopkeeper's fingers as she reached to reclaim the package. The action so startled Anne that she jumped, then turned her head to see a tall, blond man standing close beside her. His hard, unsmiling face and fierce blue eyes were fixed upon the shopkeeper. The shop had grown deathly quiet; Anne sensed that every eye and ear was attending to them.

"I believe, my good woman," the gentleman said, "that your memory is lamentably short. I saw this lady pay you. She tendered three shillings; you returned eightpence."

Anne could not take her eyes from the gentleman, so shocked was she that a stranger had come to her aid. His dress and speech clearly identified him as a person of some standing; Anne guessed that he must be in his mid thirties. His voice was pleasant, but though his words were superficially polite, beneath they held a definite challenge. He never looked at Anne, but continued to regard the shopkeeper until she responded.

"This here be no concern of yours, sir."

"Unethical business practice is the concern of every good citizen," he replied.

"Un-e-thi . . . ? What?" the woman asked.

"Dishonest," the gentleman clarified.

"Dishonest!" The woman bristled. "This be an honest shop. Ask anyone!"

"That is unnecessary," he responded, "I have seen with my own eyes just how *honest* it is." Then, ignoring the blustering woman, he turned his attention for the first time to Anne. "If you will wait here, madam, I will step into the street and locate a constable. I will be more than happy to substantiate your claim to this parcel."

Confronted by those remarkable eyes, situated in a face more handsome than any Anne had ever seen, she found herself unable to respond beyond an affirmative nod. As the gentleman turned deliberately toward the street door, the shopkeeper found a stammering voice.

"J-Just a moment, now, sir. There's no cause to call for the law. It's your word against mine, after all."

"Not quite," he returned. "It's your word against mine *and* the lady's."

"Very well, then," the woman responded angrily, "Take the goods, for we all know the law always sides with Quality. But you needn't bother bringing your trade here again for—"

"She won't," the gentleman interrupted. "Nor will I." Without another word he scooped the parcel from the counter, placed it in Anne's hands, and turned for the door.

Anne followed him quickly from the shop, knowing she must say something; but once on the street outside, all she could manage was, "Sir?"

He turned, a brow raised in inquiry.

"Thank you," she said quietly, feeling inept and foolish.

He raised a hand to the brim of his hat in a brief salute. "My pleasure, ma'am," was all he replied before he turned again and strolled off toward Piccadilly.

3

Anne turned and walked the other way as Ruth Marsh and Victoria emerged from Asprey's. Still rather shaken from her encounter with the unscrupulous shopkeeper, she listened with only half an ear to their chatter.

Ruth smiled when she saw the package in Anne's hands. "You did find something! Good! I can't wait to see."

Anne was anxious to tell Ruth about her unusual experience in the milliner's shop but did not wish Victoria to overhear. It was late that evening before she had a chance to relate it.

"How fortunate that the gentleman happened to see you pay," Ruth said.

"*And* that he was willing to step forward and say so," Anne added.

"What would you have done if he hadn't been there?" Ruth asked curiously.

"I don't know. Never have I been accused of stealing! I was so bewildered. I couldn't believe she was speaking to me. If I had tried to take the package, I am certain she would have raised the alarm. Yet to pay a second time would have been to admit she was right—when she was not. It was an impossible situation."

"What was the gentleman's appearance?" Ruth asked.

"He was quite tall, taller than my uncle George. I thought him amazingly handsome." Remembering the coldness of the gentleman's eyes as he challenged the shopkeeper, she added, "His eyes were most remarkable . . . an unusual blue, much like a deep lake in late summer."

When the topic of the handsome stranger had been exhausted, the two young women unwrapped Anne's purchases and planned how they would redecorate her dress.

Once her gown had been refurbished, Anne began a series of employment interviews that had been arranged by her aunt. Of the four interviews she was granted, none was successful. Two turned her away for lack of references, one said she was too young for the position, another said she was too old.

At the end of the week, greatly discouraged, Anne was sitting in her room setting tiny stitches along what seemed to be the endless hem of a sheet when Ruth burst in.

"Anne!" she exclaimed. "I have heard of a position. Or, I should say, Mrs. Crookshank has."

"My aunt's cook?" Anne patted the cushion next to her on the small sofa. "Sit down," she invited, instantly hopeful. "Tell me!"

"It seems Mrs. Crookshank has a cousin who works as head parlor maid to Lord Tenbury. His lordship's sister-in-law is seeking a governess for her daughter."

Anne's face fell. "A governess! But we decided I couldn't—"

"You could manage this position," Ruth interrupted. "The child is only eight, has barely left her nurse. You could easily teach her, for several years at least."

"How would I go about applying for the position?"

"Mrs. Crookshank is planning to visit her cousin tomorrow. She said she would be willing to take a letter and pass it on to his lordship's butler."

Anne promptly drafted a request for an interview and sent it with the cook the following day. Two days later she received an answer sent round from Grosvenor Square. When she saw the direction, her hopes faded; no resident of such a lofty address would hire a governess without references.

The letter offered an appointment the following afternoon at two o'clock. She decided she would not go—could not go; then in the next instant asked herself what she had to lose. A little pride, perhaps. "This is no time to let pride control your life, Anne," she could hear her father say.

Lord Tenbury looked up from his morning paper as his secretary entered the study.

"Excuse me, my lord. There has been another applicant for the tutor's position. I scheduled an appointment for this afternoon."

"Excellent, Raymond. But don't bother to bring him to me if he is as addlepated as the last, or as old as the one before him. I am beginning to believe, as Mrs. Saunders does, that there is not a single qualified tutor in this town whom my nephew has not already offended."

"What of the applicants for the governess's position, sir?"

"I should like you to see them first," his employer replied. "Those you consider qualified will be interviewed by Mrs. Saunders. She will make the final decision."

When an unprepossessing, unattended female claiming to be Miss Anne Waverly presented herself at Lord Tenbury's town house that afternoon, the butler did not hesitate to admit her. His instructions from Mr. Raymond were to show Miss Waverly to his office. He led Anne across a wide black-and-white tiled hall, past the graceful, curved stairway that ascended from its center, and past the closed doors that lined the hall's perimeter. One set of double doors to a handsome library stood open, but Anne had no more than an instant to glance inside as she passed. The butler preceded her through a door at the rear of the hall, continued the length of a narrow passageway, then opened a door on his left. He stepped aside to allow her to enter as he announced, "Miss Anne Waverly, sir."

Mr. Raymond rose to his feet and indicated a chair near his desk. "Please, Miss Waverly, won't you be seated?" Anne seated herself as he continued, "The position Mrs. Saunders seeks to fill is that of governess for her daughter, aged eight."

Anne had knocked on the mansion's street door with boldness, determined to convince these people that she was the best possible candidate for the position. But one look at Mr. Raymond's stern features was enough to weaken her resolve.

"Yes, sir," she said meekly. "That is the position for which I wish to apply."

"May I ask how you came to know of the position?"

"The governess in my aunt's house heard of it and told me."

"And your aunt is . . . ?"

"Mrs. Cressida Hodder, Oxford Street."

"Your letter did not mention any previous experience as a governess, Miss Waverly. Have you any?"

"No, sir. I lived with my father until his death last year, but I have an excellent education, and I enjoy children. I believe I could fill the position to Mrs. Saunders's satisfaction."

"May I see your references?"

"I have no references, sir, aside from a letter from my uncle, Mr. George Hodder."

His raised brows were enough to tell her that a biased opinion from a relative carried little weight with him.

"I was hoping I might be able to speak with Mrs. Saunders," Anne hurried on, "to explain my situation to her."

Mr. Raymond rose and pulled the bell rope and Anne knew her short interview was over. "I am terribly sorry, Miss Waverly, but Mrs. Saunders desires a woman with experience. You admittedly do not fill the requirement. And without references . . . well, I'm sure you understand."

"Yes. I am afraid I do," she replied, rising to her feet. "Is Mrs. Saunders at home?"

"Yes, she is," he answered, taken off guard by the question.

"Is there any chance I might speak with *her*?"

He smiled tightly. "I am afraid not, miss."

"I understand. Thank you for seeing me, sir."

Mr. Raymond crossed to the door and opened it as the butler arrived outside.

"Miss Waverly is leaving, Kimble. Please show her out."

Anne dejectedly followed the butler back the way they had come. She had told herself this was exactly what would happen, yet she felt inordinately disappointed. She realized she had allowed herself to hope. If only she had been permitted to speak with Mrs. Saunders, perhaps she could have convinced her that she was capable of doing the job. The lady was home even now, possibly behind one of these very doors Anne was passing.

Anne's thoughts were interrupted as the street door opened and a gentleman stepped into the hall. The muted light of the overcast afternoon filtered through the doorway behind him, accentuating the breadth and squareness of his shoulders.

As the butler said, "My lord," and held out his hands to take the hat and cane the gentleman offered, a footman moved to close the door. Anne stood transfixed. All thoughts of Mrs. Saunders skipped from her head in that instant, for this gentleman was the gentleman of the milliner's shop.

His hands now free, the gentleman acknowledged Anne's presence with a simple, "Madam," while she replied with an equally brief, "My lord."

This formality disposed of, Kimble moved to open the door to show the lady out, but found she had not followed him.

Anne stood regarding the man before her. He was even more imposing than she remembered. He clearly didn't recognize her. But then, why should he? He barely looked at her that day. For a moment she considered retreating, then realized she had nothing to lose.

"Lord Tenbury?" she asked tentatively.

He nodded slightly, and she continued, "Might I speak with you for a moment?" She felt she should elaborate somewhat but couldn't think what to say, especially before the servants. So she left it with the simple request, and held her breath waiting for his response.

Kimble turned back to the pair, forced now by circumstance to make an introduction he considered inappropriate. "This is Miss Waverly, my lord. She has come about the governess's position."

"I see," Tenbury responded. "Won't you come into my study, Miss Waverly. We can speak privately there."

Kimble moved immediately to a door set to one side of the hall, the stiffness of his back declaring his disapproval as loudly as any words.

Lord Tenbury paused at the door. "Have Mrs. Hearthwaite send up some tea, Kimble."

"Very good, my lord."

When the door closed behind them, Anne was the first to speak. "I apologize for taking your time, Lord Tenbury. I inquired if I might speak with Mrs. Saunders, and Mr. Raymond said it was impossible. I should like to apply for the position of governess.

Even though I am qualified, Mr. Raymond said that without references or experience, I cannot be considered."

Seeming not to have heard this rush of words, he motioned her to a comfortable chair near the windows. "Please sit down, Miss Waverly. Did you buy those flowers the day we met?"

"You *do* remember," Anne said.

"Certainly. Why should I not? They have transformed your bonnet; it is most becoming."

The bonnet was a simple straw, but the compliment nonetheless pleased her.

As she sat down, he continued. "You seem eager to secure this position."

"Yes, sir, I am. I need employment. And I believe I am well suited to this situation."

"Employment is difficult to find without references," he said.

"Yes."

"How is it that you have no references?"

"I lived with my father until he died last year. I am seeking my first position."

"How old are you?" he asked.

"Eight-and-twenty, my lord."

"Where did you live with your father?"

"In Cambridgeshire, near the university."

"And have you no friend or acquaintance there—a man of letters—a peer perhaps?"

"There is the vicar of our parish," Anne offered, wondering why she hadn't thought to ask him for a letter of introduction.

"Anyone else?" he prompted.

After a moment's thought she offered, "Sir Hugo Scoville owned the cottage we rented."

"Write to them," Tenbury suggested. "Ask them for references. Then apply again to Mrs. Saunders. If the position is still open, I am certain she will consider you. If not, you will be well armed to secure another place."

The door opened as the butler and a housemaid appeared to lay the tea. Anne rose self-consciously, the arrival of the servants making her aware of the impropriety of her private meeting with the earl.

As she backed slowly toward the door she said, "I think I won't stay for tea, my lord. Thank you for your help; I can't imagine why I never thought to ask Sir Hugo—"

"Please sit and take some refreshment, Miss Waverly," he interrupted. "I had not quite finished."

Though his words were seemingly polite, his tone was imperious, and she knew she dare not disobey if she were to have any hope of getting the position. She returned to her seat and took the delicately painted china cup and saucer the maid offered. When the servants had left the room, the earl continued as if they had not been disturbed.

"Tell me about yourself. How came you by your education?"

She told him about her mother, how she had died when Anne was six. "I was taught by my governess and by my father, who was a scholar and translator."

"Waverly," he mused. "Was your father by any chance Maxwell Waverly?"

"Yes. That's right. Did you know him?"

"He gave a series of lectures at Cambridge while I was there. I remember finding them quite fascinating. I'm sorry to hear—"

He paused as the door opened abruptly and a young man strode into the room. "I say, Nate. Would you mind if I took the grays this afternoon? . . . Oh . . . excuse me . . . thought you were alone." Turning in Anne's direction he sketched a bow. "How do you do, ma'am?"

"Allow me to present Miss Anne Waverly," the earl said. "This is my brother, ma'am, the Honorable John Saunders."

Anne reached for the hand Mr. Saunders offered

and immediately liked what she saw. He was a man in his early twenties, nearly as tall as his brother. His blond hair was a shade darker than the earl's, and his eyes gray. He smiled warmly at her, while his pleasant voice said, "Delighted, Miss Waverly. Sorry to interrupt. Didn't know Tenbury was engaged."

"Miss Waverly is interested in the governess's position," the earl said.

"That's a round one," his brother replied. "When did it become your duty to interview dry nurses?"

Once again made aware of the inappropriateness of her interview with the earl, Anne rose to her feet, wishing to be gone.

Ignoring his brother's question, Tenbury said, "Please be seated, Miss Waverly. My brother is a perennial rattle. More than half of all he says should not be attended to."

"He is correct in this instance, my lord," Anne replied. "My employment is not your concern, and I have imposed upon you long enough. I must go."

"As you wish. Kimble will see you to a hackney carriage."

"I would prefer to walk, Lord Tenbury," Anne objected. "It is only a few steps."

"Kimble will call you a hackney, Miss Waverly," he said, smiling. "Good day."

Since his tone was one that brooked no argument, she offered none, but merely echoed his "Good day," and followed the butler from the room.

A footman was sent running, and within a few minutes a hackney was waiting at the curb. She wanted to object, not wishing to spend the money when she could as easily walk, but when Kimble tossed several coins to the driver, she entered the coach without a word and in a few minutes was deposited at her aunt's door.

Even this short drive made her queasy, but she refused to let it dampen her spirits. She felt she had

31

a chance of getting this position if only she could obtain sufficient references in time. She knew she could do the job and do it well. She smiled as she mounted the front steps of her aunt's house. If her father had been there today, she knew he would have been proud.

Even with all its leaves removed, the Sheraton table in the dining salon of Tenbury House would accommodate twenty people; therefore, the Saunders family dined together at one end. Lord Tenbury occupied the place of honor at the head of the table; his brother Jack sat to his right, while his sister-in-law Arelia was on his left.

Arelia Saunders allowed half the meal to pass before she raised the question. "Is it true, Tenbury, the servants' gossip I have been hearing?"

"It is not my custom to listen to servants' gossip, Arelia," the earl replied. "You must tell me what you have heard."

"I understand that you spoke to a candidate for the governess's position."

"For once, servants' gossip is accurate. I did indeed do so."

"How extraordinary," Arelia said.

The earl allowed her comment to pass and merely replied, "Her name is Waverly, Arelia. Anne Waverly. She is in the process of obtaining references. I believe she plans to apply to you for the position. If she does, I strongly suggest that you consider her. She seems highly qualified."

"What is she like?" Arelia asked with interest.

"She is tall, dark, extremely thin," Tenbury replied. "Her features are unremarkable."

"I disagree," Jack offered. "I found her eyes quite unique. They are green and unusually alive... most expressive."

"When did you meet her, Jack?" Arelia asked.

"He invited himself into my study in the midst

of our conversation, then offended the lady with thoughtless chatter," Tenbury said.

"Not so!" his brother rounded.

"You have not completely answered my question, Tenbury," Arelia persisted, "What of Miss Waverly's character?"

"She is highly intelligent," he replied, "candid, tenacious—traits I find desirable in an educator."

"Who are her family?" she asked.

"Her parents are both dead. Her father was Maxwell Waverly, a scholar, translator of the classics. I met him years ago and admired him. His father was a baronet of an old Yorkshire family. Miss Waverly's mother was the daughter of Sir Giles Pentworth, Norfolk. That's all she told me."

"She sounds like someone I should like," Arelia offered.

"Perhaps," was all the earl replied as he appeared to lose interest in the subject and nodded for a footman to refill his wineglass.

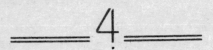

4

Anne's letters to Mr. Boone and Sir Hugo Scoville were answered within a week. Armed with these references, she applied again to Mr. Raymond and was granted an interview with Mrs. Saunders, the position of governess having not yet been filled.

If the truth were told, Arelia Saunders had several excellent applicants for the job but had purposely delayed choosing a governess on the outside chance she would hear from Miss Waverly. Mildly surprised that Tenbury had met with the woman, she was even more intrigued when he recommended her for the job.

Arelia hoped to meet Miss Waverly and discover what it was that had left such an impression upon her brother-in-law. She had never heard him describe any woman in the terms he had applied to Miss Waverly.

While Arelia Saunders looked eagerly forward to the interview, Anne traveled the short distance from Oxford Street to Grosvenor Square with a combination of anxiety and dread. She had worked diligently to secure this meeting; now that she had it, she was filled with doubt. It was true she was qualified to teach the academics, but in the arts she was well aware of her deficiencies. Trying desperately to think of some excuse that would explain her lack of musical skills, she climbed the steps of Tenbury's residence and sounded the knocker.

Kimble greeted her with an expressionless face, and she could not decide if he bore her any ill will as a result of her previous visit. He led her to a salon hung with gold and ivory paper and furnished with great elegance. Dark blue draperies were swept back to reveal a private garden enclosed by a vine-covered wall.

Seated on a sofa near the fire was quite the loveliest woman Anne had ever seen. In a morning dress of deep amethyst, her golden hair arranged to curl riotously about her face, Arelia Saunders looked nothing like the widow Anne had expected to see. Anne had had misgivings about her dress from the moment she put it on. Advancing now to take the hand Mrs. Saunders graciously extended, she was wishing both herself and her dowdy dress at Jericho.

Anne's feeling of unease did not survive five minutes in Arelia Saunders's presence. With a generous smile and a straightforward manner, Mrs. Saunders conducted a painless interview. She asked many questions, listening patiently with interest and without interrupting as Anne answered. When Anne enumerated her academic accomplishments, Arelia shook her head.

"Belinda will need little of that at present, though I should like her to start French as soon as possible. She reads well but needs a great deal of practice with penmanship. I suppose she must learn history, though I never understood why girls must do so. All those horrid foreign wars—they always bored me. She could begin mathematics—sums and so forth— whenever you decide it's necessary."

"You speak as if I have the position, ma'am."

"And so you do, Miss Waverly, if you wish it. I liked you from the moment you arrived. In fact, I was already prejudiced in your favor before we met. Lord Tenbury recommended you for the position." Seeing

Anne's eyes widen, she asked, "Does that surprise you?"

Embarrassed by both the compliment and the question, Anne hesitated before answering. "His lordship and I were interrupted that day before I could finish. There are some areas where my abilities are less than admirable."

Arelia smiled at this self-deprecation. "You surprise me. Let me guess. You don't paint."

"No, I don't," Anne admitted. "Nor do I play—anything."

"Not everyone is blessed with musical talent."

"No, ma'am, but a governess is expected to be able to offer such."

"Perhaps, but Belinda is still very young. We cannot expect her to read music before she can read English. There will be time enough later for music."

"I do sew," Anne offered, suddenly remembering one feminine talent, "Quite well."

"Now that's a blessing!" Arelia responded. "I have never set a single straight stitch in my life. The child has been working on a sampler that looks like a battlefield diagram for one of Wellington's campaigns. She needs your help and advice in that—and at once. When can you start?"

Anne could scarcely believe her good fortune. "When do you need me?" she asked.

"Tomorrow?" Arelia suggested.

"Tomorrow," Anne repeated, feeling stupid, knowing she could not possibly start tomorrow, then in the next moment asking herself why not. Nothing could be simpler.

"Good," Mrs. Saunders was saying. "I shall send the coach to collect you at two in the afternoon. Would that be convenient?"

"Yes, ma'am. You're too generous."

"Not at all. You cannot be expected to carry your trunks. At what number does your aunt reside?"

"Number twenty-three, Oxford Street, ma'am."

"Very well. You may expect the coach at two o'clock. When you arrive, Mrs. Hearthwaite will see that you are settled, and I will meet with you Wednesday to discuss your duties."

As Mrs. Saunders rose and rang for the footman, Anne realized her interview was over. She allowed herself a slight smile as she parted from her new employer. On her short walk home she practiced what she would say to her Aunt Cressida. Even though Anne suspected that her aunt would be displeased to see her leave so soon, she refused to allow the prospect to erode her triumphant mood.

When Anne arrived at Tenbury House to take up residence as the new governess, she was treated with great civility by Mrs. Hearthwaite and the other servants who came in contact with her. Having seen the position Ruth Marsh held in her aunt's home, she had been prepared to be treated as just another member of the household staff. She had no way of knowing that Lord Tenbury's staff had been carefully instructed by Mrs. Saunders at her brother-in-law's request. "Miss Waverly is a lady, born and bred, and is no less so simply because she has been forced to earn her living. His lordship desires that she be treated with utmost respect so long as she remains in this house."

Anne soon discovered that her responsibilities at Tenbury House would be neither arduous nor time-consuming. She was responsible for Belinda from the time the child rose in the morning until two in the afternoon. Beyond that, Anne's time was her own. It soon weighed heavily on her hands, for she was accustomed to her cottage chores, her rose and vegetable gardens, and most of all, her father's beloved library. She'd had a glimpse of Tenbury's library the first time she had visited the house; now she longed to browse there. But she knew it was impossible. Private rooms in the house were not for her use.

After several days of wiling away her afternoons on needlework, Anne ventured out to the lending library, in her eagerness borrowing more books than she could easily carry. With her arms overfull, the walk back was not nearly so pleasant as the walk out had been. She had covered less than half the distance to Grosvenor Square when her arms began to ache abominably, and she regretted her greed in bringing so many volumes with her. Just as she was considering setting her burden down, a carriage pulled up in the street beside her.

"Miss Waverly?"

She glanced up to see Lord Tenbury on the high perch of a phaeton drawn by two handsome chestnuts.

"It seems you have more than two arms can handle. Are you going home? May I offer you a ride?"

Anne glanced at him only briefly, then her eyes moved back to the high-spirited horses prancing impatiently, their shod hooves beating a tattoo on the flagstones. The carriage itself, graceful and fragile, rolled back and forth as they fretted. Anne's answer was so automatic that she took no time to consider what its effect might be upon the earl.

"Thank you, no, my lord. I prefer to walk." When his pleasant countenance clouded she amended hastily. "Actually what I mean to say is that I *enjoy* walking—for exercise."

"I should hate to curtail your exercise," he returned, "but I will at least relieve you of your burden."

He had only to glance at his groom, Murdock, for the man to leap into the street and lift the books from Anne's arms. She gave them up willingly, then stood by as Murdock climbed back into the carriage. "I trust your walk will be even more enjoyable now," Tenbury said.

"Thank you, my lord. I am certain it will be."

He inclined his head slightly, then dropped his hands, allowing the horses to walk on.

Anne did not enjoy the remainder of her walk. How she loathed her weakness! The simple sight of the shifting carriage was enough to make her knees tremble. What made the incident so awkward was knowing that Tenbury was largely responsible for her being hired. Now she seemed ungracious. When she arrived at the house, she found the books stacked neatly on a table in the schoolroom.

The following morning, just after ten o'clock, Tenbury made his way to the second floor and paused in the hallway outside the open schoolroom door. Miss Waverly was reading a story to Belinda—one of Aesop's Fables.

". . . for Tortoise had learned an invaluable lesson: slow and steady wins the race."

"That's a wonderful story, Miss Waverly. I liked Tortoise ever so much," Belinda said.

"He was clever, wasn't he? I have a book of my own, with this same story and lovely pictures throughout. Hare has the smuggest face. When I get my books, I will show it to you."

"I will read the story to you next time," the little girl suggested.

"I should like that," Anne replied.

Anne sat facing the open door and therefore noticed Tenbury the moment he entered. He was dressed in riding clothes—a rich brown coat and flawless buckskin breeches. She stood instantly, and her glance at Belinda brought the child to her feet as well.

"Good morning, Lord Tenbury."

"Good morning, Uncle Nate."

"Ladies," he acknowledged, smiling at his niece. "I should like to speak with Miss Waverly privately, Belinda." Then looking at Anne, "If it's not inconvenient."

"No, not at all." Anne laid the book aside, then

carefully removed her spectacles and placed them with it. "You may go play with your kitten, Belinda," she said. "I will call when it's time to do sums."

The child wrinkled her nose at the mention of sums but went obediently into the next room. Anne closed the door, then turned rather nervously to confront Tenbury. His next words surprised her.

"I was distressed to see you out yesterday unattended. Was there no one to accompany you?"

"I asked no one to accompany me, my lord."

"Why not?"

"I am the governess, sir. I need no companion—"

"That is not precisely true. You are the governess; but you are also a gentlewoman and should not walk city streets unattended. No doubt you were accustomed to walking alone in the country, but country customs will not serve here. They are neither acceptable nor safe. In future, if you desire to go out, I would prefer you take one of the maids with you, or better yet, order the carriage, especially if you intend to visit the library and bring home half their stock."

Then, rather abruptly, he changed the subject. "As I came into the room just now, I heard you tell Belinda that you would show her something when you get your books. Have you some things in storage somewhere?"

"I left several trunks, mostly books, with my vicar, Mr. Boone."

"Have you sent for them?"

"Not yet."

"Why not?"

As she hesitated, searching for a delicate way to say she could not afford to, the obvious occurred to him.

"What is his direction?" he asked.

"Mr. Jeremiah Boone, Vicar of Ripley, east of Cambridge."

"I will arrange to have your things sent on to Wiltshire," he said, "for we will be leaving town soon. Meanwhile, you have my permission to use the library here. It gets little enough use. You appear puzzled, Miss Waverly. What have I said to make you look at me so?"

"If you must know, my lord, I am amazed that you should concern yourself with me."

"I always concern myself with the people who work for me, particularly when they hold a position of influence over the younger, more impressionable members of my family. I won't detain you longer; I realize I am disrupting your study with Belinda."

When he had gone, Anne delayed in calling Belinda to her lessons as she pondered her new employer's behavior, for though his words seemed reasonable, she still found it odd that he should concern himself so closely with his niece's governess.

Anne knew she would never order the carriage for her own use, but she resolved to take a maid with her the next time she went out. She had no desire to displease the earl, thereby jeopardizing her position.

That same day, the Earl of Tenbury made a visit to White's in the early afternoon. Having given up his hat and gloves to a footman, he moved toward the lounge, stood for a moment in the doorway, then made his way toward a gaunt gentleman seated in an armchair near the windows.

The Duke of Chadwicke put aside the *Morning Post* as he indicated the chair to his right. "Good of you to come, my boy. It is to be hoped you have good news for me."

"As a matter of fact, I do, Your Grace," Tenbury replied. "Miss Waverly is safely installed under my roof. My sister-in-law has engaged her as governess to her daughter. It was the best I could do, under the circumstances."

"Damn the circumstances," the duke responded. "A more muddled business I've seldom seen. Nothing could be more awkward."

41

"Perhaps now that Miss Waverly is settled, Uncle, you can tell me why all this secrecy was necessary. You were lamentably short with details when last we spoke."

"I know, lad, and I'm sorry, but the woman decided to leave the cottage suddenly. Caught me off guard. When I heard she had bolted for London, I nearly panicked, for I knew I could not leave her to manage here on her own, notwithstanding my arrangement with her grandfather. I immediately thought of you. I knew you were in town and could be trusted to do the thing without arousing her suspicions. How did you manage it?"

"Simply enough. Once you had informed me where she was staying, I followed her on a shopping expedition and overheard enough of her conversation to know she was seeking a position. I then suggested to Mrs. Saunders that it was time her daughter had a governess—a suggestion she had not the least objection to. I managed to have Miss Waverly hear of the position through the servants' gossip. She appeared for an interview, but we nearly lost her when she came without references and my secretary showed her the door. I ended up doing the interview myself, then recommended Miss Waverly to my sister-in-law. She usually takes my advice, so all went well."

"And if Mrs. Saunders hadn't engaged her?"

"I would have found another way—companion to my mother perhaps."

"Do you think she suspects?"

"I don't believe so. The day I followed her to Bond Street, one of the shopkeepers tried to cheat her. I had no choice but to come to her defense. It was unfortunate she needed help, for I would rather not have called attention to myself. Yet when we met again, she seemed to attribute the meeting to coincidence. I believe that incident actually made our initial conversation more natural. That, and my having once met her father."

"I have never met her myself," Chadwicke said, "but by all accounts she is dull and dowdy, a bookworm, staid, prim, and not at all comely."

"At first glance, she seems to be those things," Tenbury replied, "but I do not find her dull, nor prim, nor lacking in sense."

"Well, that's something, then. You have acquitted yourself well in this, Tenbury. I am in your debt."

"Is there anything more I can do?"

"Whatever you can to make her stay comfortable. Her work won't be too demanding?"

"Hardly. My niece is only eight and possessed of a sweet nature. I cannot consider that teaching her would be drudgery."

"Good . . . good. I only hope Giles understands that I'm doing the best I can . . . considering. Of course, I have written to him, advising him of this latest development, but it could be months before we hear anything. Until then we must simply do our best."

"If I am to do my best, then I think it's time you told me everything."

"Ah, I am afraid it's a long story, Nate."

Tenbury stretched his legs out before him, crossing his glossy Hessians at the ankles. "I have all afternoon, and I don't intend to leave until I am in possession of all the details."

5

During the following week, Anne had no opportunity to explore the city, for the household was busy with preparations for its removal to the country now that the Season was ending. Anne packed not only for herself but for Belinda, a task that occupied her afternoons for three days.

On the day before their scheduled departure, Arelia Saunders swept into the schoolroom in the early afternoon. Anne was there, gathering the books she needed to return to the lending library before she left town.

"Miss Waverly. Here you are," Mrs. Saunders said by way of greeting. "Are you through packing?"

"Yes, ma'am. I finished yesterday."

"Good. I should like you to accompany me on a short shopping expedition. It will be my last chance to visit the London shops for some months. Will you come?"

"Certainly," Anne answered, assuming Mrs. Saunders was asking for her company because all the maids were too busy to leave their work. "Could we possibly return these books while we are out? I had planned to ask one of the footmen—"

"Bring them," Arelia said. "We will drop them on our way." As she left the room and hurried off down the hall, Anne snatched up her bonnet and gloves,

44

moving quickly to catch up with her employer. She had learned early in their acquaintance that one must hurry to keep up with Arelia Saunders.

The woman had boundless energy. She rose every morning at precisely ten o'clock regardless of what time she had gone to bed the night before. She ate a sparing breakfast, then left the house for a morning ride in the park. Afterward she would either be at home to visitors or take the carriage out to call upon her many friends. When she wasn't spending the afternoon with Belinda, she had numerous and varied social engagements. She would arrive home only in time to prepare for the evening's entertainment, which often extended into the early hours of the morning. Each night before she went out, she came to visit Belinda, displaying her gowns to her daughter's unending delight. "How beautiful you are, Mama!" the child would say. Anne could only agree.

As the coach lurched over the uneven pavement, Anne took comfort in knowing their destination was only a few minutes away. The books were soon deposited, and the ladies alighted before one of the city's largest fabric warehouses.

"Belinda has grown so these past months that I swear her frocks shrink each day," Arelia said. "I must order some things to see her through the summer. What do you think of this?" The jonquil sprig muslin Arelia lifted from the bolt was lovely, and Anne said so.

Arelia nodded to the clerk at her elbow and the woman scribbled on a pad. Arelia bought several other dress lengths for Belinda and one piece of burgundy French silk for herself before she asked Anne, "Have you any dresses lighter than that one?"

Anne glanced down at her plain brown dress, cut from serviceable twill. "I have several muslins, ma'am."

"I don't mean lighter in weight, I mean lighter colors. I have never seen you wear anything but brown, black, and navy."

"They are colors my father bought for me. They are practical—"

"Men should be practical, Miss Waverly; women are not expected to be." Arelia fingered a piece of pearl gray fabric. "This would make up beautifully, and would be cool for summer."

She ordered a dress length, and the woman wrote it down. As Anne would have opened her mouth to protest, the woman taking the order said, "You will look well in this, miss. Mrs. Saunders has a wonderful eye for color, that she does. You just trust her judgment."

Anne stood by silently as her employer bought several more lengths of fabric for her—sky-blue calico, russet, and burgundy muslin.

Later, in the privacy of the coach, Anne found the courage to protest. "You cannot intend all this fabric for me, Mrs. Saunders. I cannot possibly pay—"

"Nor need you. Tenbury provides livery for everyone else. I see no reason why you cannot have some attractive things."

"But ma'am, colors are not suited to a governess's position. Quiet, serviceable clothing is more proper—"

"In whose judgment? I don't agree. Children should be surrounded with stimulating things; color is one of them. Wait to see how well you will look. In the end I know you will agree with me."

Their next stop was at the dressmaker's shop. There Anne submitted to having her measurements taken and recorded while Arelia chose patterns for the yard goods she had purchased.

Beyond Anne's hearing the French seamstress spoke to her valued client. "She is too thin, this governess of yours, madam."

"Yes, Collette, I agree. Cut the dresses generously,

and I will see what I can do to put more flesh upon her bones."

The drive to Tenton Castle in Northern Wiltshire took two days—two days during which Anne suffered almost continuously from motion sickness. She traveled with Belinda and found that keeping the child occupied helped put her own discomfort at bay.

Anne did not touch her meal the night before they left. On the trip itself, she skipped meals as well, explaining to Belinda that she did not like traveling and had no appetite. Near the end of the second day, she was ready to swear she would never step into a carriage again.

Five carriages made the journey from London to Wiltshire, carrying the various members of the family as well as the servants and baggage. Anne's carriage and two others had managed to stay together on the road. When they arrived in the early afternoon, Belinda leaned up to the window, exclaiming as the familiar landmarks streamed by, "There is the church . . . and the arched bridge where Tom and I go fishing. And there is the lake. Isn't it monstrous big? And it's deep, too. We have a boat, and Tom has promised to teach me to row this summer. Do you see that oak tree there? Tom can climb it, clear to that Y near the top."

Anne made an appropriate response but was in no mood to admire the palatial splendor of Tenton Castle, a sprawling structure of gray towers, ornate turrets, and sparkling leaded windows.

Tenbury saw the coaches when they were still half a mile away and was waiting when the first one rolled to a stop before the Castle. Opening the door, he lifted a glowing Belinda under the arms and set her on the ground. He then held out a hand to Miss Waverly and frowned when he saw her pale, drawn face. She took his hand tentatively and reached one foot toward the carriage step. It was then that her

47

knees buckled, and Tenbury caught her as she collapsed into his arms.

Lady Tenbury hovered inside the great front doors as the earl carried Anne inside.

"What has happened, Tenbury? Who is this woman?"

"This is the new governess, Mother. I believe she has fainted."

"The poor thing," her ladyship said sympathetically. "Take her upstairs, Nate. I have put her in the green room next to Belinda."

When Anne opened her eyes again, she found she was being carried by Lord Tenbury as he mounted a flight of stairs. When he reached the top she said quietly, "Please, put me down, my lord."

"When we have reached your room, I will do so, Miss Waverly."

Greatly embarrassed by her position, she persisted, "It is not necessary—"

"Don't concern yourself. You weigh no more than a child; you are costing me no effort."

She subsided in silence. At the end of a long corridor Tenbury carried her through a door into a sunlit room and laid her on top of the bed. When he straightened again, Anne noticed the silver-haired lady at his elbow.

"This is my mother, Miss Waverly—the Countess of Tenbury. I will leave you in her care. I hope you feel better soon."

Anne made no reply, but when he was gone turned to the countess. "I must apologize, Lady Tenbury. I'm sorry to be a bother. I believe I must have fainted. I can't imagine why—"

"Traveling is tiresome—all that jolting about," the countess replied in a quiet, sympathetic voice. "I think it would be best if you simply rest here for the remainder of the day. I'll have cook send up some soup. After a good night's sleep, we will hope to find you much restored in the morning."

"Thank you, ma'am. You're very kind."

A short time later Anne had her soup and then slept straight through till the morning. But her sleep was disturbed by dreams—dreams of a carriage that rolled on and on, never stopping, never allowing a moment's peace.

Anne awoke when a young maid delivered her breakfast on a tray. The aroma of freshly buttered toast and tea brought her fully awake as she pulled herself up in bed.

"Good morning, miss," the maid said as she set the tray on a table and bobbed a curtsy.

"Good morning," Anne replied. "Is Miss Belinda awake? Has she eaten?"

"She had her breakfast an hour ago, miss, and has gone off with Master Thomas. Mrs. Saunders said I was to tell you there would be no lessons for her today what with the unpacking and all."

"That's probably best," Anne agreed. "She would likely be too excited to apply herself."

"So Mrs. Saunders thought, miss. She sends her compliments and hopes that if you are feeling better, you might join her in the morning room when you have finished dressing."

"I'm feeling well, thank you. Your name is?"

"Cassie, miss. Maid to Miss Belinda, and to you too, Miss Waverly, should you need me. Can I get you anything?"

"No, thank you, Cassie. You're very kind, but I'll be fine on my own."

As the maid dropped a quick curtsy and left the room, Anne hurried from her bed and surveyed her breakfast tray. She devoured eggs and tender ham as well as toast generously spread with butter and strawberry preserves. She sipped tea as she hurried into a black gown she had acquired after her father's death. She quickly fastened her hair in its severe style, then went to join Mrs. Saunders downstairs.

Outside her room, a narrow corridor laid with a crimson carpet runner stretched in both directions. Not knowing which way to turn to find the main stairs, she chose left. At the end of the hallway the corridor made a lefthand turn, then continued as before. Further along this hallway another hall crossed at right angles, while the passageway she had been following continued straight ahead. Within minutes she realized she was hopelessly lost. Fortunately, she encountered an upstairs maid who turned her in the proper direction.

She was soon descending the main stairway into the great hall, a massive room three stories high. The broad stairway, wide enough for ten persons to walk abreast, was supported throughout its descent by giant pillars rising from the floor of the hall below. Anne laid her hand along the cold marble balustrade as she slowly descended. She turned as she had been directed to a pair of doors flanked by two sets of ancient armor, while one of the footmen on duty moved to open them for her.

The morning room was a splendid combination of predominantly red carpets and pale blue furnishings. Numerous paintings covered the walls, nearly obscuring the design of the paper beneath. A moderate fire was dwarfed by the massive stone fireplace in which it burned. Over the mantel hung a life-sized, full-length portrait of a man robed in seventeenth-century splendor.

Arelia Saunders looked up as the doors opened and immediately rose to come forward and greet Anne. "You are admiring Torquil Saunders, a mere viscount when this was painted," she said. "He was faithful to the Royalist cause and created First Earl of Tenbury for his support of the king. . . . Come and sit down, Miss Waverly; you are looking positively pale. I was sorry to hear you had a difficult journey. Did you sleep well? Are you fully recovered?"

"I am feeling better, thank you," Anne replied.

"But I fear I slept overlong and neglected my duties."

"Pish! What duties can there be on one's first day in the country? It is a day meant for sleeping and recovering from the rigors of a long carriage ride. You met Lady Tenbury, I believe?"

"Yes. Briefly, when I arrived. She was most kind."

"She invariably is. Always the first to make allowances for one and always settling disputes in her quiet way. She came down to Tenton nearly two months ago with my son. Tenbury granted him a holiday in return for his promise to apply himself to his studies when his new tutor takes charge. Tom is not a model student, I fear."

"So I understand."

"Ah: The servants will talk, I suppose. I can't say that I mind gossip so long as it is not malicious."

"Has his lordship found a tutor for your son?"

"Indeed, he has. I hope to meet him this morning. He is the younger brother of our rector, a man of the cloth himself. He has recently come to stay with his brother's family and is helping with our parish at St. Stephen's. Perhaps you should stay and meet him. Then later you must meet Tom. He is always up to mischief, never having the slightest interest in anything civilized. He seldom—"

The morning room doors opened and the butler intoned, "Mr. Dennis Pearce, madam."

While introductions and pleasantries were exchanged, Anne took stock of the new tutor. Being a man of average height and build, he stood only a few inches taller than Arelia Saunders. Few costumes could be more severe than the black worn by men of the church, yet Mr. Pearce displayed the color well. His dark brown hair showed a few streaks of gray at the temples. As he greeted Anne, she noticed that his brown eyes under thick dark brows seemed uncomfortably omniscient: the sort a person dreaded on Sunday morning after having participated in wrongdoing during the week. His hand was pleasantly warm, enveloping hers firmly without crushing it.

"Was there anything specific you wished to discuss with me, Mrs. Saunders?" he asked.

"No. I merely wanted to meet you and to wish you luck. Thomas will not be an easy pupil."

"So his lordship mentioned."

"His past history does not intimidate you?"

"Not in the slightest, madam."

"Good. You don't lack for courage. I admire that."

He half smiled at this remark, his eyes never leaving her face. "I'm pleased, I'm sure, that I meet with your approval. Was there anything else?"

"Only that you should settle with Miss Waverly on a time for Tom's French lessons. She has agreed to teach the children together."

"Very well."

When he was gone Anne remarked, "What a pleasant man."

"They are all pleasant in the beginning," Arelia said. "It is remarkable what a week or two of dear Tom can do to the most amiable of men."

Anne met Thomas the following day, and during the next week saw him regularly. She found that he was, in most ways, much like the young boys her father had occasionally tutored in Ripley. Although Tom was fair like his mother, Anne saw little of Arelia's soft countenance in his features. She thought instead that he greatly resembled Lord Tenbury. He was an active boy, never seeming to sit still for a moment. Anne was rather relieved that it was Mr. Pearce and not she who would have the task of settling Thomas to his studies.

Belinda had been granted a holiday coinciding with her brother's. Anne therefore had nothing but free time on her hands. When she encountered the children, she was inclined to show an interest in whatever they were doing at the moment. Nothing could have served better for creating a bond between them.

Within a few days of her arrival at Tenton Castle, Arelia began turning the rooms inside out in an over-all cleaning effort. She had planned a house party for some twenty guests, invited to Tenton to escape the heat of the city in summer. When the maids started bustling and the dust began to fly, the children fled the Castle and Anne soon followed. Tom's friend, Will Carey, was often in their company, but he was so shy and quiet that Anne could almost forget he was there. The children took Anne to the lake and showed her their prized possession: a sturdy rowboat painted bright yellow.

"I chose the color," Belinda claimed proudly. "Tom and Will painted it."

"Which was a big mistake," Tom added. "Even on the darkest night the thing can be seen for a mile. Makes stealth impossible."

Anne could only wonder why the boys would not wish to be seen at night. She decided not to ask. It was probably better if she didn't know.

The children took her to their favorite climbing trees, which she declined to ascend with them, even though they generously offered to help her.

Of all their confidences, Anne was most pleased when they shared with her their secret swimming hole, a wide spot in the stream that was virtually inaccessible to the uninitiated. They assured her there was only a single path, which only the family knew.

"Uncle Nate wanted to clear all this brush away, but Uncle Jack wouldn't let him do it," Belinda supplied. "Uncle Jack says this was my papa's favorite place, and we should leave it just as it is."

Tom immediately changed the subject, as Anne noticed he had done several times when his sister mentioned their dead father.

"Where is your Uncle Jack?" Anne asked, remembering the warm smile and friendly good humor of the young man she had met so briefly in Lord Tenbury's study.

"He followed the Prince to Brighton," Tom supplied. "He says the country bores him, which I can't understand at all. But he did say he would come down soon. He has been teaching me to hunt on his sixteen-hand roan. I'm doing well."

"That's true," Will spoke up in a rare moment. "He only fell off twice the last time."

When Tom smiled at this revelation, Anne smiled too, realizing that a lesson with only two falls must have been great progress from the one that came before.

Anne spent an early afternoon with the children. Then, as the sun grew ever hotter overhead, she made her way back to the Castle and through the cool, dark hallways to the library. All was quiet and orderly, the cleaning finished, the first guests due to arrive in a few days. The library doors stood open, while light flooded the room from a long row of western-facing casements.

Anne had discovered that Lady Tenbury loved books but had bad eyesight, which made reading difficult. She moved to the shelves and began searching for the comedies of Shakespeare, knowing he was one of her ladyship's favorites. Perhaps Lady Tenbury would wish Anne to read to her today.

"Good afternoon."

Tenbury had been sitting in an armchair near the windows where Anne hadn't noticed him. She returned his greeting as he stood.

"May I help you find something?" he offered.

"Shakespeare. I thought perhaps *As You Like It*."

He moved to a spot several feet from where she stood and, after a moment's search, produced the volume.

"Here you are. My mother tells me you have been reading to her. It's kind of you."

"Not at all. I daresay I enjoy it as much or more than she." When Anne noticed he was regarding her strangely, she asked, "What is it, my lord?"

"Nothing. It's just that you look different somehow."

"Oh," she replied, immediately self-conscious, smoothing the front of her skirt with her free hand. "It must be this dress Mrs. Saunders bought for me. She insisted, and I could not—"

"You need not explain. I know what it is to lose an argument with Arelia. The dress is most becoming. I think, too, that your hair is altered."

Although Anne retained her chignon, Arelia had encouraged her to fix it more loosely, allowing the hair to remain fuller. Several wisps even now curled softly near her face. When she didn't answer, he changed the subject.

"Your things arrived this afternoon from Mr. Boone. I had the books carried to your room. I believe the shelves there and in the schoolroom will hold them. The horse is in the east wing of the main stables, sixth stall from the end."

"The horse?"

"Yes. I should say *your* horse." When she continued to stare blankly at him he asked, "Did you not leave a gelding with Mr. Boone?"

"Yes, but I can't believe he would send him here. Surely you told him to send only my books?"

"I told him nothing. I simply ordered a servant to fetch from Mr. Boone all those possessions you had left in his care. He returned with several trunks and one gelding."

"Oh, dear."

"Why, 'Oh, dear'?"

"I can't keep him here. I can't afford—"

"I would not expect you to pay for his keep. You will need a horse while you're here. You may as well

55

have him as any other. Belinda needs a companion when she rides, and I daresay Arelia would be glad of your company. She detests riding out with a groom at her heels."

He paused, giving her an opportunity to respond. When she said nothing, he continued. "That's settled, then."

A few moments later he departed, and Anne was left to wonder how it was that Lord Tenbury with regularity took seemingly awkward situations and in a matter of moments resolved them logically and reasonably. He spoke, and things were settled. It never occurred to her that she had any right to object.

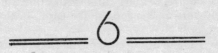

Jack Saunders descended on Tenton Castle the following afternoon. He declared that Brighton had been frightfully boring and dreadfully hot, then announced his intention to repair to the private swimming hole to wash off the thick dust of his journey with a cool swim. The boys clamored to go along and he feigned reluctant permission.

While Jack, Tom, and Will hurried off toward the secluded spot, Arelia set a leisurely pace calculated to allow her brother-in-law ample privacy for his swim. Jack avoided the shallows where the children often played and headed for the deeper water on the far side. In a matter of seconds he pulled off his boots then stripped off his shirt. Dressed only in his breeches, he plunged in without bothering to test the water.

This early in the season the stream was cold, and Jack soon had enough. When he heard Anne, Arelia, and Belinda approaching, he swam to the bank. He quickly scooped up his shirt, pulled it over his head, and was decent again before they made their way along the narrow path through the thicket.

The women sat beside him on the grassy bank. Anne watched the boys in the deep pool, gliding swiftly through the water. Soon their antics tempted Arelia and she waded in with bare feet.

"Do you swim?" she asked Anne.

"No. I never learned. I think it must be wonderful."

"My father subscribed to a swimming bath in London and considered it excellent exercise," Jack said. "He taught Tenbury and Henry and me to swim when we were quite young. We came here often in the summer."

"After Henry and I were married, I made him teach me," Arelia added. "I could teach you, Anne, if you like," she offered.

Anne only smiled, trying to envision herself paddling about as Tom and Will were. Arelia soon wandered off to play with Belinda, while the boys splashed water at each other.

"Are you enjoying your position here, Miss Waverly?" Jack Saunders asked.

"Very much. The work is easy—hardly like work at all."

"How is Tom getting on with his new tutor?"

"Mr. Pearce only started earlier this week, but so far things seem to be going well. He doesn't appear to be a man who will settle for any nonsense from Tom, and I believe Tom respects him."

"It's just like Tenbury to employ a cleric," Jack complained. "Can you imagine having him about the place all summer? I shall have to guard my tongue night and day."

"I think Lord Tenbury was interested in finding the best man for the job. I doubt if Mr. Pearce's profession influenced him unduly."

Jack smiled. "You have taken Tenbury's measure quickly enough, have you not, ma'am?"

"I know he is a master of expedience," she replied. "The remedy for most any problem seems to be written on the inside of his eyelids. He need only blink, and the solution is forthcoming."

Jack laughed aloud, but Anne soon had a more serious question for him. "I have wanted to know, but hesitated to ask Mrs. Saunders: Was Tom always a troublesome boy, or did the problems start after his father died?"

"You are much deeper than at first you seemed, Miss Waverly. The problems started just after his father died, but in the last year or so have worsened. We know he has not handled the loss well, and we have done what we can to help. We are hoping that in time, the bitterness will pass."

"Is that what you think it is? Bitterness?"

"Tom told me that he thought Henry had wasted his life—that war is a senseless endeavor. When I tried to explain that the continued freedom of the country depends on the dedication of the men in our army, he insisted that the outcome of the battle would have been the same whether his father had been there or not."

During the next two days there seemed an almost continuous stream of carriages making their way through the main gates of Tenton Park and down its long drive to the Castle. Anne learned that some of those invited were old family friends, others were acquaintances only. There were married couples, parents with daughters in tow, several widows, and a few unattached gentlemen.

"God, how I detest these little country gatherings of Arelia's," Jack complained as he and Anne stood on the balcony at twilight, watching yet another lantern-lit coach move slowly down the drive.

"Does she have them often?"

"At least once a year. She never gives up hope that one day she will invite someone who will take Tenbury's fancy. During the Season she keeps her eyes and ears open for the slightest comment he might make about a particular woman. I swear she takes notes. Then she invites a collection of people with those ladies included, hoping that the country air and relaxed setting will spur Tenbury into some action, preferably a proposal."

"Are you serious?"

"Absolutely. The sad thing is that one of these days Tenbury just might fall into parson's mousetrap, then I fear Arelia will continue the tradition to catch me a wife. How I dread the thought!"

"Does he know what she's doing?"

"Certainly he knows, and I'm sure he doesn't care. The summers here are less boring with people about, and not many men eschew the company of beautiful, wealthy women."

"Are they always beautiful and wealthy?"

"Most of the time. This year they certainly are. There are three here already who are surely on Arelia's list of possibilities. For one—"

"Wait," Anne interrupted. "Let me guess. Lady Mason. She is beautiful."

"And wealthy. Her late husband owned a respectable portion of Cumberland. A widow ripe for the plucking."

"Number two would be the daughter of the Earl of Haverham," Anne supplied. "I can't remember her name."

"Right again. Her name is Lady Constance Naismith. She's about twenty-five, still unmarried. They say she is mighty difficult to please, but Arelia must believe Tenbury could win her, otherwise she would not have been invited."

"That's only two," Anne finished. "I can think of no one else."

"Ah, you are forgetting Miss Pauline Redditch."

"But she's only a child!"

"She's eighteen. Old enough and pretty enough to tempt any man."

Anne found it hard to imagine Lord Tenbury married to any of these ladies, yet she suspected Arelia would not waste time inviting women he did not admire.

Within a few days the guests at Tenton Castle fell into a loose routine. Most of the gentlemen rose by mid morning and spent a leisurely breakfast, after which some went riding while others retired to the billiard room to talk or read the London papers.

The ladies rose later, seldom putting in any appearance until luncheon. Then they descended in their soft, nearly transparent muslins of saffron, pink, and turquoise to dot the Castle and the grounds with spots of bright color. During the afternoons they chatted in the salons or strolled about the broad lawns. Some made up riding parties with the gentlemen.

In the late afternoon the ladies disappeared to dress for dinner, a process that occupied several hours. Dinner was a long, formal affair involving many courses, carefully orchestrated by Lord Tenbury's excellent chef and overseen by Mrs. Saunders. After dinner there was congenial conversation in the drawing room, with several tables of cards. If the gentlemen preferred, they could escape female company in the billiard room, where they enjoyed that game, engaged in smoking, and relaxed with the best offerings of his lordship's finely stocked wine cellar.

Anne's days during this time also fell into a pattern, though hers was much simpler. She had breakfast with Belinda and Tom in the schoolroom. She then spent the entire morning with Belinda while Tom studied with Mr. Pearce.

Tom applied himself so well during the morning that he often had several hours free in the afternoon. Anne was relieved to see Mr. Pearce showing such good sense. Held too rigidly to a schedule, Tom would more than likely rebel again.

Often in the afternoons Anne accompanied the children on their adventures. Occasionally she rode with them, or she took them on long walks about the estate. On warm days she went with them to the stream and read in the shade while they swam. Jack sometimes rode or walked with them, saying he had little in common with "Arelia's set."

Other days Anne stayed in the schoolroom planning Belinda's lessons. Often she went to the library, a room seldom visited by Lord Tenbury's guests. There she would read or write letters to her old housekeeper, Mrs. Nesbitt, or her cousins' governess, Ruth Marsh. Lady Tenbury sometimes joined her, and they passed pleasant hours together, reading and talking. Anne ate her evening meal with the children and was usually in bed before ten o'clock, while the guests below were still at dinner.

Anne found great pleasure in her new gowns. She had never given much thought before to how she appeared to others, but when Belinda admired her gown, or Jack commented that a color became her, she flushed with pleasure. Looking at her reflection in a full-length glass, she tried to remember how she appeared only a few weeks ago. She had gained some weight, and there was a rosy glow to her cheeks. Now that she no longer scraped her hair back tightly, her face appeared fuller and she looked younger, she thought.

Her new-found pleasure tarnished somewhat in the shadow of the fine ladies invited to Arelia's house party. Against their costly gowns in brilliant colors, adorned with ribbons and lace, hemmed with rows of ornate flounces, her simple gowns paled. With their elegant coiffures, their wrists dripping diamonds, the fragrance of expensive Parisian scent following them lightly on the air, these women belonged to a different world. When Anne passed them on the stairs or in the hall, some greeted her and most smiled; several ignored her completely. Anne knew now that Mrs. Saunders had not been extravagant in dressing her. The dresses Anne had thought far too grand were perfectly suited to her position as governess.

Early one afternoon, returning from a walk in the home wood, Anne encountered Arelia leaving the

Castle on her way to the stables. She wore a dark blue habit trimmed in black braid, a bright blue feather from her hat curled charmingly against her shoulder.

"Dear Anne!" she exclaimed. "I declare I haven't set eyes on you for a week."

"You have been busy with your guests, ma'am."

"Busy? Run off my feet, more like. This type of gathering invariably wears the hostess to a thread. It almost makes one come to dread the summer."

"If you dread it so, why do you do it year after year?" Anne asked practically.

"Why? The answer is there, my girl." Arelia gazed off across the lawn to where Tenbury strolled along an ornamental water with Lady Mason on his arm. The dark-haired widow wore a pale peach gown that contoured her body like a glove. A delicate parasol of the same color shielded her head and her complexion from the harsh sunlight. Tenbury, however, seemed not to mind the sun, for he was bare-headed, his pale hair catching the light as he bent his head to smile at the lady.

"Look at him," Arelia continued. "He's so handsome—so much like Henry. . . . " She paused, but before Anne could reply spoke again. "He has much to offer a woman. He should marry. What he is waiting for I cannot imagine; he will be thirty-five this fall."

"Perhaps he had rather not be wed. Not all marriages are happy," Anne offered.

"True. Yet he has a responsibility. He needs an heir."

"But surely Tom—"

Arelia shook her head, interrupting Anne in mid sentence. "No. This is not what I expect for Thomas. Henry and I had property in Kent. It's there for Tom when he needs it." She looked past Tenbury and his companion to the expanse of park and forest beyond. "All this should go to Tenbury's son. That's the way it has been for generations; that's the way it should be. . . . Dear me. I must go. Lord Wilmington is waiting."

As Arelia bid farewell and hurried off, Anne turned and entered the Castle, making her way to the library. Lady Tenbury was there. Anne greeted her and moved directly to the shelves, searching for a specific book.

"Will you read to me today?" her ladyship asked.

"Certainly, my lady. What should you like to hear?" Anne found the volume she sought and began paging through it.

"What do you have there?" Lady Tenbury asked.

Anne smiled and crossed the room to sit near the countess. "*The Odyssey*. I was just speaking outside with Mrs. Saunders."

When she paused, Lady Tenbury encouraged, "About?"

"About marriage," Anne replied. Continuing to turn pages, she did not notice how Lady Tenbury's brows rose with interest. "Homer has some thoughts about marriage," Anne said. "Ah! Here it is." She read aloud:

"May the gods grant you all things which your heart desires, and may they give you a husband and a home and gracious concord, for there is nothing greater and better than this—when a husband and wife keep a household in oneness of mind, a great woe to their enemies and joy to their friends, and win high renown."

"I think that very true," her ladyship said when Anne had finished. "Don't you find it appealing? My marriage was so."

Anne smiled, "I can believe *your* marriage was, Lady Tenbury, for you are 'gracious concord' itself."

"La, child! You flatter me. Whose marriage were you discussing—yours or Arelia's?"

"Actually, Arelia was discussing Lord Tenbury's marriage."

"I see," her ladyship responded. "I, too, would like to see him happily wed. I think most mothers wish to see their children comfortably settled. But I am not anxious that he be in a rush."

"Do your children need to marry for you to consider them settled or happy?" Anne asked.

"I think companionship and commitment are important. Loneliness can be overwhelming. I felt it keenly when my husband died. Thank the Lord I had three strong sons to help fill the void."

And one of those is already gone, Anne thought to herself.

"But you did not answer my question earlier, Anne," the countess said. "Do you find Homer's concept of marriage appealing?"

"I suppose so. I have never thought much about marriage. All the years I lived with Papa, I readily accepted my life with him. By the time he was gone, it seemed to me that any opportunity for marriage was long past." Anne was gazing steadily out the window, an almost forlorn expression in her eyes.

Very quietly Lady Tenbury said. "Allow me to quote you a bit of the same *Odyssey* you hold: 'Surely these things lie on the knees of the gods.'"

The unhappy squeal of a cat—close followed by a pitiful wail from Belinda—brought Anne instantly to her feet and to the partially open library door. Belinda was sprawled across the floor of the front hall, her calico kitten gripped tightly in her outstretched hands. Towering above her with a look of mingled disgust and reproach was Lady Mason, still on Lord Tenbury's arm. Clearly the woman and the child had collided; to Anne's eyes, Belinda had come off the worst.

By the time Anne covered the few steps to the scene, Tenbury had lifted Belinda to her feet. He carefully peeled the frightened kitten from her clothing and handed it to Anne. Belinda shrank timidly against Anne's skirts when her eyes encountered the scowling visage of Lady Mason.

Seeing that Belinda's instinctive apology had frozen on her lips, Anne said, "I am sure Belinda is most sorry, my lady. She must have been chasing the kitten and didn't see you."

Lady Mason, without acknowledging Anne's apology or even looking at Belinda, turned to Tenbury and said, "What one most dreads about coming to the country is the necessity of encountering children. With what governesses are paid these days, you might think they would at least be able to keep the urchins out from underfoot. I realize this must be your niece, Tenbury, but don't you agree that children should be confined to the nursery?"

Anne stood with the kitten clutched to her breast, one arm about Belinda's shoulders, as she listened with unbelieving ears to this speech. She could do nothing more than stare at the lady, totally at a loss for words even had she been able to summon the courage to utter them. Her eyes moved from Lady Mason to Tenbury, whom she found regarding her with a stern expression. Unable to withstand his scrutiny, she dropped her gaze to the floor. Tenbury answered Lady Mason's question after only the slightest pause.

"I don't agree at all. I believe children should be wherever their adventurous feet carry them. Within reason, of course." He reached down and took Belinda's chin in his hand, tipping up her tear-stained face. "I think your kitten has had enough excitement for one day, Belinda. Perhaps it would be best if you took her outside to play."

The child was smiling as Anne escorted her out the door and down the steps. Anne was grateful that the earl made so little of the incident, but she was prepared to pity both Belinda and Tom if Lady Mason ever became the next Countess of Tenbury.

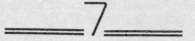

7

Early the following afternoon, dressed demurely in her gray gown and straw bonnet, Anne set off to walk to the village. There had been a cloudburst during the early hours of the morning, but it had cleared away, leaving blue skies with thin white clouds above. Near the puddles left by the rain, house martins were busily collecting mud for their nests. Along the hedgerows Anne noticed the frail wild roses in bloom, while in the fields beyond, the farmers were busy cutting the first hay of the season. The sweet scent of freshly mown clover greeted Anne on a gentle northerly breeze. Further on she recognized a patch of blackberries in blossom—she would bring Belinda to pick them later in the summer.

She was nearly halfway to the village when Tenbury overtook her in his curricle. He pulled his pair to a standstill beside her. "Well met, Miss Waverly. I have been wanting a word with you. Are you on your way to the village? Let me drive you."

"Thank you, sir, but—"

"I know, you prefer to walk. Unfortunately it is difficult to conduct a conversation between a carriage and the ground." By a quick count he realized this was the fourth time she had refused to drive with him. Nettled, he was in no mood to indulge her.

"Perhaps we could speak another time, my lord."

"The present time is most convenient for me, Miss Waverly."

When she still hesitated, he added. "May I add that I am not accustomed to having persons in my employ gainsay me, ma'am. Please get into the carriage."

The groom jumped down, vacating his seat. Anne unhappily took the hand Tenbury held down to her.

As Murdock set off back to the Castle, Tenbury put his horses in motion, and Anne summoned all her willpower to calm her anxiety. She had just finished luncheon . . . she must not allow herself to be ill now.

"Could you let the horses walk, my lord? The day is so pleasant."

He cast a sideways glance at her. Her face had lost its color, and her eyes were dull. Suddenly suspicious he asked, "Do you fear open carriages? You need not. I've been driving more than twenty years and have yet to kill a passenger." Then remembering one day long ago and feeling the need to be totally honest he said, "There was a broken arm once . . . Henry." When she turned her horrified gaze to him he added, "But we were racing recklessly, and the pair we had that day were never so steady as these. What do you need in the village?"

"Sewing needles," she replied.

"You won't have much to choose from here. I will drive you to Winthrop. There you will have an excellent selection." Then, without consulting Anne, he turned eastward at the crossroad and proceeded toward Winthrop, a town some three miles distant.

He smiled at her continued silence, trying to think of a way to relax her. "This is the pair I most often drive in London. Steady as they come. Nothing disturbs them—carriage horns, sheep. I've had birds rise up under their noses, and they never broke stride. See what a smooth trot they have?" He allowed the pair to trot, and the increased speed caused a correlating decrease in Anne's equilibrium.

"Please stop the carriage, my lord," she whispered at length. "I must get down." Before he could respond or reply she reached forward to grasp the reins in front of his hands, pulling back with all her strength. The horses, moving at an extended trot, were brought up short by this brutal usage. Both stopped almost immediately, the near one rearing onto his haunches in protest. Taken totally by surprise, Tenbury was busy for some moments in calming his outraged pair. He noticed only that Miss Waverly leaped from the carriage before it had completely stopped, forced her way through the hedges at the side of the road, and disappeared.

When the horses were finally quiet, Tenbury glanced in the direction Miss Waverly had gone. There was no sign of her.

"Miss Waverly," he called, "Are you all right? I cannot leave the horses."

When there was no answer, he called again, "Miss Waverly!"

"Give me but a moment, my lord."

When she finally emerged from the hedges, she appeared even paler than before. She stopped at the side of the carriage, refusing to look at him. "With your permission, Lord Tenbury, I should like to walk back to the Castle."

He had been prepared to rip up at her for mishandling his horses, but one look at her pale countenance drove all anger from him. "Why didn't you tell me you suffered from motion sickness?"

"It isn't the sort of thing one advertises. 'How do you do. I suffer from motion sickness.'"

He smiled. "Of course not, but when I insisted, surely you could have said something."

He jumped down from the curricle then and went to the horses' heads. "Shall we walk on to Winthrop? It's only a little more than a mile, and I happen to know you are a vigorous walker."

She took the free arm he offered her for support, and they continued down the relatively deserted country lane. Occasionally they passed a farmer's cart or a lone horseman, but if anyone thought it unusual for them to be walking when they had such a slap-up rig to drive, no one indicated as much. They just smiled or nodded as they went on their way.

"It's nothing to be ashamed of," he said.

"Isn't it? Well, I *have* been ashamed of it. All my life."

"You've been troubled always? Since childhood?"

"Yes."

"Like as not you don't really suffer from it anymore; your illness could be learned."

"I'm not sure I understand what you mean."

"The very real fear you had as a child manifested itself in the sickness," he explained. "After a time you became so accustomed to the two things going together—the motion and the illness—that once the fear was gone, the illness stayed on, more from habit than for any physical reason."

"Are you saying the problem is only in my mind?"

"I'm saying it could be, and if it is, it could be cured. All those times you refused to drive with me—this was your reason?"

"Yes."

"And the day you arrived at Tenton, your illness then was due to the same thing?"

"Things were rather worse that day for I hadn't eaten."

"Hadn't eaten that day?"

"Hadn't eaten for the entire trip."

"What foolishness! Better to eat moderately and cast up your accounts if you must, than to starve yourself to the point of fainting. I believe you refine too much upon this. I have seen men sick with fear before a battle and sick with horror afterward. Our bodies betray us from time to time. There is no cause for shame in that."

When they arrived in Winthrop, Anne made her purchase while Tenbury waited for her in the street outside. As she emerged from the shop, he said, "There is a posting inn at the edge of the town that has tolerable food. I think you should have another lunch."

Anne was inclined to object until she realized she was truly hungry. They walked together to the Duck 'N' Drake where an ostler took the horses and Tenbury ordered a private parlor and a simple meal.

"This can't be prudent, sir," Anne objected. "Won't people think it odd?"

"They will think I have driven my niece's governess to town for some needles and have stopped to eat. I am well known here, Miss Waverly. My credit can withstand a simple luncheon and a drive, or rather walk, in broad daylight."

They shared a shepherd's pie followed by a bowl of strawberries and fresh cream. Since the maid serving them was often in the room, they had little opportunity for conversation during their short meal.

The curricle was at the door as they stepped from the inn into the street. Tenbury looked up to the sky where the thinly scattered clouds were once again thickening.

"It appears as if we may have more rain," he said.

Anne glanced anxiously at the clouds, thinking of the long walk home that lay before her. Tenbury extended a hand to her and she raised questioning brows.

"Allow me to hand you up, madam. I promise a sedate walk every step of the way home and an instant stop should you require one."

With this assurance, Anne climbed into the carriage, and they were soon on their way back to Tenton Castle.

"You are already worried about parting with the lunch you just consumed," he said before they had gone a hundred yards.

She turned toward him in surprise, her thigh contacting his on the seat. "How did you know?"

"It's elementary. When you enter a carriage, any carriage, the first thing you think of is the illness you have suffered in the past. You worry it will happen again. That worry sets your nerves on edge, tenses every muscle in your body, and leads you to make yourself sick. I have promised to walk the horses. Forget your luncheon, as you have long forgotten your fear of carriages. Instead, enjoy the scenery, the fresh air, my excellent company, and witty conversation. If you will but relax, I believe your illness will vanish."

Wanting to believe he was right, Anne tried to do as he asked. The day continued pleasant, for even though the clouds thickened, the rain held off.

"When we met earlier, I mentioned there was something I wished to discuss with you," Tenbury said. "I feel I should apologize for Lady Mason's behavior yesterday."

"It is not your place to apologize for her, my lord."

"No. It's not. But I am certain she will never do so herself, and I am convinced you are owed an apology. I know this will probably be hard for you to understand, but she doesn't even realize she said anything offensive. Many women of her class—our class—disparage children and governesses. Such comments are commonly heard and widely accepted."

"That doesn't make them right."

"No. Yet I doubt you or I will be able to do much to change things. So I apologize for her tactlessness and hope you can make allowance for it and put it behind you."

It was on the tip of her tongue to ask what he

could possibly admire about such a woman, but she realized how inappropriate the question would be.

"Arelia tells me that Belinda is doing well in her studies," he continued. "What of Tom? Have he and Mr. Pearce made progress?"

"Yes. You made the perfect choice in Mr. Pearce. He is a natural teacher, most sensitive to Tom's . . . moods."

"Is he often moody?"

"Not always. The last few days he has seemed rather restless, though."

"Tomorrow is June eighteenth," Tenbury said. "Three years since Waterloo. That's where Henry died."

"I see."

Anne was quiet for some time afterward, and Tenbury didn't interrupt her thoughts. As they turned onto the drive of the Castle, he spoke at last. "We are home, and now I will ask: Did you feel the least ill on the way?"

"Not at all. But you kept me talking. I had no time to think of it."

"Precisely. You had no time to think. I will take you up again some day. I expect you will soon discover that your motion sickness is a thing of the past."

Later the same evening, Anne spent nearly an hour in the schoolroom reading through one of the Greek histories her father had translated. Finally she found the passage she sought. Taking a quill and paper, she copied the words, then blotted the page carefully.

When she went to Tom's room, she found him in bed but not yet asleep. "Could I talk with you a moment?" she asked.

He nodded and she came to sit on the edge of the bed. "Tomorrow is the eighteenth," she said, "but I imagine you know that." When he only nodded again, she continued. "I was wondering if you would take me tomorrow to visit your father's grave. I thought since it was the anniversary, and I have never been there . . . I would like to go."

"All right. I suppose I could take you there."

"Good. There is something else. I have been in the schoolroom searching for something I remembered reading once. I found it and copied it out for you. It was written by the Greek historian, Thucydides, several hundred years before the birth of Christ. I should like you to read it tonight before you go to sleep." She handed him the page as she rose from the bed. "Good night, Tom. Sleep well."

"Good night, Miss Waverly."

When the door had closed behind her, Tom unfolded the paper.

Fix your eyes on the greatness of Athens as you have it before you day by day, fall in love with her, and when you feel her great, remember that this greatness was won by men with courage, with knowledge of their duty, and with a sense of honor in action . . . So they gave their bodies to the commonwealth and received, each for his own memory, praise that will never die, and with it the grandest of all sepulchers, not that in which their mortal bones are laid, but a home in the minds of men, where their glory remains free to stir to speech or action as the occasion comes by. For the whole earth is the sepulcher of famous men; and their story is not graven only on stone over their native earth, but lives on far away, without visible symbol, woven into the stuff of other men's lives. For you now it remains to rival what they have done and, knowing the secret of happiness to be freedom and the secret of freedom a brave heart, not idly to stand aside from the enemy's onset.

Tenbury and Arelia descended the front steps side by side. "Where were you after luncheon?"

he asked. "Miss Redditch searched everywhere for you. She said you had agreed to show her the Roman ruins."

"Oh, dear," Arelia responded. "I completely forgot about her, but I must be forgiven, Nate. You cannot imagine my shock when Tom asked me to accompany him and Miss Waverly on a visit to Henry's grave. To my knowledge, Thomas has never been there, so I was quite taken aback."

"Did you go?"

"Certainly, I did. It was a moment of some revelation. He's growing up too fast, Tenbury. There is so much of Henry in him, yet he is nothing like Henry. . . . Do you understand what I mean?"

He paused halfway down the steps, pulling on his riding gloves. "Yes, I believe I do, though it sounds antithetical when you phrase it just so."

"I can't help thinking Miss Waverly is in some part responsible for this change in Tom," Arelia said. "I believe it was a fortunate day for us when she applied for her position."

"I couldn't agree with you more. Did you leave Tom and Miss Waverly at the cemetery?"

"No. We walked together to the summer house, and they went on to the lake. Tom offered to take Miss Waverly boating. Here comes Lady Naismith. I don't believe I have ever seen a woman sit a horse so well."

They both watched as Lady Constance Naismith trotted her black gelding toward them from the stables. She was twenty-five but looked younger. Being the Earl of Haverham's only child, she had been cosseted from birth. Her beauty she took for granted. Her red hair was drawn back from her face and fastened in the nape of her neck, but already tiny curls had escaped to bounce against her shoulders in the breeze. Her riding habit of emerald green hugged the generous curves of both hip and breast, accentuating her excellent figure and perfect posture.

Gold braid in double rows adorned the lapels, cuffs, and hem, while peeking from beneath her skirts a shiny silver spur glinted on her left heel. The horse fussed, and she flowed gently with him, as if anticipating his motion instinctively.

Tenbury could not fail to appreciate the picture she presented as he first helped Arelia to the saddle, then turned to mount his sleek bay. Bringing his horse up beside Lady Naismith, he asked, "Can that piece of flash jump, or is he strictly a park horse?"

She smiled saucily and quipped in reply, "He will jump higher and run faster than that brute you bestride, my lord."

One of the gentlemen who had just joined the party laughed at this, asking Lady Naismith if she would favor a small wager to support her claim. Tenbury listened with only half an ear. Far across the meadow toward the lake, he saw a tiny figure emerge from the wood, and began running toward the Castle. He watched a few seconds longer, then said to Arelia, "Take the party and be on your way, Arelia. I will catch up."

When she looked a question, he only shook his head and motioned for her to be off. She did as he asked, while he set his horse in the other direction, toward the ever-growing figure that he now recognized as his nephew. As the horse and boy converged in the meadow, Tenbury realized his instinct had been correct—Tom was running with a purpose. In a few seconds they were within hailing distance.

"Uncle Nate," Tom yelled breathlessly. "I . . . need you . . . at the lake . . . the boat . . . overturned . . . she can't swim."

There was no need for Tom to say who *she* was. A cold fear enveloped Tenbury as he slowed his horse and reached down to haul the boy up behind him. "Did she stay with the boat?" he demanded. "Is she holding on?"

"Yes. But she's frightened; she wouldn't let me help her."

"You did the right thing, Tom. Coming for help was the right thing."

Tenbury didn't speak again as the bay thundered at full speed across the meadow and through the thinly spaced trees surrounding the lake. The boat had overturned in deep water perhaps two hundred feet from shore. Anne was perfectly still, gripping the keel with both hands, holding her head and shoulders above the water.

Tenbury and Tom came off the horse together. All Tenbury said was, "Hold the stallion, Tom," as he pulled off one boot, then the other. His coat followed, landing in the reeds near the shore as he waded waist deep before swimming out to the boat.

When he reached it, he too took hold with both hands to rest from his exertion. He moved closer to Anne in the water, but she showed no sign of having noticed his arrival. Her eyes were closed, and she was gripping the keel so tightly that her fingers had turned white.

He tried to speak as casually as he could for clearly the woman was terrified. "Miss Waverly. If you will let go now, I can take you to shore."

She opened her eyes and looked at him. "My lord, I seem to be in a dangerous situation."

"Not anymore. Let go the keel, and I will swim you to shore." He moved his hand to cover her fingers, thinking he might remove them for her. To his amazement he was unable to budge them. They seemed fused to the boat bottom.

"Miss Waverly . . . Anne. Remember how you overcame your fear of the carriage? I want you to do that now. Look at me."

When she did so, he said, "I want you to relax as you did then. Do you remember the day I carried you up the stairs at the Castle? You were very light. You will be even lighter in the water. Please trust me. Let go of the boat."

He put an arm around her waist from behind and pulled her back. When she contacted his solid body behind her, she leaned against him, then finally freed the keel.

"You can help most by remaining as still as possible," he said. "Try not to move."

That should be easy enough for her, he thought, since her limbs had to be numb from shock and the effects of the cold water. She cooperated as well as he could wish, and before long he felt his feet touch the soft mud of the lake bottom. With his arm around her they struggled through the water until they were waist deep. He then lifted her and her soggy, clinging skirts free of the surface and carried her to the shore.

As he continued to carry her beyond the shore line, she finally spoke. "You may put me down now, Lord Tenbury."

"I will carry you to the Castle."

"It's more than a quarter mile to the Castle, sir."

"I can rest if I need to."

"Please put me down," she insisted, struggling in his arms.

When he ignored her, she snapped, "Why do you always insist on using your superior strength to get your own way?"

In that instant he lowered her to the ground. As soon as she stood steadily, he removed his arm from her shoulders.

"Do I do that?" he asked.

"Invariably."

"You're cold."

"In which case walking will warm me. It is June, not November."

Tom, who had stood holding the horse and his breath while his uncle effected Miss Waverly's rescue, now remained silent, not understanding the meaning behind the angry exchange of words.

Without speaking again, Tenbury moved to where he had dropped his boots and pulled them on with difficulty. He then fetched his coat, tossed it over his horse's withers and mounted. His fine lawn shirt was plastered to his powerful torso, but the lady was in no mood to admire his musculature as he rode his horse to within a few feet of where she stood.

"If you have no further need of my services, madam, I will bid you good day."

Turning his attention to Tom he said, "You did well, Tom, and should be proud of your quick thinking. Perhaps you should accompany Miss Waverly to the Castle. I predict she will have difficulty walking with those wet skirts."

Tenbury turned his horse again and cantered off in the direction of the stables.

When his lordship's valet was summoned to lay out dry clothes, he exclaimed at Lord Tenbury's condition.

"What happened, my lord?"

"I have been rescuing a damsel in distress, Hadley, but I fear most of the distress has been mine."

"How is that, sir?"

"I am, as you see, soaked to the skin. I have ruined these buckskins and most likely this shirt as well. But most distressing of all, I have missed an opportunity to race my Orion against Lady Naismith's black gelding."

"I can see how you could feel cheated, my lord," Hadley replied, handing Tenbury a towel with which to dry himself. "But these situations often have compensations. Surely the lady you rescued has pledged her undying gratitude?"

"On the contrary, my dear Hadley. The lady, I regret to say, did not even thank me."

8

When Tenbury finished dressing, he went downstairs to the library. It would be some time before the riding party returned. He felt no desire whatsoever to join them.

He took a newspaper to a comfortable armchair near the windows, yet found his thoughts too troubled to concentrate. He was trying to imagine the Duke of Chadwicke's reaction had Miss Waverly managed to drown herself today. Tenbury knew the duke well enough to know that no excuse would be acceptable if any harm came to the woman while she was in Tenbury's care.

"She's a plaguey nuisance," he mumbled, then mentally counted the days till the end of his responsibility for her. Her accusation that he dealt unfairly from a position of strength rankled, but he was far from willing to admit she could be right.

He was still in the library half an hour later when laughter sounded in the hall outside before the doors opened to admit Jack and Anne. Their laughter ceased abruptly as Tenbury rose from his chair.

Anne had changed her sodden gown for one of soft blue. Since her hair was wet, she had gathered it simply with a broad ribbon at the base of her neck. It hung in damp waves down her back. She put her hands to the ribbon now, wishing her hair was properly dressed.

"You see, Jack, that you were wrong," she said uncomfortably. "We *did* meet someone."

"Only Tenbury," Jack answered irreverently.

"We came down the back stairs," Anne explained, "certain we would meet no one. I apologize—"

"No need," Tenbury cut her short. "I am not offended by loose hair. It's rather lovely, in fact."

"So I told her," Jack agreed. "When she said it would take hours to dry, I told her it would be silly to sit in her room on such a day." Walking to the long windows that opened onto the terrace, he set one slightly ajar, allowing the warm breeze to invade the room.

As Jack walked away, Anne took a few steps closer to Tenbury and said quietly, "I didn't thank you earlier for helping me; you must think me ragmannered."

"I think you were overwrought at the moment, ma'am. One can be forgiven certain lapses at such a time."

"You are generous, sir. Nevertheless, I should like you to know that I appreciated your help."

"To a point."

She looked past him to where Jack, seemingly ignoring them, had taken up Tenbury's paper and begun reading.

"You're right. I do not like people to do for me what I am capable of doing myself."

"And you are most capable, Miss Waverly, are you not?"

She drew herself up. "I like to think I am."

"Then I suggest that if you intend to pursue boating, you should learn first to swim. It is a skill everyone should possess. If you will excuse me, it is time I dressed for dinner."

When he had gone, Anne and Jack talked together for nearly an hour before Anne excused herself to go speak with Mrs. Saunders. She found her dressing for dinner as well.

"Do you remember the day at the stream when you offered to teach me to swim?"

"Yes, of course."

"Were you serious?"

Arelia turned from a perusal of her hair in the looking glass to confront Anne directly. "Certainly, I was serious. Why? Do you wish to learn?"

"Yes. Very much." Anne then related the incident with Thomas at the lake. Arelia paled at the telling.

"Dear Anne," she said, when Anne had finished. "You could have drowned."

"I suppose I could have just after we capsized. But Tom was so clever. The moment my head came above water, he was there to grasp my hand and lead it to the boat. Once I had hold of it, believe me, I had no intention of letting go. We were far from shore, and Tom could see I was terrified, so he swam back and ran for help. He was so brave; I am proud of him."

"No less am I, and so I shall tell him."

"Lord Tenbury told him he had done exactly as he ought."

"That should have pleased Tom," Arelia approved. "Tenbury is as close to a father as the boy is ever likely to have."

"Why do you say so? You might marry again."

"Perhaps. But I have found there is a problem when you have had a ten-year marriage to a good man. You find yourself comparing each suitor to what you had before; invariably they are found lacking." In an abrupt change of topic, a habit Anne had learned to expect of Mrs. Saunders, Arelia said, "When shall we begin the lessons? If it is as warm tomorrow as it was today, we will meet at the stream. I am engaged to ride with Lord Wilmington after luncheon. Shall we say two o'clock?" She didn't wait for an answer as she forged ahead. "I must warn the children to stay away. It will be our private time. All right?"

"Yes. It would be wonderful; if you're certain you can leave your friends."

"I love to swim. And I must admit I am already tiring of our guests. It will be good to get away from them." Arelia soon hurried off, declaring she would be late for dinner.

Anne went slowly back to her own room, hoping the following day would be a fine one. Having faced her fear of carriages, and feeling she was well on her way to overcoming her difficulties with them, she was eager to tackle her incompetence in water.

The next day was warmer than the previous one had been. Anne and Arelia met at the appointed time and at Arelia's suggestion stripped down to their chemises in order to have maximum mobility in the water.

"There is no one to see, and even if someone did happen along, we are decent enough in these so long as we stay in the water."

Anne knew this to be true. In the water they were completely covered in white from neck to ankle. Once out of the water, however, she hurried to reclaim her clothes, for a wet chemise adhering to the skin was considerably revealing. After the first day, when she had been anxious for fear they might be seen, Anne relaxed somewhat, and by the third lesson she had gained enough confidence to sit with Arelia in the sun until their underclothes were dry. Only then would they resume their gowns and return to the Castle.

Anne recognized that her "lessons" were far from what she considered a lesson should be. Much of the time she and Arelia were together they would simply talk, or paddle playfully in the water. Yet she realized that as the days passed she was actually learning.

If she wanted an example of a true lesson, she

had only to sit in on one of Mr. Dennis Pearce's sessions with Thomas. Not only was the man adept at dealing with children, he was an accomplished teacher and a brilliant scholar as well. Often, when the children were finished for the day, he and Anne talked for hours about the history and literature they both loved. She soon learned that his grasp of the classics was almost as broad as her father's had been; he soon learned that she could step in and take over his Latin class with Thomas if need be. He was continually amazed at the scope of her education.

"I have never known a woman who could do more than quote a few words in Latin. You should be proud of your knowledge of the language."

"I do well enough. Yet I believe I would trade some of my proficiency in language for a tiny bit of musical talent. I have started Belinda on the pianoforte, but it won't be long before she knows as much as I do."

"Perhaps I could help," he offered. "I play."

She looked her surprise. "You do?"

"Yes. Does Belinda like music? Will she practice?"

"I believe so. She has set to with a will on the simple things I have given her so far. How is it that you learned to play?"

"My mother played beautifully," he said. "I remember many an evening as a young boy, listening to her until I fell asleep in one of the big chairs near the parlor fire. When my sisters took lessons, I asked to take them, too. Neither of my parents objected. When I went away to school, I continued to study."

"Will you play for me sometime?"

"I don't know how appropriate it would be."

"We need not use the pianoforte in the grand salon. There is another at the far end of the east wing. Didn't you know? It was placed there to keep monotonous practice from bothering the family and guests. It is almost as fine an instrument as the other and is perfectly tuned."

From the day Mr. Pearce learned of the pianoforte in the remote corner of the Castle, he often went there in his spare time to play, while Anne occasionally followed to sit and listen. His was a talent she had always jealously coveted, but one for which she had no skill. She had often of an evening heard the lady guests singing and playing after dinner for the assembled company. All their efforts paled into insignificance when compared with the exceptional talent of Mr. Pearce.

The warm days of early summer passed pleasantly for Anne. She enjoyed her governess duties and the time she spent with both Dennis and Jack. She shared adventures with the children. She continued to read to Lady Tenbury, and had womanly discussions with Arelia that were like nothing she had ever experienced, for she had never had a close female friend near her own age before.

One Wednesday morning she and Belinda finished their lessons early. They planned to ride before luncheon with Mrs. Saunders, so she could see for herself how Belinda's horsemanship was improving. When they arrived at the stables, however, they were greeted by an apologetic Murdock. He had Belinda's pony and Mrs. Saunders's mare saddled and ready, but Anne's horse was still in his stall.

"I don't believe you'll be wanting to take him out, Miss Waverly," the groom said. "He's winded and has been hard used."

By this time they all stood beside the loose box that housed Anne's brown gelding. He was heavily sweated over the neck and shoulders and in the flank. As he turned in the stall, a collection of welts were visible on his left side.

Anne drew in her breath in dismay while Arelia exclaimed, "What is the meaning of this, Murdock? This horse has been cruelly spurred. Who is responsible?"

" 'Twas Lady Naismith, Mrs. Saunders. Her black

came in lame yesterday, and she ordered me to saddle Miss Waverly's gelding for her this morning. I told her Miss Waverly would be needing the horse herself, but she made little of that. Said she would have him back in plenty of time. I didn't know what I should do, ma'am. I had orders from his lordship to do as his guests asked, within reason. Her ladyship being such a bruising rider, I never imagined she would treat a horse so. She never did so to her black. Though I've seen her wear the spur, there has never been a mark on him, I swear."

Anne spoke for the first time. "She would have no need to spur the black, Murdock. He is a horse of great spirit. My Brownie is only an old friend. My father bought him for his temperament, not his speed. Though he jumps willingly, he has never been fast nor particularly strong. No doubt her ladyship found him a lackluster mount."

She had moved into the stall and was gently stroking the neck of her weary, mistreated horse. Although Anne was distressed, she didn't feel she had any right to criticize one of Lord Tenbury's guests. Arelia was not so circumspect. When Tenbury rode into the stable yard a few minutes later, she beckoned him to them and wasted no time in giving her opinion of Lady Naismith's behavior.

"It's unforgivable, Tenbury. She had no right to take the horse without permission, but to abuse him is the outside of enough."

Tenbury inspected the horse carefully. "I think with a few days rest and some light exercise, he will be fine," Tenbury announced. "There should be no scarring from the spur, though I agree there can be no excuse for such cruelty. Saddle Zephyr for Miss Waverly, Murdock. She hasn't been out for a few days and could use the exercise." Then to Anne he added, "It's sometimes hard to break her cleanly from a walk to a canter, but otherwise she is easy to handle. You will have no problem with her. I promise you nothing like this will happen again."

Tenbury followed Murdock to another stall where the groom began saddling a handsome chestnut. They spoke quietly for a few moments before Tenbury left the stables.

Anne enjoyed her ride on the well-mannered mare, and Arelia was impressed by the progress Belinda had made. Toward the end of their ride the skies began to cloud over; they barely made it home in time to avoid a drenching.

The rain continued throughout the day. Anne kept to her room and the schoolroom, but by evening found herself restless. She went downstairs to the library and found Jack there.

"The weather has driven all of Arelia's guests indoors," he complained. "This afternoon I narrowly escaped being a fourth at Mrs. Overset's whist table. Tonight it's silver loo!"

"Poor Jack. Shall I read to you from where Tom interrupted us yesterday? It was Ben Jonson, remember?"

"Yes, I remember. Something about drinking."

She scowled at him. "It was not about drinking. It was metaphorical."

"Whatever you say. Though by now you should know you're wasting your time. You will never improve my mind; it is past hope."

She ignored him and began where they had been reading last:

> Drink to me only with thine eyes,
> And I will pledge with mine;
> Or leave a kiss but in the cup
> And I'll not look for wine.
> The thirst that from the soul doth rise
> Doth ask a drink divine;
> But might I of Jove's nectar sup,
> I would not change for thine.

"More about kissing," Jack said, when she had finished. "It seems everything we read lately has to do with kissing. What was that line the other day? 'Give me a kiss and to that kiss a score,' and so on into the hundreds, wasn't it?"

"Yes."

"And then there was that piece of Swift," he continued. "How did it go?"

" 'Lord, I wonder what fool it was that first invented kissing!' " Anne quoted.

"Yes, that was it," Jack agreed. "Have you ever noticed how much is written about kissing?"

Anne nodded. "I never thought much about it in classic literature, but even in novels there seems to be a great deal."

"You read novels?" he asked.

"Your mother lent me several of hers."

"My *mother* reads novels?"

"Yes. Shouldn't she?"

"I suppose she may if she likes. I just never thought . . . Why is it, do you think, that one can never imagine one's parents being passionate? You know—kissing, and so forth?"

"I don't know, but you're right. If I try to think of my father in that light . . . it seems quite ridiculous. Though I must admit, I'm not much of an authority on passion and such."

"Nor am I."

"You must at least know about kissing," she insisted. "You have certainly done some."

"Of course, I have . . . some. Haven't you?"

"No. None . . . never. There was never anyone. No men; at least, none who ever tried."

"Do you wish there had been?"

"Truthfully? Yes. It's rather depressing to read year after year about passion, kissing in particular, and not have the slightest notion what it's like. It's even more depressing to think I may live my whole life and never have the experience."

"I find that difficult to believe," he said.

"Why do you? I'm twenty-eight years old, Jack. I'm not likely to marry. So—"

"If you'd like, I could."

"Could what?"

"Kiss you."

"Kiss me?"

"Yes, if you like. I'm not an expert, but I've done my share." He moved his hand to the side of her face, gently tucking a stray curl behind her ear. "I think I should rather like to kiss you. It would be an honor. Could we dispense with these spectacles?" he asked, as he gently removed them and set them aside.

"I need them for reading—"

"We won't be reading just now."

Their eyes met as his hand slid to cup her chin and turn her face up to his. His mouth was warm and tender, and she knew in that first instant that kissing deserved all the praise it received inside literature and out. It was wonderfully unique—an indefinable sensation unparalleled by anything she had ever experienced before. As her untrained lips parted beneath the pressure of his, his kiss deepened and his hands moved against her back, pulling her closer.

This idyll was brutally interrupted by Tenbury's brusque voice from the doorway, "It's past your bedtime, Jack, isn't it?"

The couple drew apart. Neither of them spoke and Tenbury soon continued, "When I gave you the run of the house, Miss Waverly, I did not expect you would forget your place in it."

Jack rose to his feet, a flush of anger in his cheeks. "There is no call for that remark, Nate. You have not the least notion what's happening here."

Tenbury answered with a sarcastic smile. "*Au contraire*, my dear brother. It is quite obvious."

Anne rose to leave, knowing it would be impossible

for her to voice a reasonable explanation of their behavior in the face of Tenbury's disapproval. She had best leave it to Jack to explain.

Jack took her arm to detain her. "You need not go."

"I wish to."

He smiled. "All right. But don't forget your book."

As he held it out to her, she hesitated. "It's his lordship's."

"Tenbury won't miss it," Jack insisted. "Take it with you. I'll see you tomorrow. I enjoyed our talk tonight."

When she was gone, he turned on his brother. "Why do you treat her so? She is as well born as we."

"Only on her father's side. Her mother's family included any number of dirty dishes. Truly, Jack, don't you think she's a trifle old for you."

"Are you interested in hearing an explanation of what you saw?" Jack parried.

"I'm sure any explanation you had to offer would be vastly amusing, but I don't need you to explain a scene a child could understand."

Jack turned away and strode angrily toward the door. Tenbury's next comment stopped him with his hand on the knob. "I only intend to say this once, Jack. I won't have any dependent under my roof abused, coerced, or deceived by a member of my family."

Jack's only answer was to slam the door, leaving his brother alone in the library.

What was Jack playing at? Tenbury wondered. Despite his warning, he had never considered his younger brother the kind of man who would take advantage of a governess's vulnerable position within the household. But if it wasn't that, then what? Could Jack be seriously attracted to Miss Waverly? She was four years older than Jack.... Still ...

Tenbury could only hope that the Duke of Chadwicke would conclude this business promptly before the situation with Miss Waverly grew any more complex.

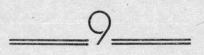

9

The rain continued through the night and into the next day. Arelia stopped in the schoolroom as Anne and Belinda were finishing their lessons.

"I should like you to bring Belinda to the drawing room tonight after dinner," Arelia said. "Several of our guests have asked to see her, so I thought she should put in an appearance. She need not stay long."

"I shall be happy to bring her down. Is there anything special you would like her to wear?" Anne asked.

"Perhaps the pink, with the lace ruching?"

"She looks well in that," Anne agreed.

Arelia soon left and made her way toward the housekeeper's room via one of the narrow back stairways. On the first floor landing she paused, cocking her head to one side as she listened attentively. Barely perceptible strains of music drifted on the still air. Forgetting the housekeeper and the menus for the moment, Arelia moved down the corridor toward the little-used east wing of the Castle. The volume of the music increased as she advanced. It was soon discernible as a piano sonata, a piece unfamiliar to her, yet as beautiful as any she had ever heard.

She paused at the closed door of the parlor, not wishing to disturb the pianist. Yet as she listened to the well-executed piece, she became more and more curious to know which of her guests possessed such proficiency. She opened the door silently, regarding her son's tutor with almost equal amounts of amazement and admiration.

She was slightly to the side and behind him, yet he must have sensed her presence, for he glanced up, then stopped playing abruptly as he saw who stood there. He pushed back the bench and rose. Her lemon-yellow gown seemed to bring daylight into the darkly paneled, heavily draped room. He had the fanciful impression that her golden hair was itself a ray of sunshine.

She advanced immediately to protest. "No! Please don't stop. It's beautiful. I have never heard it before."

"It is Mozart. A lesser-known piece."

"And more difficult to play than some," Arelia added. "Please sit down," she encouraged. "I will sit myself, then you may be comfortable." She perched on the edge of a nearby chair, then said, "I would love to listen to the end. Unless you had rather not have an audience?"

One look at her appreciative face was enough to tell him she was sincere, so he reseated himself and picked up the piece where he had left off.

She sat silently. The one time he glanced at her she had her eyes closed, her head leaning back against the chair.

He finished with a flourish and, as the vibrations of the last chord died away, Arelia leaped to her feet, clapping her hands as an exuberant audience of one.

"Wonderful! Wonderful! What a splendid gift you have! Why have you never mentioned it? Do you come here often?"

Typically, Arelia's comments and questions came too quickly for the listener to reply to them all. Mr.

Pearce did as most people did in conversation with her—he answered the last question she asked.

"I have been coming a few days only, for I just learned from Miss Waverly that this instrument was here. I hope you don't mind."

"Mind? Of course not. Why should I mind? I only wish you would play in the salon where there would be more ears to hear you. You have only the mice for an audience here."

"How can we know they are not appreciative?" he asked.

She smiled. "How, indeed? While I have the opportunity, I have been wishing to speak with you . . . about Tom."

"Yes?"

"I want to thank you for the miracle you have wrought in him, for it is little short of that, I assure you."

"I don't understand, ma'am."

"I must tell you truthfully, sir, that I had little confidence you could do any better with Tom than all the others."

"All the others?"

"The other tutors who came before you. Surely Tenbury told you of them?"

"His lordship told me he needed a tutor for his nephew. He said the boy had been sent down for a series of pranks and what the school termed an 'uncooperative attitude.' "

"He didn't tell you about the other tutors? How like Tenbury! There were six of them—six highly qualified men who could do nothing with Tom. They all quit; several informed me that my son was the most trying student they had ever encountered."

"Lord Tenbury did say Tom was having difficulty accepting his father's death . . . that he refused to apply himself."

"We kept him out of school more than six months after Henry died," Arelia said. "Then he asked to go

94

back, but he never settled in. This unusual behavior began . . . the mischief . . . so unlike him."

"Grief is a strong emotion and can exhibit itself in many ways," Pearce offered. "The period of mourning a loved one is different for everyone. What of you? Do you mourn your husband still?"

At first taken aback by the question, Arelia realized that somewhere in the middle of the conversation, Mr. Pearce had converted from tutor to clergyman. She found she didn't mind as she tried to answer truthfully. "Yes. I suppose I do. I can talk about him now, with Jack and Tenbury, and the countess. I couldn't do so for a long time. Tenbury had to tell Tom and Belinda when the news first came. I couldn't do it. Couldn't bring myself to say the words 'your father is dead.' Even now, after all this time, they are still painful."

She was looking down, clasping her hands tightly. Stepping close, he said quietly, "Tom has those same feelings—loved his father as you did, misses him as you do. His belief that lives are wasted by war convinced him that his father died without reason, that his life was forfeited with no reward. I think now that he is older, he is starting to understand why a soldier becomes a soldier, and why wars can be necessary. Perhaps that is why his attitude and his work are improving."

"Is there anything I can do to help?" she asked.

"Say the things you couldn't say three years ago. Tell him about the pain and the loss you feel, then maybe he'll share his feelings with you."

She smiled at him, unshed tears making her blue eyes glisten. "You have given me good advice; I shall try to follow it. I'll leave you now so you may return to your music. Perhaps I can come another time . . . to listen."

He nodded as he walked her to the door. "Please do. You are always welcome."

Arelia walked down the corridor until it turned. Then she stopped and waited. Within a few moments Mr. Pearce began to play again. This piece was much different from the last—slow and melancholy; Arelia didn't recognize the composer.

When the gentlemen had joined the ladies in the salon after dinner, Anne brought Belinda down to formally meet some of the guests. She had helped Cassie dress the child carefully in the frock Arelia suggested. In the bright pink dress, with her blond curls bouncing against her back, Belinda looked delightful. Anne dressed herself in the best gown she owned, the burgundy muslin Mrs. Saunders had purchased for her.

By this time, Anne recognized most of the house guests. She took Belinda to Arelia's side, relieved to see that Lady Mason, who had such uncomplimentary things to say about both children and governesses, was on the far side of the large room.

While Lord Wilmington, a particular friend of Arelia's, engaged Belinda in conversation, Anne took time to observe the other guests. They were all dressed formally, the ladies in richly colored evening gowns, the men in dark coats and knee breeches. In her simple gown, Anne felt plain indeed.

Lady Naismith, who had used Anne's horse without permission, was stunning in deep blue satin. The three men included in her small group appeared to hang on her every word.

Lord Tenbury, dressed in severe black and white, sat beside Miss Pauline Redditch, the youngest and prettiest of Arelia's three candidates for the position of future Countess of Tenbury. The earl's mother was seated near the hearth, where a small fire had been kindled to chase away the dampness of the evening. Since Arelia had taken Belinda in hand, Anne excused herself and went to greet her ladyship.

"Sit with me, Anne," Lady Tenbury invited. "I so enjoy your company."

While the countess chatted, and Anne supplied an occasional response, Anne stole another look at Lord Tenbury. Something about him tonight drew her eyes. He was as handsome as ever, his clothes fitting his form to perfection. His blond head in the candlelight glowed tawny, while his pleasant smile appeared often for Miss Redditch.

Anne then transferred her gaze to Miss Redditch. If the petite brunette could capture the heart of the elusive earl, she would be a fortunate woman.

Anne had not seen Tenbury since he had interrupted her kiss with Jack. She wondered if Jack had somehow managed to explain. If not, it was more than likely that Tenbury was still displeased with her.

It was unfortunate he had walked in when he had, for she had been enjoying her first kiss. She tried to remember it now and found that recalling the moment was difficult. Her gaze returned to Tenbury and focused on his lips. They were smiling again—barely separated, showing a narrow line of fine, straight teeth.

Were all kisses the same, she wondered? Would kissing Tenbury be much the same as kissing Jack? A moment later she raised her eyes to find the earl returning her regard. She flushed and turned aside to Lady Tenbury, forcing herself to make a response to something the countess said.

The next time she looked up she groaned inwardly, for Lady Mason was making her way toward the countess. Anne considered the woman both rude and insensitive, but knowing there was no escape, she simply looked down at her folded hands and hoped the lady would ignore her. She did not see Lord Tenbury excuse himself to Miss Redditch and cross the room toward his mother.

"Countess," Lady Mason gushed, "You are wise to sit near the fire, for the evening has grown chilly."

"The Castle has ever been a drafty place," the countess replied. "I always keep a shawl near me, even during pleasant weather."

"I wonder, Miss . . . I'm sorry, I can't recall your name."

Anne looked up in dismay as she realized Lady Mason was addressing her. "Waverly, my lady," she supplied.

"Yes, of course, Miss Waverly. Would you mind fetching a shawl for me? I left one on the bed in my room."

Anne stood. "Certainly, my lady. Which room is yours?"

"The queen's room, I believe it's called. Two doors past Lady Tenbury's apartments, on the opposite side of the hall."

As Anne would have walked away, she found that Tenbury was standing behind Lady Mason's shoulder.

"Please sit down, Miss Waverly," he said quietly.

"I was just leaving, my lord. Lady Mason—"

"I heard her ladyship's request." Turning toward the door Tenbury caught the eye of a footman standing there. In a moment the man was at his side. "You may give your instructions to this man, Lady Mason," he said coolly. "He will be more than happy to fetch whatever it is you need."

As Lady Mason stood in rigid silence, Anne thought she would do as Tenbury suggested and give her instructions to the footman. But suddenly, without a word, she turned and walked away.

With a nod Tenbury dismissed the footman. When Lady Mason was out of hearing Anne said quietly, "I will fetch the shawl. She told me where it is."

"That will not be necessary, Miss Waverly," Tenbury replied.

"But I think she is offended, sir."

"If she is, it is her own concern. You are not a servant; I will not allow my guests to treat you as one."

"Tenbury is right, my dear," the countess added. "We have footmen three deep to do such tasks."

Tenbury spoke again. "You are still standing, Miss Waverly."

"Yes, sir. I must go. Belinda has stayed long enough; it is well past her bedtime."

"Take her, then," the countess remarked, "but when you have seen her upstairs, you must return. You have already enlivened my evening, as I knew you would."

"I don't think . . . Perhaps we could meet tomorrow, Lady Tenbury," Anne said.

"If my mother requests your company tonight, Miss Waverly," Tenbury remarked, "I don't see any reason for you to deny her."

"No, sir," she conceded. "I will be back, ma'am, as soon as may be."

When Lady Mason had walked away, undisguised anger on her face, the Earl of Haverham moved to her side.

"You are unhappy with our host, my lady?"

"Tenbury has the oddest notions," she offered. "He treats that mousey woman more like his light o' love than a governess. I merely asked her to fetch a shawl for me. To hear Tenbury, one would think I had asked her to walk to China for it."

As Lady Mason continued in the same vein, Haverham found it curious that someone besides himself had noticed the unusual solicitude Tenbury showed his niece's governess. Haverham himself had seen them driving together; then there was the rumor flying about that Tenbury had deserted a riding party to rescue the governess from an overturned boat on the lake. Probably nothing to it . . . yet . . . if Tenbury left a mistress behind in London, perhaps he discovered that Miss Waverly had talents

99

beyond those necessary in the schoolroom. Such an unobtrusive, quiet woman was not Haverham's usual style, yet one woman was much like another in the dark, he reasoned.

After the governess had taken the child away, then returned to sit with the countess, Haverham made his way to Tenbury's side. A few well-worded questions should yield him the information he sought.

Tenbury was watching Anne, thinking of her kiss with Jack and what it could have meant, when Haverham approached him. He listened with only half an ear to the man's comment and answered without thinking.

"I say, Tenbury, I believe your niece's governess is not all she seems."

"You are absolutely correct, Haverham. There is a great deal more to Miss Waverly than meets the eye."

Anne retired late that night and was wakened from a sound sleep when someone pulled back the coverlet and began climbing into the bed with her. Half asleep she asked, "Belinda? Couldn't you sleep?"

"Not Belinda, my dear, but Haverham, at your service."

He chuckled at his own joke, but Anne hadn't heard the words. At the first sound of his voice she scrambled for the far side of the bed. Thinking he must be drunk or sleepwalking, or at the very least in the wrong room by mistake, she said, "My lord, I am Miss Waverly; you are in the wrong room."

"Not at all. I am exactly where I wish to be."

As he crossed the bed and exited on the same side she had, she moved around the end to the opposite side again, keeping the bed between them. Since she preferred to leave both her bed curtains and her draperies open at night, his shadowy form was revealed in the dim light passing through the windows.

"You will leave my room instantly, sir," she demanded.

When he chuckled, her belief that he had made a mistake was replaced by fear. She realized she had erred in coming around the bed, for now he stood between her and the door.

"Must we play at cat and mouse?" he asked. "Your employer told me plainly that there is a great deal more to you than meets the eye. I am anxious to find out what that is."

"My employer?" she asked, aghast at his suggestion.

"Yes. Lord Tenbury himself. I'm not certain he actually offered you to me, but we needn't tell him. This can be our little secret."

He made his move then, quickly around the foot of the bed. Anne attempted her only route of escape, over the high side of the bed itself. He caught her easily, and they landed together on the soft ticking. She considered screaming but feared frightening Belinda, who slept in the next room. Haverham was not a large man; perhaps she could still get away. As she struggled with him she soon realized that regardless of his size he was much stronger than she.

Kicking her legs frantically, she managed to contact some delicate spot, for he swore and momentarily slackened his hold. She rolled away, but as her feet touched the floor he reached out and grabbed at her shoulders. As his pull swung her toward him, the sleeve of her fragile gown tore away in his hand. His face was immediately before hers now, and she sensed rather than saw the lasciviousness there. He pulled her against him, trapping one arm between them. Her right arm, however, remained free, and she raised it until her fingernails contacted the warm skin of his cheek. Arching her fingers with a will, she pulled with all her strength.

Haverham uttered a cry of pain and simultaneously released her. She sped for the door, through it, and down the corridor to Arelia's room. When she found Arelia's door locked, she hurried down the hall toward the countess's apartments. Before she got that far, she saw a soft glow beneath Tenbury's door and without hesitation opened it and slipped inside.

Tenbury was sitting, writing, at a desk; a branched candelabra stood at his elbow. He was completely dressed with the exception of his evening coat, which had been thrown upon the bed.

He rose in amazement as a breathless Anne closed his door and leaned against it. "Miss Waverly! What is the meaning of this?"

It seemed for a moment as if she would not answer him. She wore only a simple white nightgown and even the dark waves of hair, which fell in disarray over her shoulders, could not hide the fact that the garment had been torn away from her left shoulder. Her feet were bare, her face so pale she appeared ghostly.

"L-Lord H-Haverham. He implied that you offered me to him."

"What?" he thundered. "Don't be ridiculous." He pulled a quilt from the bed as he advanced on her. "Here, cover yourself."

Looking down at her torn gown, she gasped, then leaned away from the door as he reached the blanket behind her and pulled the ends together across her chest. He continued to hold the ends in closed fists as he demanded. "What happened?"

"I woke to find him crawling into my bed."

"Did he hurt you?"

"No. I scratched his face and got away."

"Good," he nodded approvingly. "Come along. You cannot stay here. I must take you back to your room." When he reached to open the door, she held back. "Don't worry," he assured her. "We will be certain the room is empty, and you will lock the door behind me. He would need an ax to get through it. How did he get in, in the first place?"

"It wasn't locked. I never lock it. I didn't realize there was a need to."

With the coverlet clutched about her shoulders and dragging on the carpet behind her, Anne followed Tenbury silently through the dark halls back to her room.

As Tenbury had expected, the room was empty. He lit a number of candles to assure her all was safe. The bed was destroyed, covers and sheets had been dragged about in all directions. "Fix your bed and go to sleep. Meet me in the library tomorrow morning promptly at nine."

"But I have lessons with B—"

"At nine, Miss Waverly."

"Yes, sir."

"I think you should wash the blood from your hand," he added.

She followed the direction of his gaze to where the bloodied fingers of her right hand clutched the blanket.

"Come bolt the door behind me and say nothing of this to anyone," he said.

She did as he bade her, while he waited outside until he heard the bolt slide home. He then walked silently down the corridor to the head of the stairs. He was angry enough to throw Haverham from his house, bag and baggage, along with his daughter and her silver spur. But prudence won out. Rousing the Castle at two A.M. would only spawn the type of scandal he most deplored.

When he finally went to bed, he didn't sleep well. Once when he awoke, he imagined he saw Miss Waverly leaning against the inside of his door. She had looked so vulnerable in her bare feet with her hair loose and disheveled. Yet she had acquitted herself well. She had put the lecher to rout. He was proud of her.

10

The following morning, Tenbury learned from his butler that the Earl of Haverham had left the Castle at dawn, claiming some urgent business in town. Tenbury thought it more likely he was on his way to his country estates, there to hide his face until the wounds inflicted by Miss Waverly had time to heal.

She appeared promptly at nine in a wheat-colored gown of sprig muslin, with a simple green ribbon adorning the high waistline. She closed the door and stood just inside it. Her dark hair was dressed carefully. Her wide green eyes regarded him steadily.

"You look tired," he said. "Please sit down."

She took the chair he indicated, sitting very straight on its edge, her hands folded in her lap.

"Did you get any sleep last night?" he asked.

"A little. Despite knowing the door was bolted, I kept imagining I heard it opening. It's silly, I know."

He walked a few steps away, then turned to face her. "You said something last night that I should like you to explain—something about my offering you to Haverham. What did you mean?"

"I knew you would ask me, and I have been trying to remember exactly what it was he said. I believe he said you told him there was a great deal more to me than meets the eye."

"I may have said some such thing. I can't remember. It's true enough in any case, but clearly he chose to misconstrue my meaning."

"But it *isn't* true," she objected. "I am exactly what I seem—a governess—plain and simple. Why would you wish him to believe I was anything more . . . or less?"

"I had no wish to discuss you with him," Tenbury replied. "He raised the subject, and I answered him. I don't remember clearly what was said, but nothing inappropriate, I assure you. Are you certain *you* didn't say anything that might have led him to believe—?"

"Certainly not! How could you think that?"

"I think it because I saw you with Jack. Remember?"

"Jack explained, didn't he?"

"No. I told him no explanation was necessary."

"Well, it is necessary! We weren't kissing for the reason you think we were kissing."

"Really? And what reason is that?"

"You know. Because we wanted to."

"You were kissing, then, because you didn't want to?"

"No, of course not. We were kissing . . . as an experiment."

"I see."

"Do you? Truly?"

"No. But somehow I feel any further explanation would only confuse me more."

"Lord Tenbury, I believe you are being purposely obtuse in this matter."

"Very well, ma'am, I will come to the point. Are you in love with my brother?"

"Certainly not!"

"Then you should not have been kissing him."

"I have already explained—we were not kissing for that reason!"

"I think this the most ridiculous conversation I have ever taken part in," Tenbury said. "Perhaps it *would* be best if you simply explained why you were kissing my brother."

"I mentioned to him that I had never been kissed—and probably never would be—and he offered."

"To kiss you."

"Yes. And then you walked in—"

"And interrupted."

"Yes. Which was perhaps unfortunate."

"Undoubtedly. And tell me this, Miss Waverly. What sort of conversation could you and Jack have been having for this topic to arise in the first place?"

"It's rather hard to explain. I had been—"

"Wait! Never mind. I think I had rather not know."

"As you wish, sir, but I promise you, it was all quite innocent."

"I believe you," he said, then with a subtle change in tone added, "Last night, however, was not. Haverham is gone, but I should still like you to bolt your door at night so long as any guests remain in the Castle." He walked to her and stood before her chair. "The family has grown fond of you. We would be distressed if any ill befell you." Taking her chin he turned her face toward the windows. In the better light he could see dark circles beneath her eyes. "You didn't sleep, did you?" His gaze dropped from her eyes to her lips, which were slightly parted. "Did Haverham kiss you?"

"He tried. I managed to avoid him."

"If he had, you would not have liked it." He released her chin and walked to the windows, gazing out into the light fog that had replaced the previous day's rain. "Of all the vices in men," he said, "I despise most the one that leads them to believe they have a right to use and abuse women, utilizing the advantage of superior strength. You lodged such an accusation against me that day by the lake. Do you remember?"

Her face troubled, she rose and went to him. "It's not the same."

"I think it is. Perhaps the same evils are present in us all, and how we manifest them is merely a matter of degree."

He took out his pocket watch and checked the time. "I must go. You will remember to lock your door? And you will have Cassie sleep in the room with you if you are at all uneasy?"

She smiled at his concern as she nodded in assent.

Then he smiled down at her, the wonderful smile he had shared so often with Miss Redditch the previous evening. "And if you should ever want to practice kissing again, don't hesitate to ask me. I have had a good deal more experience than Jack."

He was gone before she could reply. He was teasing, of course, yet it was some time before she could get the image of kissing him out of her mind.

" '*Veritas nunquam perit.*' Truth never dies."

"Very good, Tom," Mr. Pearce said. "I believe that will be enough for today. We will continue on page seventy-eight tomorrow."

Tom was gone instantly, leaving Mr. Pearce and Anne alone in the schoolroom.

"What are you reading?" he asked.

"Herodotus. Listen to this: 'This is the bitterest pain among men, to have much knowledge but no power.' Do you ever feel so, Dennis?"

"Sometimes. You?"

"Yes. More than sometimes. Since my father died, I have accepted that I have little or no power, especially regarding my future. All the knowledge in the world won't gain me security or a place where I belong."

"You belong here."

"For now. But in a few years Belinda won't need me. Then I must move on."

"Tom will go back to school, too. Soon, I think," he said.

"Yes. But it's different for you. You have an independence. You will take on students or a parish because you wish to, not because you must."

"You would rewrite the quotation then to say: 'This is the bitterest pain among men, to have much knowledge but no money.' "

She laughed. "Yes. I believe it's truer that way. But money and power have always been close partners."

"And when they come together often accomplish more evil than good."

"No sermons today, Dennis," she teased. "The sun is finally shining, and I have a swimming lesson with Arelia."

"How are you progressing?"

"Well, I think. I can cross the stream by myself; I can tread water for five minutes. By the end of summer I will be as adept as any trout."

"You and Mrs. Saunders have grown quite close," he said.

"Yes, we have, and I find it remarkable. I've never had a close friend before, but I always assumed friends would have much in common. Yet Arelia and I are nothing alike."

He thought them more alike than she realized but didn't say as much. "She seems to spend a good deal of time with Lord Wilmington," he remarked. "Perhaps she is planning to remarry."

"She wants to marry again. She makes no secret of it. But I know she has turned down four offers since the beginning of the year. Personally, I think she is searching among the wrong type of men."

"What do you mean?" he asked.

"When I first met her in London, she went from

party to party night after night, and I would expect that men flocked around her, attractive as she is. Yet none of them measured up. This summer she has invited those same frivolous people here. She doesn't seem to remember how she met Henry."

"Her husband?" he asked, "How did she meet him?"

"Jack told me they met here at the Castle. Henry was down from university on winter holiday, and she was invited to a hunting party with her parents. He was walking along in his hunting jacket with three dead rabbits slung over his shoulder. She nearly rode him down on a bridle path and evidently ripped up at him for walking where he shouldn't have. It was only later that she realized he was a son of the house. He was a younger son, headed for a career in the army, but he had something special that she saw and loved."

"Which makes it all the more tragic that he died so young."

"Yes. And though she insists she would like to marry again, I wonder if she will ever find a man she can love as much."

After the early morning fog burned off, the day grew hot, and the swimming lesson was not only instructional but refreshing.

Afterward, when Arelia returned to her guests, Anne and Jack went for a long walk together, then Anne joined Lady Tenbury in the library before dinner. She ate alone in the schoolroom and completed some sewing before Arelia entered the room.

"Anne. I want you to come with me."

"Oh, Arelia, please, not the salon again. I'm not dressed, and I don't—"

"No, no. They're all still eating. I excused myself for the evening. Said I had the headache, which was a lie. Have you ever known such a hot day?"

"It has been hot, but—"

"Come along, it's dark, time to go."

Dragged by the arm, Anne left the Castle with Arelia. They walked together through the twilight. The oppressive heat of the day still hovered over the ground, for there was no freshening breeze to dispel it. The women soon arrived at the private bathing pool. Before Anne could ask why they had come at this time of night, Arelia started to remove her dress.

"You can't mean to swim in the dark?" Anne said.

"Not only in the dark," came her companion's answer, "but in the nude!"

"In the . . . Arelia, you can't be serious!"

"I am. Henry and I often did this. There is nothing as exhilarating—well, almost nothing," she added. "Hurry out of your things or you will be left behind."

"But we cannot! What if someone sees?"

"It's dark, goose. Who will see? Besides, all the time we have been coming here to swim, we have never seen anyone."

"That is because you warned the children they must stay away."

"The children are in bed, Anne. I never guessed you could be so milk-livered! Take off those clothes and come in." There was a flash of pale skin in the moonlight as Arelia dove into the water. Anne stood alone on the bank, trying to imagine how it would feel to be in the water, completely free of any encumbrance. She wished she could be as uninhibited as Arelia—she wanted to be.

"Coward," Arelia called, as she splashed back toward Anne.

That was the word Anne needed to hear. Within seconds she had stripped off her dress and chemise and followed. As Arelia had promised, the water was wonderful. She was right; there was no other feeling quite like it.

"Did you really do this with your husband?"

"Occasionally, on a summer evening, when it was hot, and we couldn't sleep."

"Often, in literature, lovers are uninhibited, but I was taught and have always believed that we English are different."

"In what way?"

"That we adhere to rigid rules of behavior, those that are considered proper; that husbands visit their wives at an appropriate time and at other times—"

"And at other times show no interest? Don't you believe it. My marriage wasn't like that. Henry and I did outrageously inappropriate things. Even here once . . . we . . . our last summer together . . . "

Her voice trailed off in the darkness, and Anne regretted having led her into sad memories.

"I'm sorry, I never meant . . . I have no right to speak of these things."

"Don't be silly. You're old enough to say what you please, especially to me, and you may ask whatever questions you like. I don't mind them."

"It's not proper to wonder about such things."

"It may not be considered proper," Arelia countered, "but I believe all women think about them, whether they are willing to admit it or not."

"All women? Even women like Lady Mason?"

Anne heard Arelia chuckle in the dimness. "All right, I yield that point. *Not* all women and most definitely *not* Lady Mason. I can just hear her, can't you? 'Children and husbands must be borne—two of life's necessary evils. One must keep a stiff upper lip and face one's trials with fortitude.' I must have been mad to think Tenbury could possibly fancy her. She's worse than a plague of pox."

Later, as Anne and Arelia walked past the terrace on their return to the Castle, a man rose from the steps where he had been sitting.

"Mr. Pearce," Arelia said.

111

"Good evening, ladies. I hope I didn't startle you. I have been sitting here listening to Miss Redditch at the pianoforte."

"She is not so good as you," Arelia commented.

He neither agreed nor disagreed but only said, "Her style differs from mine."

Even in the darkness, Anne could sense a restraint in Dennis—a subtle change that came over him whenever Arelia was present. At first merely suspicious, she was now nearly certain that Dennis admired her flamboyant friend. Thinking how much he had to offer when compared to Arelia's London beaux, Anne excused herself on the slimmest pretext and hurried up the steps to the door, leaving them alone in the moonlight.

"Your hair is wet," Dennis commented when they were alone.

"We have been swimming," Arelia replied, then added provocatively, "in the nude."

Dennis smiled, pausing a moment before he replied, "Whenever we talk, you seem to enjoy saying things intended to shock me. I am not so easily scandalized."

"I have always been uncomfortable with members of the clergy," she admitted. "My faults and shortcomings seem greater in the presence of good and worthy men."

"Those of us called to do God's work are no more worthy than any other. It is our work, our profession. And just as a barrister doesn't win all his arguments nor a doctor cure all his patients, so a minister doesn't always do what is right. We serve God and our fellow man, and when we fail, we seek forgiveness as all sinners must."

"You are an unusual cleric, Mr. Pearce."

"And you, Mrs. Saunders, are an extraordinary woman."

Two days later, Anne went early to Arelia's room, hoping her friend would have something positive to say about the conversation she had shared with Dennis on the terrace steps.

Arelia's bedroom door was opened by her maid, who barred Anne's way.

"Mrs. Saunders is not feeling herself this morning, miss. I fear her headache the other evening may have been a forewarning of something more serious."

Knowing the headache had been feigned, Anne was puzzled. "May I see her?"

"Perhaps later, miss—"

"Let her in, Barrett," Arelia's voice came from within the room, "and send down for some tea."

As the servant left, Anne entered to find Arelia still in her nightgown, seated upon a couch near the windows. Her face was pale, and her eyes looked tired, as if she hadn't slept.

"It's because of the swimming, isn't it?" Anne asked, going to Arelia and sitting beside her. "You have taken a chill."

Arelia patted her hand reassuringly. "No, it is not because of the swimming, and I have not taken a chill. It is a small stomach complaint, nothing more."

Anne rose to her feet. "A stomach complaint could mean the influenza. One of the downstairs maids sickened with it last week. Perhaps you should have the doctor see you."

"I'll be all right," Arelia insisted.

"But I have never known you to be ill."

"It is true that I am generally very healthy, but I assure you—" Arelia broke off as Anne stood and moved toward the door. "Where are you going?"

"To find Lady Tenbury and ask her to send for the doctor. Better to be safe—"

"Anne! You will do no such thing!" Arelia's angry tone stopped Anne before she reached the door; she turned back, puzzled by her friend's vehemence. "I

113

do not want any fuss made over me, for I am not ill. I have done something very foolish. I am anxious, and I did not sleep, but I do not have the influenza."

At that moment the maid returned. While she arranged the tea on a small table, Anne walked to the windows and drew back the draperies. A light fog lay over the park and the woods beyond. When the maid had gone, she turned her back to the window, leaning against the sill.

"Can you tell me what you did that was so foolish?"

"I agreed to meet Lord Wilmington in the rose garden at midnight last night." When Anne frowned, Arelia defended herself, "He was most charming at dinner. I suppose I had a bit more wine than I should have. But for whatever reason, I made the assignation."

"Did you keep it?" Anne asked.

"Certainly, I did. And it was lovely. We sat in the garden under the moon. The fragrance of the roses was heavenly. He pays the prettiest compliments I have ever heard." She paused then, but Anne would not let the subject rest.

"I see nothing in this to lose sleep over," Anne remarked.

"It was what came next that I regret. He embraced me, and I returned his embrace. We kissed. But in the midst of our embrace we were interrupted."

"By whom?"

"Mr. Pearce."

"Oh, dear! Did he say anything?"

"He said 'Excuse me,' and proceeded on his way."

Anne digested this information for a few moments before she said, "But surely he must recognize your attachment to Lord Wilmington. We have all seen it. I don't think he'll say anything, Arelia. Whether he approves or not, your affairs are not his concern. Besides, he is in your employ. I doubt he would wish to

114

incur your displeasure and jeopardize his position here."

"I don't think he will say anything, either," Arelia said. "That is not what worries me."

"Then, what does?"

"I didn't realize, until this happened, just how much I value his good opinion. It distresses me to imagine what he must think of me now."

"He thinks you are in love with Lord Wilmington," Anne replied.

"But I'm not. That's the unfortunate part, don't you see? The irony is that Wilmington has been pursuing me for nearly a year, and all that time my behavior has been above reproach. But the moment I give in to temptation, who is there to witness my transgression but the minister himself."

As Arelia rambled on, a suspicion began to grow in Anne. If Arelia cared so much for Dennis's opinion, she must be forming a strong attachment to him. Anne's theory was strengthened by Arelia's next comments.

"I know you have grown fond of Dennis."

"I have," Anne replied. "We are good friends . . . but only friends. It sounds to me as if you wish more than friendship from him."

"I doubt if even friendship is possible now."

Arelia grew silent, then; and try as she might, Anne could coax her to say no more. Even when Anne insisted that Dennis was an understanding and forgiving man, Arelia held her peace, for she understood something that Anne did not. She knew that for a man, some things were harder to forgive than others.

11

Two days later, after luncheon, Anne stood at the window of the schoolroom staring down at the long row of carriages in the drive. Most of the guests were leaving. It was another hot, sweltering day. High, thin clouds did little to filter the melting rays of the sun, which beat down relentlessly. Horses impatiently pawed the ground, raising small clouds of dust, while busy footmen hurried about with heavy trunks and portmanteaux, heaving them high onto the tops of the coaches and strapping them securely in place.

"In less than an hour we shall have the Castle to ourselves again," Tenbury said from the schoolroom doorway.

"Are you sorry to see them go?" Anne asked.

"No."

"Nor am I. Yet I fear Arelia might be."

"Her matchmaking plans for the summer have failed again," he said. He moved into the room and paused before a comfortable chair. "Do you mind if I sit?"

"Please do," she replied as she sat on the window seat behind her. "You are aware, then, of Mrs. Saunders's hope."

"Of course. Arelia is not devious. Covert actions have never appealed to her. Yet I fear I am a great

116

disappointment to her. She insists I am impossible to please, and perhaps she is right; perhaps I am too exacting. Tell me, Miss Waverly: What did you think of Arelia's candidates?"

"It is not my place to comment on my betters, my lord."

"Rubbish! Why do you speak so?" he asked angrily.

"Because it's true," she defended. "Lady Mason is the daughter of a duke, wealthy and beautiful—"

"Who has no sense of humor, an inflated estimate of her own worth, and a deep-seated dislike for children," he finished.

"That *would* be a drawback if one wanted children," Anne admitted.

"Indeed," he replied simply.

"Well," Anne tried again, "Lady Naismith is well connected, rides with great skill, and sings like an angel."

"She also has a cruel streak, a total disregard for the feelings of others, and a father who is a loose screw. To refer to such people as your betters is to insult yourself."

"Everyone has faults, Lord Tenbury. I can list mine just as you listed them for Lady Mason and Lady Naismith."

"Oh, yes," he agreed, "you have faults. Not the least of which is a low opinion of yourself. Fortunately you also have initiative, which is a good thing, for without it you would in all likelihood be with Mrs. Hodder still, ruining both your health and your eyesight by sewing for her until midnight and beyond."

Anne hadn't thought about her aunt for weeks and found it curious that Lord Tenbury should even remember her name. "How did you know I sewed for my aunt?"

"You must have told me."

"I don't remember doing so."

"I doubt you remember much about our first interview. It was rather unorthodox."

She felt unorthodox was a mild description of that meeting. It all seemed so long ago.

"Speaking of interviews," he continued, "I came specifically to speak with you about Arelia. She has been acting strangely the last few days, and I wondered if you knew why."

"Strangely?" Anne asked, parrying the question.

"She has claimed the headache two days running. I can't remember her ever suffering from such a complaint before. Last night she came down to formally bid our guests farewell, but she retired soon after dinner. She says nothing is amiss, yet I have not seen her at all today."

"She is having some personal problems, my lord, and doesn't care for company just now. We all need periods of tranquility from time to time."

"I have never known Arelia to need it; she is by far the least tranquil person I know."

"She is, nevertheless, troubled at present," Anne said. "I was thinking I might talk to Dennis—Mr. Pearce—about it."

"Do you think he could help?"

"I'm not sure. The problem . . . is a perplexing one."

"Nevertheless, I hope you know you can depend upon me, should the need arise."

"How can I not know it, sir, when you have come to my aid on numerous occasions? You assisted me that day in the milliner's shop; you made it possible for me to apply for this position; you came quickly when the boat capsized. I do not distrust you, nor doubt your abilities, but the matter is a private one—"

"And more easily confided to the clergy," he finished for her.

"Yes," she replied, pleased that he understood.

Tenbury rose from his chair and walked to the window. Several of the coaches had rolled away while they talked. "There goes Miss Redditch," he remarked. "I will miss her sweet hands upon the harp."

"And won't you miss her otherwise, my lord? It is difficult to fault her. She is beautiful, personable, accomplished, well read, an heiress—"

"She is also very young, and I find I have lost all interest in the infantry. I believe I prefer a woman who has mellowed."

She raised her face to his, and for a brief moment their eyes held while she wondered what he meant by what he said, and he wondered why he had said it.

In the next instant the spell was broken as a footman spoke from the doorway. "Excuse me, my lord. Lord Spafford would like a word with you before he leaves."

When Tenbury had gone, Anne returned to her work while the row of waiting carriages continued to carry the guests away.

Nearly an hour later, Lady Tenbury went in search of her eldest son, determined to discuss a subject that troubled her greatly. When she found him in the library, she came directly to the point. "I wish to speak with you about Miss Waverly, Tenbury."

He had lowered the paper he was reading when his mother entered the room; now he folded it and put it aside. "Certainly, Mother. What is it?"

"I have grown fond of Miss Waverly in the short time she has been with us, and because of that fondness I feel I must speak. What is she to you?"

"She is my niece's governess."

"She is more than that."

"Yes. She has become a companion to you and a friend and companion to Arelia."

"When I left town," Lady Tenbury persisted, "there had been no mention of a governess for Belinda. Then, before the cat could lick her ear, Belinda had a governess—a governess, I might add, who was hired in the strangest fashion."

At this point Anne arrived at the library door, hoping to find Lady Tenbury there. As she paused outside she clearly heard the earl's voice. "That may well be, Mother, but you must admit that regardless of the way she was hired, she has filled the position admirably."

Anne turned away. Were they discussing her? Then she paused again as she heard Lady Tenbury's next words.

"Perhaps I must phrase my question more plainly," her ladyship said. "What is Miss Waverly to you, personally?"

Anne considered eavesdropping to be disgraceful, but her interest in his answer kept her rooted to the spot.

"She is nothing to me personally."

"You will never make me believe that," his mother replied. "I saw the compassion in your eyes as you carried her upstairs the day she arrived here. I know you drove her in your carriage, and I was there when you stepped in to protect her from Lady Mason in the salon the other evening."

"Very well, Mother. I should have known better than to try to deceive you, at least. You are correct; Miss Waverly was hired under unusual circumstances. She was hired by my contrivance. I have a specific reason for wanting to keep her within my control and under my protection."

Anne's slippered feet carried her silently away from the library and up the stairs to the privacy of her bedchamber. Why did Lord Tenbury say she was hired by his contrivance? If anyone had contrived it was she—refusing to follow the butler to the door, forcing him to make an introduction, and then asking Lord Tenbury for an interview. His last words puzzled her even more, for although she rather liked the thought of being under his protection, she didn't care for his presumption that she was within his control, and she couldn't even begin to imagine what his *reason* might be.

At one point she regretted not staying to hear more, but had she done so she would have learned nothing, for when the countess asked Tenbury to explain himself, he said he regretted that he could not. The matter was a confidential one, between himself and another party. With that her ladyship had to be content.

The more Anne thought about Tenbury's words, the more confused she became, until she had so many more questions than answers that she concluded eavesdropping was indeed the evil it was purported to be.

By that evening Arelia decided she'd had enough of her self-imposed solitude. Mr. Pearce could think what he wished of her. If he insisted upon walking about the gardens after midnight, then he deserved to be offended by what he saw. If she met him about the Castle, she was determined to be civil but distant—she was the employer, he the employee. That was all they were to each other.

For the next two days she took great care to avoid him, steering clear of those places where he was most often found. She never went to the east wing again to listen to him play, though she imagined it often enough—imagined his broad shoulders as he sat at the pianoforte, his dark head slightly bent in concentration, his long, nimble fingers gliding so knowledgeably over the keys.

When they finally met by chance outside the salon one evening, she greeted him with a forced smile but had difficulty meeting his eyes. His response was cool, diffident, and in that moment she knew that the friendship, which had begun so promisingly, had ended.

A week of cool, rainy weather gave way to another warm spell. Standing on the terrace at twilight, Tenbury watched Tom and Will Carey coming back from a swim with their hair wet and damp towels draped over their shoulders. He smiled as he remembered how often he and Henry and Jack had done the same. Twenty minutes later he stood on the bank of the private swimming hole. Like Arelia, he had always found a bathing costume too restrictive; he dressed only in a pair of old knee breeches that he kept for swimming.

He swam steadily for ten minutes, finding the water as wonderfully refreshing as the boys had after a hot, humid day. Then, he lay on his back in the shallows, watching the moonlight play over the gently swaying tree branches. Crickets chirped in the long grass nearby, while across the stream in a backwater, several frogs chatted back and forth. Occasionally the undergrowth rustled as a hare or badger scurried by. Soon, however, Tenbury heard the distinct sound of footsteps proceeding along the path to the stream. He waited silently, his eyes focused on the clearing where the path ended.

When the unmistakable figure of Miss Waverly emerged, Tenbury fully expected Arelia to be only a step behind. It soon became clear, however, that Miss Waverly had come alone. She glanced out over the pool, looking directly at the spot where Tenbury was. When her eyes traveled on, he knew she had not seen him in the shadows. He knew he should speak, but if she had come for a swim—why should he ruin it for her?

One by one, Anne undid the buttons of her simple gown, slid if off her shoulders and stepped out of it. She hung it carefully over a nearby tree branch. Dressed now in only her white chemise, she sat to remove her slippers and stockings. When she stood again she hesitated, glanced around at the dark woods, then lifted her hands to one of the ribbons fastening her chemise. Tenbury held his breath. If she decided to take off more, he would be forced to reveal himself. She turned her head as another small animal scurried through the bushes, then, retaining her chemise, waded into the water. She swam the length of the pool several times before she moved in Tenbury's direction. He knew he must speak now, for his voice would frighten her much less than her coming upon him in the dark.

"Good evening, Miss Waverly."

Her progress was halted immediately as her feet sank to touch bottom and her heart pounded with momentary fear quickly dispelled by a familiar voice.

"Lord Tenbury!"

"I didn't mean to frighten you, but when you started coming my way I had to say something."

"How long have you been here?"

"Here at the pool? About half an hour. I was resting here in the shallows when you arrived."

"Why didn't you speak then?"

"Because, I assumed, and correctly, that you came to swim, and I did not wish to spoil your pleasure."

Clearly she was thinking how close she had come to disrobing completely, as she said accusingly, "You were watching me."

"Yes. And had you decided to swim *au naturel*, I would have warned you, I promise. I am not a *voyeur*, Miss Waverly. I suppose Arelia taught you that trick?"

"We did swim so once."

"And did you enjoy it?"

"This is not a proper conversation for us to be having, my lord."

"I suppose not. Yet in the dark on such a night, one is tempted to ignore the rules of the drawing room."

He stood then and moved from the shallows into deeper water. His legs in the black breeches blended into the darkness, but his chest was clearly visible as he waded into the water in the moonlight. Anne averted her eyes and backed away until the water closed over her shoulders.

He stopped several feet from her as he said, "You swim well for having practiced only a short time. But your arm position could be better." Before she even realized what he was doing, he had taken her by the shoulders and backed her into shallower water. Stretching one of her arms in the air he bent it carefully. "The arm should be just so, while your head is here." He moved her arm in relation to her head. "Try it."

Too overwhelmed by his casual directions to object, she did as he asked.

"Good," he approved. "Don't you feel it works better?"

"Yes, I do. You're right. Thank you."

"Try several strokes together. See if you can maintain the style that long." Again she did as he asked while he swam alongside. She took a breath just as a wave from him broke against her face. She gulped and sputtered, lost her concentration, and went under. The water was not deep, and her feet soon found the bottom. Even as they did, she was aware of his hands at her waist, steadying her.

She pushed water and wet strands of hair from her eyes then instinctively reached to hold him away—to let him know she could stand without help. Her open hands encountered the cool, firm muscles of his chest, and she snatched them away as if they had contacted an open flame. She looked up into his face, to tell him he need no longer hold her. What she saw there temporarily froze the words in her throat, for his face held an expression like none she had ever seen before. Even in the dim light, she could see that his eyes were searching hers, as if they, too, were seeking answers.

With great effort, she managed, "You . . . you may let me go now, Lord Tenbury."

"Must I? I had much rather not."

The hands at her waist moved around to the back and pulled her against him. Now her hands had no choice but to come again to his chest. She rolled them into fists, so she wouldn't have to feel. . . .

One of his hands came to her shoulder, then slid to the side of her neck, the thumb tracing the line of her chin. Slowly, her hands unclenched, until her sensitive fingertips lay against his smooth skin.

When his thumb traced her lower lip, her eyes moved to watch his mouth. She thought he said her name once—so quietly she couldn't be certain. As he bent his head, she focused on his lips, then closed her eyes as his mouth met hers. She could never remember clearly afterward whether she had returned his kiss. She couldn't remember how long the kiss lasted—she only knew that it didn't seem long enough. Her hands, at first so tentative, had begun caressing his wonderful skin. They traveled over his shoulders, around his neck, thereby flattening her chest against his with only a wet layer of thin fabric between.

When the kiss ended, Tenbury held her face for a moment in both hands, certain now that she would not attempt to flee from him. Realizing he had chosen a poor place to make love to a woman, he took Anne's hands and started to lead her to the shore. "Let's get out of the water."

His words seemed to break the spell she was under. She pulled her hands away, refusing to go with him, feeling as if she had just wakened from sleep. "You go, my lord. I will come out when you are gone."

"What's this? I don't admire coyness, Anne."

"Not coyness, sir, but modesty," she protested, trying to hide the thrill she felt when he used her name.

"Modesty be damned," he replied, holding out a hand to her. "Come."

She backed off a few steps in the water. "I will not, Lord Tenbury, for I do not wish to." When he advanced toward her, she added, "And you will not compel me, for you have assured me that coercion is a trait you despise in men."

"Very well, madam. You win. I will go back to the Castle to change, and I will wait for you there."

She only nodded in the dimness, agreeing with what he said *he* would do. She had no intention of seeing him again tonight. She would return through a servant's entrance and make her way up a secondary stair to her room. There she was determined to stay until she could adequately digest the happenings of the past hour.

Safely in her room, Anne stripped out of her wet clothing and took down her hair. She was soon warm and dry in a fresh gown, but she was far from comfortable. She sat in the window seat near an open casement. The scent of the rose gardens below wafted softly on the warm evening air, while the nearly full moon rode high in a clear sky. She realized it was still shining on the creek that ran through the forest, still shining on the pool where she had so recently been. Had she really been there? What took place was so unexpected, she could easily believe it had been a dream. Yet no dream was ever so real, so sensual; no dream would leave her lips trembling and her eyes moist.

A gentle scratching at her door startled her. When she opened it, she found a footman standing outside. "Lord Tenbury would like you to join him in the green salon, miss."

Anne's hands went instinctively to her hair, hanging damp and loose. "Please convey my apologies to his lordship, and tell him I have retired for the evening."

"Very good, miss. Good night, miss."

When the footman had gone, Anne returned to the window and her contemplation of the evening's events. Six months ago she would have believed that if a man kissed her as Tenbury had—it was the same as a proposal of marriage. She was no longer so naive. Tenbury had kissed many women. He admitted as much when he said he had more experience kissing than Jack. Yet he had never married. Nor had Jack.

Perhaps Tenbury kissed her for the same reason Jack had—to give her a memory to file away. Yet Tenbury's kiss was very different from Jack's. While she felt amazement, pleasure, and exhilaration with Jack, there was something most unsettling about the experience with Tenbury. In his arms, sharing his kiss, she felt nearly powerless, as if all her strength, all her reason had flowed into him, and she herself disappeared. Looking back on the experience, she realized she cooperated in everything he did, followed where he led, never for a moment hesitated, never resisted him.

Anne yawned behind her hand as the moon set. As she crawled into bed and drifted off to sleep, she thought she finally understood what is was to be truly ruled by passion.

═══12═══

When Anne awoke the following morning, a misty drizzle was falling outside her windows. The sudden change in weather only served to reinforce her feeling that the fantastic events of the previous evening had never taken place. While her senses insisted she had been kissed by the Earl of Tenbury, her more rational being declared that nothing could have been more unlikely.

She had difficulty concentrating on her lessons with Belinda and was relieved when noon finally arrived. After luncheon she remained in her room, fearful of going below stairs and encountering the earl. Yet even though she dreaded their next meeting, she tried to imagine what that meeting would be like. Would he smile at her and speak to her tenderly as he had the night before? Or would he treat her as he always had, with friendly reserve? If he regretted his actions, perhaps she would find him cold or aloof. After much consideration, she reached no conclusions. She admitted to herself that her understanding of the romantic overtures of men in general, and Lord Tenbury in particular, was slim to nonexistent.

Later that afternoon, castigating herself for a coward, Anne made her way to the library. She spent an enjoyable hour with Lady Tenbury until

Tom, kept in by the weather, begged her to join him in a game of billiards.

"You know what a poor player I am, Tom," she protested.

"That's why I like to play you, Miss Waverly. I cannot beat Uncle Jack or Uncle Nate or Mr. Pearce."

When Lady Tenbury chuckled, Anne replied, "You can't imagine how flattering it is to be sought after because you are the worst at something."

"How will you improve if you don't practice?" Tom asked. "Don't you always tell me so?"

"Hoist on your own petard, my dear," Lady Tenbury mumbled as Anne laid her book aside and rose to leave with Thomas.

Anne was still smiling as she followed Tom across the great hall toward the corridor that led to the billiard room.

"A moment of your time, Miss Waverly."

Anne paused and turned at the sound of Tenbury's voice from above; he had just started down the last flight of the staircase.

"You go ahead, Tom, and set up the game," she said. "I will be along directly."

As the boy walked away, Anne moved to the bottom of the stairs and watched Lord Tenbury descend. He wore a dark blue coat, blue-and-white striped waistcoat and drab buckskins; he held his leather driving gloves in one hand. At the door, Kimble held his lordship's hat in readiness, while through the leaded windows flanking the doorway, Anne could see the earl's curricle and team in the drive.

By the time Tenbury arrived at the bottom of the stairs, Anne's pulse had quickened, and her palms were damp. She gripped them together painfully as he stopped beside her, then forced herself to look up at him. He was not smiling, yet his manner did not seem diffident.

Tenbury glanced past her shoulder at the butler and footmen standing nearby before he said, "I am leaving for London in a few moments, Miss Waverly. I was hoping to see you before I departed. This journey is urgent, otherwise I would not choose to leave at this particular time."

Did she imagine the slight emphasis he placed on the words "particular time?" Was she also imagining an unusual light in his eyes, something indefinable, seeming to be there one moment and gone the next?

"We must discuss at length the topic we touched upon so briefly last night," he added cryptically.

Did he think she had been too bold? Had he expected her to repel him? Did he mean to dismiss her from her position because of her improper behavior? These questions were only a few of the many that presented themselves as she answered as casually as possible, "Certainly, my lord. There will be time enough when you return."

He regarded her a moment longer, seemed about to say something more, then appeared to change his mind. He pulled on his gloves and collected his hat from Kimble. When he said good-bye, she echoed a response, then stood in the hall and watched him mount into his curricle and drive away. He had promised they would discuss the incident further. But how many days would pass before that conversation could take place, and to what end would the discussion lead?

On Sunday morning, Anne, Arelia, and Lady Tenbury drove to the service together, covering the short distance to the village church in one of Lord Tenbury's open carriages.

Dennis Pearce's older brother, Basil, had been rector of St. Stephen's parish for more than fifteen years. His wife of nearly two decades and his brood of eight children occupied two full pews. Almost of a height with Dennis, the rector was of stockier build and displayed a slight paunch. His hair, once dark, was mostly gray. Though the tone of his voice was uncannily similar to Dennis's, the Reverend Basil Pearce had a mellower approach to language than his younger brother. He spoke quietly, sometimes lapsing into a monotone, an unfortunate habit that served to lull certain of his parishioners into a state of somnolence.

The Reverend Pearce often spoke on traditional texts, and today was no exception. He based his sermon on the text of Matthew chapter twenty-four, verse forty-one: "Watch and pray, that ye enter not into temptation: the spirit indeed *is* willing, but the flesh *is* weak."

Arelia Saunders's uneasiness began the moment the text was read. Why was it, she wondered, that the sermon so often seemed to be written specifically for her? Surely there were other sinners in the congregation besides herself. She sat very straight in the pew, schooling her face to polite interest. She knew Dennis was somewhere among the listeners; since he was nowhere in front of her, he had to be behind. She would not give him the satisfaction of seeing her discomfort.

The too-long sermon dealt primarily with the question of temptation and the power of prayer, but the flesh was mentioned often enough to make more than one parishioner squirm.

When the service was over and the congregation spilled out into the overcast morning, Arelia said in a quiet aside to Anne. "Such a marvelous way to start the week, don't you think? It's always so refreshing to hear how miserably we fail, no matter how hard we try." Then she smiled archly as she added, "Though, granted, some of us don't try so hard as others."

Before Anne could respond, they arrived at the carriage and Arelia spoke again. "If the two of you don't mind, I think I should like to walk back to the Castle. I feel I need the exercise after sitting so long."

When neither Anne nor her ladyship made any objection, Arelia turned toward the path leading past the cemetery and into the wood beyond. It was a walk of nearly three-quarters of a mile.

Since the day was overcast and the hour still early, there had not been enough warmth to burn off the dew. Arelia's thin shoes were soon wet through from the damp grass, but she didn't mind. She watched as a large squirrel scampered to a low branch, then sat to enjoy one of last season's acorns, his sharply clawed paws skillfully turning the shell as he nibbled his way inside. The wood was lovely. Wild summer flowers bloomed in great profusion on the woodland floor, while overhead the song thrushes called incessantly through the still morning air. Why, surrounded by such beauty, did she feel so close to tears?

Arelia walked on rapidly until she heard a voice call from behind, "Mrs. Saunders, please wait."

She raised a gloved hand quickly to brush the tears from her eyes as Dennis jogged up behind her. "I thought you drove to church this morning?"

"We did," she said, not looking at him as he walked beside her. "I chose to walk home."

"Alone?" he seemed surprised.

"Yes, alone," she answered, more sharply than she intended. Realizing he had not taken his eyes from her face since he caught her up, she said, "You are staring, Mr. Pearce."

"If I am, it's because I can see that something is troubling you," he replied. "Is there anything I can do?"

"Please, spare me the sympathetic vicar's manner," she said bitterly. "I have had enough pious posturing this morning to last me a month. Tell me, did you suggest the text for your brother's sermon, or was it lucky coincidence?"

"Do you really believe I would do that?"

"It wouldn't surprise me," she said, "particularly after what you saw in the rose garden the other night."

There was a pause before he replied quietly, "I was afraid that had distressed you. You have been rather . . . distant lately." When she didn't answer after several moments, he said, "In that text our Lord has gone to the Garden of Gethsemane. He has asked the disciples to watch and pray with Him, but they have fallen asleep. He isn't speaking specifically about temptations of the flesh."

"Does the context matter so much?" she returned. "The verse still speaks of temptation and the sins of the flesh. And if that one doesn't suit, I am certain you could quote me a dozen others that deal directly with the subject."

Reaching out he took her arm to stop her and turn her to face him. "You sound as if you are angry with me. Why?"

"Angry? Yes, I suppose I am angry. What were you doing in the garden at that hour of the night?" she demanded.

"I couldn't sleep; I was on my way down to the kitchens to warm some milk. It is much shorter to cut through the garden."

She half laughed in response. "Warm milk! Most men would pour themselves a large brandy. But you're not like most men, are you, Mr. Pearce?"

"I hope not," he answered.

When she could no longer sustain his regard, she began walking again.

"I don't know why you should care so much that I saw you together," he continued. "It is not my place to judge your behavior, and I have not done so. If you love Lord Wilmington and intend to marry him—"

"I do not love Lord Wilmington, and I do not intend to marry him," she interrupted.

This surprised him more than anything she had said so far, for he had been assuming that her forthcoming marriage was a *fait accompli*.

Without pausing to think, he spoke on impulse. "Then why were you—?"

"I simply yielded to temptation. It was just as your brother said in the sermon, a weakness of the flesh."

When he didn't reply, she said, "I see I have finally succeeded in rendering you speechless. Would it help my case any if I were to tell you that I would have regretted my actions even if you hadn't seen us? I know it is wrong to raise false hopes in Wilmington."

"Regret and repentance are necessary for forgiveness," he said, then added unexpectedly, "which I need as much as you."

"*You* need forgiveness? For what?"

"That night you believe I was . . . what? . . . dismayed? offended? disappointed? Later, perhaps, I was. But my first feeling, my first emotion was none of those. The first thing I felt when I saw you together . . . was jealousy."

It was now her turn to stop walking and stare at him.

"It didn't last long," he continued. "I pushed the feeling quickly to its proper place. But it was there. Very strong and frightfully real. So you see, the sermon spoke as much to me as it did to you. None of us is safe from the desires of the flesh. Sin surrounds us every day; we must always be on guard against it."

Carefully hiding the hope his little confession raised in her, Arelia asked Mr. Pearce if she might have the support of his arm over a particularly rough portion of the path. He complied and she linked her arm through his, resting her fingers lightly along his strong forearm.

"It seems we both harbored some misunderstanding about that night, sir. I once thought we could be friends. Perhaps it is still possible."

He agreed it was possible, and they lapsed into a companionable silence as they walked along, both occupied with their own thoughts, sifting through the conversation they had just shared, drawing inferences from it.

Dennis was relieved to think Mrs. Saunders would not be marrying Lord Wilmington after all, while Arelia had reason to hope that her newly discovered attraction for Mr. Pearce was reciprocated.

There was nothing unusual about Monday morning, nothing to forewarn Anne that this was a day that would totally change her life. She rose at the normal time, dressed in her sky blue calico, and shared a fruitful morning of study with Belinda. At eleven o'clock, Tom and Dennis joined them for a French lesson. It too, went smoothly. Dennis was in better spirits and so was Arelia. Anne didn't have to guess why. She had seen them arrive home together after church. Clearly, they had come to some understanding.

After luncheon, Anne sat alone in her room planning Belinda's lessons for the remainder of the week. Since her windows faced the rear of the Castle, she was not privileged to see the emblazoned post-chaise-and-four that arrived and deposited a distinguished-looking man. Her first hint that a visitor was in the Castle came when Kimble knocked quietly at her door. Anne said, "Come," then rose in surprise when she saw who stood there. Kimble had never come to her door before, in fact she couldn't ever remember seeing him above the first floor.

She hurried to the door, certain that whatever brought Kimble to her must be of importance. "Yes, Kimble what is it?"

"You have a visitor, Miss Waverly. He has sent up his card."

Anne lifted the delicate, gilt-edged card from the silver salver Kimble held in his hand.

"The Duke of Chadwicke!" she exclaimed. Suddenly suspicious, she said, "This is some sort of hoax, Kimble, isn't it?"

"Certainly not, miss. The gentleman arrived just a few moments ago. You can see the coach in the drive if you disbelieve me."

"But there must be some mistake. He cannot wish to see me."

"I assure you, miss, he was quite specific. Asked for you by name. Said he understood you were employed here as governess to Mrs. Saunders's daughter."

Realizing that if Kimble was telling the truth, she was keeping a duke waiting, Anne hurriedly followed the butler downstairs. In the great hall several footmen in crimson-and-white livery stood at attention near Lord Tenbury's servants. She had no time to consider what this visitor might want with her before Kimble opened the doors of the salon and announced her.

"Miss Waverly, Your Grace."

Anne took a few steps into the room as Kimble pulled the doors together behind her. She found herself confronted by a thin, elderly gentleman dressed severely in black and white. He raised his quizzing glass and surveyed her critically from head to foot.

"How do you do, Your Grace," she muttered as she curtsied deeply, then stood irresolutely.

"Well, come, girl, come closer. I will not bite you, after all. Come and sit near me, so I may sit as well. I hate standing about. Awkward business, standing about."

Anne moved to the chair he indicated and seated herself, while he continued, almost without drawing breath, "I daresay you're wondering who I am and why I'm here. I know your grandfather, you see." As he paused and sat near her, Anne had the unmistakable feeling he was as uncomfortable taking part in this interview as she was.

"Which grandfather?" Anne asked, when he seemed unlikely to enlighten her.

"Sir Giles—Giles Pentworth. Knew him as a boy, was a close friend till he went overseas. Our properties marched with one another. Still do actually; the boundaries haven't changed in nearly two hundred years. It is on behalf of your grandfather that I am here, Miss Waverly."

"I have never met my grandfather, Your Grace. He went out to India shortly after I was born. He never communicated with us."

"I hesitate to disagree with a lady, but he did communicate! Told me he wrote to your father on more than one occasion, asking if there was anything he could do for you—the only child of his only child."

"My father never told me."

"Your grandfather may be far away, Miss Waverly, but I can tell you this—all these years he has kept track of you. That's where I come into his plan. Years ago, when he left, he asked me to keep an eye on you, and I have done so. I had an arrangement with your rector, Mr. Pomeroy, and in more recent years, Mr. Boone. Twice a year they would write me, telling me how you went on. These letters I forwarded to your grandfather."

"But why didn't he write to *me*?"

"He had no wish to intrude. He and your father had never been on the best of terms, and when your father made it clear that he wished no assistance, Giles respected that decision. But now that your father is gone, God rest his soul, your grandfather

137

wishes to settle some property on you, property that he intended for your mother."

When he paused for breath, Anne could think of nothing to say. To imagine that her grandfather had gathered news of her all these years! And she'd never known nor even suspected.

The duke continued, "You must understand, Miss Waverly, that Sir Giles is a nabob. Not six months after his father died, he took his inheritance and invested it in India—gems, spices, rare and costly fabrics. He cared not one jot for those who looked down their noses at him for daring to go into trade. He has amassed a fortune, and he wishes to share it with you."

When he paused politely to allow her to respond, she felt foolish and thick headed. "You must forgive me, Your Grace. It's just that this is all rather hard to take in. My father regretted that Sir Giles was in trade, and his comments led me to believe that grandfather barely subsisted. Now you are telling me that he is a wealthy man?"

"I am telling you that Sir Giles is an *extremely* wealthy man. Giles doted on your mother. She was his only child to survive infancy, and he had great plans for her. Since she was only nine-and-twenty when she died, her death was a severe blow. When he learned of your father's death, Giles got the notion to make over to you, on your twenty-ninth birthday, those properties he intended for your mother. I have his solicitor waiting in another room. It lacks a week till your birthday, but it will take at least that long to sign and process all the papers transferring the various properties to you."

"Exactly what properties do you speak of?"

"The ancestral home, which adjoins mine in Norfolk, will descend upon your grandfather's death to his closest living male relative—your cousin three times removed. But to you, Sir Giles has already deeded Pentworth House and its revenues, situated on a two-thousand-acre estate in Lincolnshire; he has also made over to you his London house, in Charles Street, I believe. Nothing fancy, but respectable. Giles was never fond of London, but his wife was often there for the Season before they left for the East. Both properties are free from mortgage and in excellent condition. The London residence is closed. Pentworth House has a skeleton staff and an excellent steward. I have given orders for it to be totally turned out and readied against your arrival, should you decide to visit there, or indeed go there to live."

"Go there to live?" Anne repeated. Most of what he had just said was floating somewhere in the air over her head, refusing to sink in.

"It is your home now, if you wish it. You cannot continue as a governess now that you are a woman of independent means."

Anne rose from her chair without speaking and walked to the windows facing the front of the Castle. *A woman of independent means.* Before she could even begin to assimilate the thought, the duke spoke again.

"There is one other item about which you must be informed. Your grandfather invested much of his capital in precious gems. These are safely deposited at Barclay's in London. At their last appraisal their estimated worth was near one hundred thousand pounds. He wishes you to have these as well, either to set into jewelry or to preserve as an investment for your future."

Anne turned from the windows to regard him with renewed consternation. "How can this be? Is he such a wealthy man?"

"He is, though few know it. He keeps to himself and, though he lives comfortably, is not particularly ostentatious. His heir, for instance, knows nothing of the existence of these gems."

"But why should he give me so much when he doesn't even know me?"

"He is nearly eighty years old, and you are his only close blood relation. To whom else should he give it?"

"I can't imagine. I just never dreamed . . . Could I write to him, to thank him?"

"Certainly. I can give you his direction. I know he would be pleased to correspond with you."

"What will I ever do with such wealth?" she asked.

"Enjoy it, husband it well, use it for good if you can, and don't be deceived into thinking only good can come of it. Great wealth can be a curse as well as a blessing. People who never noticed you before will fall over themselves to be gracious. Men who wouldn't give you a passing glance will pay compliments to your eyes and tell you your wit and intelligence are second to none. Wealth will attract fortune hunters as carrion attracts crows."

═══13═══

The Duke of Chadwicke allowed Anne very little time to assimilate his extraordinary news before he sent for the solicitor to join them. Mr. Murphy was short and slight. He walked with a hurried step and carried a document case that appeared too heavy for him.

After formal introductions were made, the duke continued, "Murphy has administered your grandfather's estate for many years, Miss Waverly. If you take my advice, you will continue to employ him. He is intimately acquainted with the details of your property and highly qualified to advise you concerning it. He needs you to sign a few documents today. As your grandfather's representative in this matter, I have reviewed them carefully, but we will explain each to you as we proceed."

Nearly an hour later, the gentlemen formally took their leave. When Mr. Murphy had collected his various papers and fastidiously stowed them away, the duke bid Anne farewell, encouraging her to contact him if she had any further need of his services. The two men left the Castle together, climbed into the coach, and were soon on their way.

Anne stood at the windows of the salon and watched until the coach disappeared from sight. She thought for a moment how easy it would be to believe she had imagined the whole thing, for it had seemed as unreal as Tenbury's kiss in the dark woodland pool. Yet when she looked down at the leather pouch in her hand, a pouch containing five hundred pounds in small notes and golden guineas, she knew it had really happened. She had never seen so much money at one time in her life. When she had objected to taking it, both gentlemen were adamant. They insisted she would need money for new clothes, for travel expenses.

Anne was still standing at the window when both Arelia and Lady Tenbury entered the salon, demanding to be told how it was that Anne came to be acquainted with the Duke of Chadwicke.

"He is Tenbury's uncle," the countess offered, "but I have not seen him in years. He seldom leaves his estates in Norfolk."

"I don't know him," Anne replied. "I never met him before today."

"What did he want?" Arelia asked. "You sat so long with him we were nearly overcome with curiosity."

"His Grace has brought me wonderful news, something I never suspected. It seems he is a trusted friend of my maternal grandfather. He informed me that when I turn twenty-nine on the fifth of August, I will be in possession of an independence." It was an outrageous understatement, but she could bring herself to say no more.

"Why, Anne!" Lady Tenbury exclaimed. "What good fortune!"

"Indeed, ma'am. I am most fortunate."

"I'm not so sure I agree," Arelia said, half-teasing. "If you have an independence, you will leave us. I'm not certain I care for that."

"Leave you?"

"Well, you would hardly wish to continue as governess," Arelia reasoned. "Did he tell you how much you would have?"

"It seems there is an estate, and a modest London

142

residence, and some income as well."

"That settles it, then," Arelia said, a broad smile showing her pleasure at her friend's wonderful news. "Your days as a governess are over. Belinda must have a holiday until I find a replacement for you. I am so happy for you, Anne!"

Another hour passed before Anne was able to escape her well wishers and go off on her own. It seemed no amount of time would be sufficient to take in all that had happened in the last few days. Her life was changing suddenly, radically, and she wasn't at all certain she wished it to. These last few months at Tenton Castle had been some of the fullest she had ever known. Although she had been content with her father, she had never had the opportunity to make friends her own age—friends like Jack, Dennis, and Arelia.

If she were to leave the Castle, she thought she would miss Arelia most. She had spent less time with her than with the others, yet their friendship was special. She had shared many of her private thoughts with Arelia, and Arelia had confided equally in her. It was a friendship such as sisters shared—a friendship she had never expected to have.

Anne spent the remainder of the afternoon in her room, finding that her head ached from all the information it was being forced to deal with, for the more she pondered it, the more unbelievable it seemed. Since she was looking forward to a quiet meal in her room and an evening of solitude, she was distressed when Lady Tenbury sent a message inviting her to join the family for dinner. Not certain what she should do, she went to find Dennis to seek his advice. She briefly explained her new-found wealth, once again making light of its size and extent.

"If there is a problem in all this, I don't see it," he replied. "Weren't you just telling me a few weeks ago that you hated the thought of having no control of your life? Now you will have; you should be delighted."

"Of course, I am pleased," she responded, "but what should I do about Lady Tenbury's invitation to dine with the family?"

"You should go."

"But how can I? Yesterday the governess, today a guest at dinner. I would feel most uncomfortable."

"Anne, you are not a servant here; you never were. You were a gentlewoman forced to earn her living, but a gentlewoman all the same. The position didn't change who you are."

"Perhaps not. But I feel as if it did. Arelia didn't ask if I wanted to stop teaching, she simply assumed I would. She said Belinda could have a holiday until I was replaced. If I no longer have my post, then there is no reason for me to stay. I can see Arelia was right when she said I would leave. I must leave; there is no place for me here."

When she looked at Dennis, she found him regarding her steadily, but he did not reply. "You agree with me, don't you?" she asked.

"Yes. I understand how you feel. You are caught in an awkward situation."

"I can be uncaught simply enough. I have money; I have a home to go to. The duke said it has even been prepared for me. How do I hire a coach to carry me there, Dennis?"

"The Duck 'N' Drake in Winthrop hires post chaises. For a few pence I could send a village boy with a note."

"Will you write the note for me? I wouldn't know what to ask for."

"How far do you plan to go?"

"To Lincolnshire."

"When would you like to leave?"

"Tomorrow, as early as possible."

144

"Anne, are you sure? Perhaps you should take more time to consider."

"I am sure, Dennis, of only one thing—I no longer belong here. I will do my thinking elsewhere."

Anne joined Arelia, Jack, and Lady Tenbury in the drawing room before dinner. She came at the last moment, hoping they would all be there before her.

All three looked up as she entered, and she decided to speak at once. She addressed Lady Tenbury, "I thank you for your kind invitation to dine with you, ma'am, but I regret I must decline it. With your permission, I should like to leave tomorrow, and I must do all my packing tonight." At Lady Tenbury's pained expression, Anne added, "You have been most kind to me, all of you, but I need time alone to adjust to this change in my circumstances."

She could think of nothing further to say. It was Jack who recognized her discomfort and rescued her from having to say more. "Of course, you do. We understand. But you must promise that when you have settled your affairs, you will come back to visit."

She smiled at him but made no promise.

Noticing the omission, Arelia stepped closer and said, "You were always much more than an employee here. Go if you must, but know we shall all miss you."

Very near tears by this point, Anne quickly excused herself and hurried to her room. There she carefully packed her belongings into trunks and cases. Near midnight, both mentally and physically exhausted, she crawled into bed and was soon asleep.

At nine the following morning, Dennis stopped at her room to inform her that the earliest the posting house could send a coach was eleven o'clock.

"Kimble says the footmen can carry your things down now, if you like."

"Thank you, Dennis. They are ready."

By ten o'clock Anne's belongings were stacked in the great hall. She had said good-bye to the children and to Arelia, Dennis, and Lady Tenbury. She was not anxious about the carriage ride ahead and had even allowed the cook to pack her a lunch, which she had every intention of eating. Attired in a modest tan traveling dress, she sat in the library with Jack, awaiting the arrival of the hired post chaise. They were not speaking of her reasons for leaving; they were reminiscing instead about all the things they had done together that summer.

Lord Tenbury was in a foul temper. He had been driving almost continuously for four days on a fruitless mission. He had driven first to London, then to Norfolk, in search of the Duke of Chadwicke, only to learn upon arriving at the duke's residence that His Grace was away from home on a visit to Tenton Castle!

So Tenbury had journeyed back to Wiltshire. Just outside Winthrop, he was forced to collect his team to a trot as he came up behind a slow-moving post chaise. He waited impatiently for the only straightaway wide enough to pass, then swore irritably when he saw there was a vehicle approaching in the opposite direction.

At each crossroad, where there was a possibility that the coach might turn off, it proceeded stubbornly on his route. When it slowed to turn in at the gates of the Castle, he swung his team around it, cantered them the wrong way down the drive normally used as an exit from the park, and arrived at the Castle first.

Jumping down from the curricle, he mounted the steps quickly and demanded of Kimble, "Are we expecting visitors?"

Given no opportunity to welcome Lord Tenbury home, Kimble was forced to answer, "No, my lord.

I believe this is the coach hired by Miss Waverly. She is leaving today."

"Leaving?" Tenbury stepped into the hall. He stood for a moment contemplating the pile of baggage stacked there. He slowly stripped off his driving gloves and handed them to Kimble, then glanced through the doors as the hired coach pulled up before the Castle. "Pay off the post boys and send that vehicle back where it came from," he ordered Kimble. "If Miss Waverly plans to travel, she will do so in my coach, with servants I can trust. Where is she?"

"I believe Miss Waverly is in the library, sir, with your brother."

While Kimble stepped outside to dismiss the hired chaise, Tenbury walked the short distance to the library doors.

Anne rose instantly when she saw him on the threshold; she had hoped to be gone before he returned. As he advanced, she noticed his blue coat was wrinkled and his breeches creased, while the customary shine of his boots had been obscured by dust, and his fair hair disordered by the wind. His eyes looked tired, but beyond the fatigue was something else.

"Excuse us, Jack," Tenbury said abruptly, never taking his eyes from Anne's face.

A shiver of fear raced through Anne at those words, an emotion she had never before connected with Tenbury. She wanted more than anything for Jack to stay in the room, but she would not ask him to defy his brother.

"I'll see you before you go," was all Jack said before he left them alone.

"Kimble tells me you are leaving," Tenbury stated.

"Yes. A great deal has happened since you left the Castle on Friday, my lord. I can't think where to begin."

But she did begin, telling him she'd had a visitor

and who the visitor was. Several minutes into her dialogue, Anne had the impression the earl wasn't listening. His eyes had a vacant, far-away look, much like the one a teacher sees in the eyes of a student who is not attending. She paused, for some reason suddenly remembering the words she had overheard Tenbury speak to his mother. "*She was hired by my contrivance. I have a specific reason for wanting to keep her within my control.*" That memory, coupled with Lady Tenbury's revelation of the kinship between Tenbury and Chadwicke, raised a sudden suspicion. "None of this is news to you, is it, Lord Tenbury?" she asked.

She watched carefully as his eyes and thoughts focused on her, returning from wherever they had been. He didn't answer but walked away to the windows and stood looking out, offering her only his profile to study. After a moment she followed him there, standing directly before him so she could read his expression clearly.

"You knew I was to receive an inheritance," she accused.

"Yes, I knew."

"When did you know?"

"From the beginning."

"How did you know?"

"Chadwicke told me. That's where I've been these past days. I went to his home in Norfolk. I intended to ask his permission to tell you about the inheritance myself. But my trip was in vain."

"Because he had already left to come here."

"Yes."

"When you say you knew from the beginning, when precisely was that?"

"Before we met. I planned to have you hear of the position in my house. I arranged to have you hired."

Her eyed widened in surprise. "To what purpose?"

"Chadwicke was concerned when you moved to London. He wanted to be certain you came to no harm, that you found a safe refuge until the day he was free to tell you of your grandfather's plans. He enlisted me to help him."

"So I wasn't hired for my qualifications after all. When Mr. Raymond sent me away, that was all a plan, a game so I wouldn't suspect."

"No. That was a point where my plans went awry. Raymond knew nothing of my design. I did not expect you to come without references, so I did not foresee that he might dismiss you."

Now it was her turn to walk away. She sat on the edge of a nearby chair, shaking her head in disbelief. "But why couldn't you simply tell me the truth? Why was all the deception necessary?"

"Pentworth wanted nothing said until all was arranged. Chadwicke actually knew few of the details until recently, though he suspected the property would be considerable."

"Then all these months, when I thought you were being kind to me, you were filling the role of *duenna*—a watch-dog to the Pentworth heiress! Is that right?"

"Not precisely."

"But wait," she said, as another thought intruded. "You said you knew everything before we met, but that is not possible. We first met in the milliner's shop. You were not there by design."

"I was," he confessed. "I followed you that day. I overheard you tell your companion you were seeking a position. I then acted on the information."

"So you came to my aid that day only because you were protecting my interests?"

"That is partially true, yes."

"Come now, Lord Tenbury. Only partially? I viewed you that day as some sort of guardian angel, while the truth is you only helped me because you felt obligated. Your gentle concern for my lack of recommendations—it was all a sham. You hired me, or undoubtedly forced your sister-in-law to hire me, despite my qualifications being less than adequate. Your apprehension when I walked about the town, your solicitude when you discovered my motion sickness, even your heroic rescue at the lake—you didn't do any of those things for Anne Waverly, your niece's governess—you did them for Anne Waverly, heiress-to-be. You could not allow this heiress to drown in the lake, nor permit her to fetch and carry; she must not work too hard, nor too long, nor too strenuously.

"I *trusted* you, from the first. I thought you sensitive and caring and gentle. You were there when I needed you; you smoothed out the rough places, had all the answers, made me face my fears, allowed me to respect and admire you. And all the while you were deceiving me, never concerning yourself with who I was, but only what I was worth."

When she finally paused he said, "Much of what you say is true; I cannot deny it. At first I did see you merely as a responsibility—even an inconvenience. But at some point, between then and now, things changed."

Suddenly she rose from her chair and lifted her reticule from a nearby table. "I'm sorry, Lord Tenbury, but I must go now. There is a coach waiting for me."

"I sent it away."

"You sent it away! You had no right," she snapped.

"If, when we have finished our discussion, you still want to leave, my coach and servants will take you wherever you wish to go."

"As far as I am concerned, we have finished our discussion, sir."

"I suspected you would be angry when you learned the truth," he said, "but I didn't think you would be so unfair as to refuse to hear my explanation."

"I *have* heard your explanation."

"About my reasons for employing you, yes. But we have not discussed Thursday night."

When he mentioned the night they had kissed, she felt herself blushing, but when she tried to walk away, he took hold of her arms above the elbows.

"I hadn't meant for it to happen," he said. "When it did, I was uncertain how to proceed. I wanted to tell you then how I felt, but found I couldn't with so many secrets between us. That's why I went to speak with Chadwicke. I thought if I could first explain to you about the inheritance and the part I had played in your being here, then it would be easier to explain what happened that night."

She was listening to what he said, but finding it difficult to concentrate. His hands, despite all she now knew of him, felt warm and wonderful. His voice was like the sweetest music. He was so close, inches from where he had been that night, pressed tightly against her.

"Anne." The single word was half-caress, half-pleading question. She looked into his fervent blue eyes. How easy it would be to lose herself in them.

No doubt sensing her weakness, he lowered his head to kiss her, but the moment contact was made, she pulled away.

"I think it would be best if we simply forget what happened that night, Lord Tenbury. I was kissed by a man I thought I knew. But I was wrong. I don't know you at all, and I don't believe I wish to. I have said good-bye to everyone, and I should like to leave the Castle—immediately."

As he stood regarding her in silence, she felt he was about to argue, but he said only, "I will have a coach at the door in fifteen minutes."

He moved toward the door then but stopped before he reached it. "There is one thing you must believe. No one besides Chadwicke and myself knew anything about this—not my mother, nor Arelia, nor Jack. There is nothing false in their feelings for you." He left the room without looking at her again.

Tears sprang to her eyes as she stood there alone. She wasn't sure why, but she believed him, and she was grateful he was the only one involved. At least the relationships she had shared with the other members of his family had not been a lie.

In the hall Tenbury ordered his chaise-and-four brought to the door immediately. Then he instructed Kimble to speak with the maid Cassie. "Tell her she has five minutes to pack. She is to accompany Miss Waverly to Lincolnshire. If she wishes to remain there in Miss Waverly's employ, she is free to do so."

Tenbury shut himself in his study, leaving strict orders that he should not be disturbed. He withdrew from an inside coat pocket the special license he had collected as he passed through London. As he propped it against his ink stand and reached for the brandy decanter, he wondered briefly what had led him to believe that a woman as principled as Anne Waverly would ever consider an offer of marriage from a man who had so completely betrayed her trust.

——14——

Anne's journey into Lincolnshire took the better part of two days. She ate a meal at each stop and though she suffered not at all from motion sickness, she suffered greatly from heart sickness.

During her interview with Lord Tenbury, she had wanted nothing more than to be gone. Now, even though she tried again and again to force all thought of him from her mind, that meeting kept coming back in bits and pieces to haunt her. She had accused him of much, he had admitted much, yet there was so much more that had been left unsaid, so many questions unanswered.

He said he had wanted to tell her how he felt. What did that mean? She realized now it could mean almost anything. Why hadn't she asked him to explain?

Did he know the extent of her wealth? She had failed to ask him that. After consideration, she decided he probably did. She also thought she understood his actions the evening in the pool. She had no great beauty, but it was possible she had more wealth than Lady Mason, Lady Naismith, and Miss Redditch combined. Certainly enough wealth to make her palatable as a wife. Tenbury had never shown any interest in the lively butterflies Arelia paraded before him year after year. Had he concluded that an extremely wealthy, quiet wife, who would sit at home and allow him to go his own way, would suit him best?

Her most unsettling memories of their last meeting were the emotions that took control when he touched her. How was it that he still had such power to attract her? Why for that brief moment had she considered yielding to him? Passion, she decided, was a complex and fearsome thing. But Anne Waverly—reasonable, intelligent woman that she was—had no intention of allowing such an emotion to rule her reason again.

The Duke of Chadwicke had told Anne little about Pentworth House beyond the fact that it was well managed; therefore, she was pleasantly surprised when she arrived there. Approached through a heavily wooded park, the red brick manor nestled on the far side of a small clearing. It was compact and rectangular, two stories overall with a third story rising above the central portion. A raked gravel drive, retained by a skillfully constructed stone wall, turned in a gentle arc before the house. From a break in the center of the wall five shallow steps descended to a natural pond surrounded by carefully scythed lawn and wildly colored flower beds.

Inside the house all was clean and orderly. A crisp housekeeper curtsied and greeted Anne with a smile, then invited Lord Tenbury's servants to spend the night. When they departed the following morning, Anne was left with only Cassie in a house full of people she didn't know.

Yet the transition from stranger to mistress did not take long. Anne met her steward and saw immediately that the duke had been correct about him—he appeared to be an honest, able, industrious man. All the servants at Pentworth seemed pleased to have the house occupied again, while Anne was happy to involve herself in any activity that came to hand, for the busier she stayed, the less time she had to think of Tenton Castle and the friends she left behind. Pentworth House had been decorated with both taste and style; she found it suited her well.

Anne wrote to her old vicar, Mr. Boone, to discover if his widowed sister-in-law, Mrs. Sophia Boone, would be interested in coming to Anne in the position of companion. Mrs. Boone was approaching fifty, but she and Anne had always been compatible; Anne was certain they could cohabit comfortably. If she must have a companion, she preferred Mrs. Boone to anyone else.

Sophy Boone, nearly as pleased at the opportunity to help Anne as to relieve her brother of the burden of her support, purchased a ticket on the mail coach and was with Anne within a few days of receiving her letter.

Anne spent the month of August settling in to her new home. She wrote to Belinda, Tom, Lady Tenbury, and Arelia, but only Belinda and Lady Tenbury answered with any regularity. When Arelia did write, she dashed off a quick note only, always apologizing for being a poor correspondent, admitting she was not good at friendships over long distances. Anne was not offended nor surprised by this. It would have been uncharacteristic for Arelia to sit for any amount of time laboring over the composition of a letter.

All who wrote to Anne mentioned the earl occasionally; none of them knew that he and Anne had quarreled. And, of course, with each correspondence she received from the Castle came Tenbury's frank, scrawled across the corner. She couldn't recall ever seeing his signature before; now she had a collection of them tied with a ribbon in her desk drawer. It was a bold, self-assured hand. Sometimes when a letter arrived, she would gaze at the signature and try to imagine him writing it there.

It was a short note from Arelia in early September that started Anne thinking about a visit to London.

Arelia stated that she and Lady Tenbury were going to the city soon. She suggested that Anne open her house and come up for the Little Season.

The efficiency of the staff at Pentworth House left Anne with little to do. It was tempting to think of browsing in some of the London shops she had merely glanced into. She had always dreamed of visiting the museums, the libraries, the theater, perhaps even the opera. Her aunt had kept her too busy for these entertainments on her first visit to London; if she went now, she could do as she wished.

With Arelia's letter in her hand she went in search of her steward. She found him in his office and, as was her custom, came directly to the point. "Mr. Romney, how long would it take to prepare my London house for occupancy?"

"If I could take some experienced staff with me and be authorized to hire more when I arrived in town, I would say less than a week."

"Could you spare the time now to undertake the project?"

"I can leave tomorrow."

Anne was not surprised at his willingness to leave immediately, for she had encountered this spirit of cooperation at their first meeting. Knowing next to nothing about land or property ownership, Anne had determined at the outset to make her wishes known, then allow those who were experienced to implement them for her. She explained to Mr. Romney the way she wished her household to run, then left the hiring of a complete staff to him. She defined what she needed in terms of carriages and horses, but left the choosing of the vehicles and animals entirely to others. Now she simply stated that she wished her London residence prepared, and she knew without question that when she arrived there, all would be orderly and proper.

Throughout the whole process she tried to listen and learn, but she soon discovered that the change from isolated country spinster and governess to lady of property would not be accomplished overnight. Her bank account might place her among the wealthiest women in England, but in her mind and heart she was still the scholar's daughter.

Having the money at her back gave her a wonderful sense of freedom and an almost childlike delight in shopping, but it added little to her self-confidence. Nor did it add to her sense of security, for somehow she believed that if wealth could come so easily, without warning, then it could disappear just as easily.

Sometimes at night, she would dream that the gems had been stolen and the house reduced to ashes. She saw herself tired and hungry, using her last coins to take a coach to Tenton Castle. She stood on the steps in the rain as Tenbury answered the door; she begged him to take her in, to allow her to be governess again. He never answered her, but only stood there with an inscrutable expression on his face.

At this point the dream would invariably end, the image of his face slowly trailing away, disappearing into a mist of light and shadow. And in those first moments after he was gone, despite the trauma of loss—loss of her wealth and loss of her home—it was not those feelings that held the uppermost thought. Instead she longed to hear him speak, was frustrated time and time again by his silence. If only the dream would continue a moment longer, what would he say to her?

Anne and Sophy Boone arrived in London to find the house in Charles Street modest in size but lavishly decorated. Handsome paneling and stylish paper brightened many of the rooms, while throughout the house, floors were spread with priceless Oriental carpets.

Costly Eastern vases sat in niches that appeared to be designed specifically for them. The salon exhibited a collection of jade and ivory figurines crafted with amazing skill. Anne was admiring these when Mr. Romney arrived home from one of his many trips to the employment agency.

"We found those in one of the trunks in the attic," he said. "I don't know if you admire Oriental art, but I thought they were rather spectacular."

"They are . . . indescribable," Anne replied, setting aside a small unicorn with tiny, delicate hooves.

"There are numerous crates and boxes in the attics, Miss Waverly. It seems your grandfather collected a great many things. Some of the crates shipped from India have never been opened."

"He can't intend me to have them."

"Sir Giles's instructions state clearly that this house and its contents are entirely yours," her steward insisted.

"Well, if my grandfather went to all the trouble to collect these, then we shall make every effort to display them as lovingly as he would."

A short time later, while Anne continued to explore her salon and Sophy knitted comfortably near the windows, Anne's new butler, a dauntingly sober figure hired only two days earlier, announced from the doorway, "Mrs. Arelia Saunders, miss."

"Arelia, I did not expect to see you so soon!" Anne exclaimed as she moved forward with both hands outstretched to welcome her friend.

"Your note said you would arrive this morning. I hoped I would be your first visitor."

"And so you are. You look wonderful; what a charming gown!" At this flattering tribute to her aquamarine morning dress, Arelia did a pirouette before she came further into the room to be introduced to Anne's companion. Since Mrs. Boone was not a gregarious person, she soon returned to her knitting, content to listen as the two friends caught up on each other's news.

"How are the children?" Anne asked.

"They are well. Busy with their studies. I have never known Tom to apply himself with such energy to anything. Mr. Pearce has worked wonders with him."

"And Belinda?"

"She was uncomfortable for a time with Miss Twitte, but I think she is getting on much better now. She misses you."

"I miss her, too. But she writes to me nearly every week. What of Mr. Pearce, Arelia? Have you remained friends?"

"We have. I often listen to him play. We went for a ride together once and even walked to the lake one evening after dinner."

"You like him more than a little, don't you?" Anne asked tentatively.

"I do, yes. I find myself liking him more each day. Unfortunately, I believe he finds me frivolous. He keeps me always at a distance; there is a reserve. Perhaps he . . . " She hesitated, conscious of Mrs. Boone listening to every word. "Perhaps he has not forgotten the rose garden."

"But I thought you said he understood?"

"He said he did."

"Then, I believe you should take him at his word," Anne offered.

"Perhaps," Arelia returned. "Time will tell."

"Has Lord Tenbury come to town?" Anne asked carefully, trying to sound as if Arelia's answer would be of only passing interest to her.

"No. He and Jack left last week for the horse races. I believe they planned on going first to York, then to Newmarket for the St. Leger. I can't precisely recall. Tenbury has been moody of late. Snaps at a person for no apparent reason. Imagine this: he informed me that I need not bother to clutter the Castle with beautiful women for the hunting season. 'I am weary of your matchmaking schemes, Arelia,' he said. He told me to invite what friends I wished and he would invite his, but that I should leave my matrimonial candidates to someone else, for he'd had his fill of them."

Then, typically, Arelia changed the subject suddenly. "What are you doing this afternoon? Will you come with me to Collette's? I am having a new ball gown fitted. I should love you to see it. And if you plan on attending ton parties yourself, we will keep Collette busy cutting gowns for you."

"Perhaps I shall not be invited to parties."

"No chance of that, dear Anne, no chance at all."

During the following days, Anne took part in what she afterward described as a frenzy of shopping. With Arelia as her guide and adviser, she was certain she visited every fashionable shop the city held. She was equally certain she purchased something from each of them.

Every day parcels and packages arrived at her house, delivered from the dressmakers or the milliners or the cobblers. Into the empty drawers of her dressing room were stowed stockings and filmy underclothing, gloves and scarfs and delicate dancing slippers. In seemingly no time the huge, nearly empty wardrobes were brimming with gowns of every description—walking dresses, morning dresses, evening gowns, and ball gowns of blue and orchid, apricot, indigo, and vermilion.

Anne's first public appearance was at a small dinner party held by Lady Tenbury at Tenbury House and including only twenty of her closest friends. Anne had chosen to wear a gown of Prussian blue that made her eyes appear darker green. She stood before the full-length mirror in her bedchamber, admiring the dressmaker's skill in fashioning the gown.

Tiny pleats fell from a high waistline banded by a piece of wide ribbon, which was drawn into a bow at the back. Short puffed sleeves emerged from a modest neckline to overlay long sheer sleeves that buttoned at the wrist, while row upon row of delicate ruffles whispered about her ankles. A pair of slippers, short gloves, and a single strand of pearls with matching earrings completed her ensemble.

Anne stood for a long time regarding the woman in the reflection. Here was a woman she knew well, but a woman the polite world had yet to meet. Clearly she remembered the duke's warning that she would be treated differently now that she was a woman of substance. It wasn't that she didn't believe him; she only hoped in her case, he might be wrong. As frightening as it was to enter a stratum of society heretofore unknown to her, it was even more frightening to think she would meet with mendacity or hypocrisy there.

In her early twenties Anne had attended a few small parties with her father in Cambridgeshire, including several at Sir Hugo Scoville's. She had danced with the young gentlemen who asked her, but she was shy, so enjoyed most to sit and listen to others talk, seldom taking part in a conversation herself. At Lady Tenbury's party she found she was no longer tongue-tied. When the gentlemen seated to her right and left at dinner addressed comments to her, she was more than willing to converse with them. As a result, the evening passed pleasantly.

Having introduced Anne in this subtle way to some of the leaders of society, Lady Tenbury suspected that within a few days Anne would receive invitations to various functions. This was indeed the case.

Since Anne had offered nothing definitive about her circumstances, it was left to the London rumor mill to fill in the unknowns concerning this new arrival on the social scene. At first the curious had little to go on: Miss Anne Waverly, formerly of Cambridgeshire, had recently come into an inheritance. She was acquainted with the Saunders family, in itself an excellent recommendation. As she was often seen in company with Lady Tenbury or Mrs. Saunders, clearly the relationship was of some standing. A trifle of information was added when someone said they were familiar with the estate Miss Waverly had inherited in Lincolnshire. Tidy little property, free and clear, they said. After several of the more curious made morning calls on Miss Waverly at her residence in Charles Street, they reported that she was surrounded in her gracious home by priceless Eastern art objects. Once even this meager information had circulated the town, it was clear to one and all that a single woman in possession of such property was someone worth noting.

Anne, not a master at pretext or dissembling, accepted all her new acquaintance on an equal footing, without prejudice. She saw none of the deceit and dishonesty the duke had warned her of. She smiled at those who smiled upon her and enjoyed her acceptance into Arelia's world.

When she was formally introduced to several of the guests who had been present at Tenton Castle in the summer, their reactions varied. She was certain Lord Wilmington knew her instantly, but after only a slight flicker of surprise, he took her hand gallantly at Arelia's introduction and proclaimed himself pleased to make her acquaintance.

When Anne realized she was to be seated near Lady Mason at a dinner party she spoke to Arelia in an anxious aside, "What shall I do if she recognizes me?"

"It's not likely she will. Persons of her self-importance consider it beneath their dignity to remember the names and faces of insignificant others. But if she does, you need only tell the truth: you were a governess who came into an inheritance." But when Anne was introduced to Lady Mason, the lady greeted her with a rigid, uninterested smile, and not the slightest spark of recognition.

It was nearing the end of September before the Earl of Tenbury and his brother Jack arrived in London. After a brief greeting to his mother, who happened to be home when he arrived, Tenbury went off to White's to enjoy the afternoon with friends he had not seen in several months. Seated with a group of men, they first discussed the results of the St. Leger, run several days earlier. Within a few minutes, however, one of the men asked Tenbury if he could shed any light on the worth of the new heiress.

"Which heiress would that be, Peabody?"

"Miss Waverly, of course. The whole town is wondering."

So Miss Waverly had come to town. Tenbury was surprised but took care to hide it as he asked, "Why should I know more than the next man?"

"She seems thick as thieves with your sister-in-law and has driven out more than once with Lady Tenbury. I assumed you might know—"

"I have little interest in the fortunes of my mother's friends, Peabody. I fear I cannot supply the information you seek."

"I told you he wouldn't know," the man beside Peabody said sourly. "It's been kept mighty close. But you can bet it's considerable; the plain ones always have the heaviest purses."

It was on Tenbury's lips to say he did not find Miss Waverly in the least plain, but he thought better of it. No one seemed aware that she had served in his house as governess. It would be best if he admitted to a slight acquaintance only. He must warn Jack to be on his guard for questions about Anne.

Peabody's friend soon spoke again. "I don't know why you're interested. She'll take a title in the end; they always do. Why should she settle for the likes of us,when she can make herself a lady. I've put my money on Farringdon. Of the three, he has the best chance."

"Of the three?" Tenbury asked politely.

"The three who have set a bet upon the books."

Instantly angry and again forced to hide it, Tenbury adroitly led the conversation to another subject. Later, after Peabody and his friend were gone, he had recourse to White's betting book and after a brief perusal found the entry the men spoke of. "Farringdon, Crilley, and Blake wager five-hundred pounds each, the losers to pay the winner upon the announcement in the *Gazette* of his engagement to Miss A. W., newest heiress on the town."

Those three! He would be surprised if they could scrape together five hundred among them. Farringdon held the highest rank, viscount, and was most often bailed out of his gambling embarrassments by an over-indulgent father. When he did inherit, Tenbury had no doubt he would run through his fortune in record time. Crilley was a baronet with mortgaged lands he had never set foot upon. His extravagant living had outrun his income for years. Tenbury was not the least surprised to find him pursuing an heiress. Blake was an impoverished Adonis of thirty who periodically allowed himself to be kept by older, wealthy women.

Taken altogether, they were not a wholesome lot. Tenbury wondered if Arelia had sufficiently warned Anne about them. She might be wealthy, but she didn't know chalk from cheese when it came to dealing with men.

Suddenly uneasy at the club, Tenbury collected his hat and gloves and called for his carriage. Arelia would be home to dress for the evening. He must speak with her.

15

When the earl returned to Tenbury House, he found Arelia resting in her sitting room before undertaking the rigors of a ball that evening.

She was, as always, pleased to see him. "Tenbury! So you have finally come to town. How were the races?"

"Much like all races," he replied shortly. "Arelia, I must speak with you about Miss Waverly."

"You know she has come to town, then."

"I could hardly help but know. Within minutes of arriving at my club I was parrying questions about the size of her fortune."

"I'm not surprised. It is the latest on-dit. The mere lack of information seems to make people all the more curious."

"What have you said?"

"Nothing. How could I? I know nothing. I would never be vulgar enough to ask Anne, and if she did tell me anything, I would never share it with sordid tattlemongers. Why are you letting it trouble you? I'm sure it is the same with every new heiress. People wish to know everything. They will eventually lose interest, and the gossip will subside."

"It troubles me because I do not like to see bets laid at the club about people I care for."

"They are placing wagers about Anne?"

"About who will ultimately lead her to the altar, yes."

"Nate, that's awful!"

"Is she aware—does she know she has false admirers?" he asked. "Have you warned her?"

"I have not. But the Duke of Chadwicke did. She told me so. And I believe she took his warning to heart. She is not a foolish schoolgirl, Nate."

"No, but she is both innocent and inexperienced, and she has no one to protect her. She has no idea of the snares that might be laid for her by those anxious to acquire her wealth. How long has she been in town?"

"A little more than two weeks."

"Have you seen her with Crilley, Blake, or Farringdon?"

"I saw her dancing last night with Viscount Farringdon. But she dances with many men."

"What of the others?"

"I believe she drove out once with Lord Blake."

"And Crilley?"

She shook her head. "I can't remember. There is always a crush of people at social gatherings. I haven't been in the habit of watching her."

"Well, if you value her, you would be well advised to keep watch over her. You might warn her as well, particularly about those three."

"Are they the ones who placed the wager?"

Avoiding a direct answer, he replied, "Not a word about this, Arelia, to anyone. If you see Jack before I do, warn him that he may be questioned about Miss Waverly."

That evening, Tenbury decided to accompany Arelia and his mother to the Margate's ball. He considered Miss Waverly's decision to come to London an unfortunate one, yet he could not resist attending on the chance he might see her. Her verbal disapproval of his behavior had seriously damaged their relationship, but it had in no way diminished his feelings for her.

Tenbury did not see Anne among the ball guests, but within an hour after their arrival, he found Arelia at his side.

"Walk with me, Tenbury," she said, "I must speak with you."

She took his arm, and they strolled together from the ball room into an adjoining reception room that was less crowded and offered more privacy. "I have just learned from a mutual acquaintance that Anne attended a masquerade tonight at Vauxhall Gardens with Lord Crilley."

"What?" Tenbury asked in an astonished undertone. "Who else made up the party?"

"Lord and Lady Summer."

"I don't know them."

"Nor do I."

"I can nearly guarantee you they are intimates of Crilley, however," he replied. "I fear I must leave, Arelia. Please make my apologies to my mother."

As he tried to turn away, Arelia kept his arm. "Nate. You had best stop first in Charles Street to discover what color she is wearing. Otherwise it could be impossible in a large crowd—"

"That's an excellent notion; I will do so." He patted her hand briefly, then was gone.

In Charles Street he learned from Cassie that Anne had indeed gone to a masquerade. Though the girl could not confirm the names of the people who accompanied Anne, she did offer the valuable information that her mistress was wearing a pale blue dress covered by a dark blue domino.

Stopping briefly at his own home to collect a black domino and mask, Tenbury soon arrived at Vauxhall Gardens. There he addressed his strong young footman Sidney. "I may encounter some problems here this evening. Stay alert. Should I need you, I will whistle—

so." He then gave a quiet example of the tones he would use, should he require the footman's assistance. Sidney nodded as Tenbury moved away and disappeared into the crowd.

The earl soon realized his task would be harder than he at first suspected. Many of the ladies' dominoes covered them so completely that it was difficult to distinguish the color of the gowns beneath. Crilley, however, was tall and fair; therefore, Tenbury was able to eliminate all those couples in which the man was either dark-haired or short. For a time he watched one likely couple dancing, then knew he was wrong when the lady's domino swung open to reveal a gown of light pink. Another couple he dismissed when he realized the lady did not share Anne's mannerisms. The tilt of her head, the movements of her hands weren't Anne's.

Finally, when he was nearly ready to admit that his quest was hopeless, he heard a lady laugh, and his pulse quickened. He turned in the direction of the sound and discovered two couples sharing supper in a booth nearby. As he watched the lady, he became convinced she was Anne. Though her eyes and the top half of her face were hidden behind a mask, he could not mistake the well-defined chin, the straight line of teeth when she smiled, the delicate lips. Retreating to a place from where he could watch without being observed, he determined to chaperone Miss Waverly until her escort returned her safely home.

Nearly twenty minutes later, the foursome vacated their box and strolled off into the dimly lit gardens. Tenbury followed a safe distance behind. At the first division of the path, the second couple split off, allowing Anne and her companion to proceed alone. Tenbury closed the distance between them. When Lord Crilley helped Anne to a seat in a secluded arbor, Tenbury quietly made his way behind it, creeping close enough in the darkness to both see them and hear their words. He had never purposely eavesdropped in his life, yet he felt no compunction now.

"Are you feeling better?" Crilley asked.

"Yes. Thank you. I can't imagine why I should feel faint. If I could sit a few moments, I'm sure I'll be better directly."

"Perhaps we danced too much. You are fatigued. Shall I take you home?"

"Maybe that would be best." Looking up, Anne seemed to realize for the first time that they were alone. "Where are Lord and Lady Summer?"

"I suppose they walked on," he answered. "Come. I will take you to my coach and have you home in no time."

As he began to draw her to her feet, Anne resisted. "I cannot go alone with you, my lord. We must wait for your friends." She put her hands up, holding her head between them. "I feel so odd; could it have been something I ate? . . . The wine?"

She had commented on the bitterness of the wine at supper. The other three had laughed, saying that Vauxhall masquerades were infamous for their mediocre wine.

"You are astute, Miss Waverly. Perhaps your wine did have an ingredient that ours lacked. You are looking not at all well. Perhaps you would allow me to support you? Try to relax . . . "

When Tenbury heard no response from Anne, his role as passive chaperone ended. As he moved quickly to the path, his shadow fell across the soft beam of light penetrating the arbor from a lantern hung along the tree-lined pathway. Crilley looked up to see a black-clad figure confronting him. He came to his feet instinctively, trying to hide Anne's drooping figure behind him.

"So sorry to disappoint you Crilley, but I fear you will detain Miss Waverly no longer tonight. She is not, as you assumed, without a protector."

Then from the darkness of the shadow, a powerful fist emerged to meet Lord Crilley's jaw. He staggered for a moment under its impact, then his knees buckled. Tenbury quickly caught him under the arms to keep him from falling backward over Anne, then deposited him to one side of the bench. Tenbury stripped the mask from his face and seated himself beside Anne, taking her hands and waiting until she looked at him. "It was perhaps unwise to come here with him," he said. "If you will come with me now, I will take you home."

Even though Anne's thoughts were muddled, Tenbury's offer to escort her home seemed more acceptable than Lord Crilley's similar suggestion a few moments ago. Despite her last meeting with Tenbury, and the bitterness of her words then, Anne never doubted she would be safe with him. As she rose shakily to her feet, he took her arm. She walked unsteadily for a few steps, leaning heavily on him for support. Clearly losing patience with their slow progress, Tenbury bent to lift her in his arms. Anne's instinctive objection died on her lips, for she had no will to utter it. To be spared the effort of walking was a sublime relief, for her feet seemed leaden and her limbs numb. She gratefully relaxed against him. Reaching her arms about his neck and nestling her head into his shoulder, she closed her eyes.

Tenbury deserted the lighted pathways, making his way carefully through the darkest portions of the gardens to the edge of the carriage drive. There, in the relative quiet along the road, he whistled shrilly three times, then waited. Within a few moments his coach approached slowly down the drive. When it was close, he stepped from the shadow of the trees into the moonlight. As the coachman pulled to a stop beside him, Sidney hurried to help his master put the lady safely inside. "To Miss Waverly's house in Charles Street," Tenbury said briefly, pulling the door shut

170

from the inside. Sidney swung onto the coach as it moved off into the streets of Lambeth.

One small lantern burned within the coach, casting a flickering sallow light over its interior. Anne was leaning back in the corner while Tenbury sat beside her, her limp wrist in his hand. Her pulse was slow and steady. He suspected she had been drugged but had no way of knowing what Crilley had given her or how long its effects would last.

"You foolish girl," he said aloud. "Don't you know you're no match for them?"

His words penetrated the haze, and Anne's eyelids flickered open. "I didn't know you were in London," she said.

"I arrived earlier today."

She nodded but was unequal to conversation. "I'm so tired," she said.

"Rest then. You'll be home soon."

She closed her eyes and didn't speak again. Tenbury continued to hold her hand in his, even though he had determined that her heartbeat was regular, for he had discovered that each time he held her, he was less willing to let her go.

By the time the coach arrived in Charles Street, Anne had fallen asleep. Tenbury ordered Sidney to watch over Miss Waverly as he walked to the front door and knocked. He asked once again for Miss Waverly's maid. When Cassie appeared, he explained as briefly as possible. "I cannot carry her in the front door and risk being seen. Go through the house and unbolt the rear entrance. We will bring her up from the mews."

When he was gone, Cassie hurried to do his bidding, while the coach made its way round to the stables. Tenbury carried Anne unseen through the walled garden behind the house and up a secondary stair to her bedchamber. "I believe she has been drugged, and she may sleep for some time," he told the maid. "I don't know what she will remember when she wakes.

Tell her what she needs to know, to set her mind at ease. Keep this to yourself; the fewer people who know about it, the better."

Sometime during the night, Anne passed from the artificial sleep effected by the drug she had been given into a natural slumber. She awoke just after nine o'clock with a slight headache.

She turned her head to see Cassie busy laying out her morning gown. She had a vague memory of a nightmare—had she just wakened from one? Then she remembered the masquerade. She could recall being afraid. . . . She couldn't remember coming home.

"Cassie?"

"Good morning, Miss Anne. You had planned to call upon Lady Tenbury this morning. Should you like the primrose or the coral?"

"Cassie. What happened last night? I don't remember coming home."

"It was late, miss, and you were weary."

"No. It was more than that. I was walking in the garden with Lord Crilley, and I felt faint. I actually thought I had been . . . I can't remember what happened. How did I get home? *When* did I get home?"

"Please don't distress yourself, Miss Anne. You were home just after one o'clock. A friend saw you with Lord Crilley and stepped in to help when he realized the danger you were in. He brought you home safely."

"It was Lord Tenbury," Anne replied, vague memory returning.

"Does it matter, miss? You are safe; that is all that should concern us."

"I didn't think he was in town."

"His lordship came to the house not long after you had gone," Cassie supplied. "He asked if it were true that you had attended a masquerade. When I said you

172

had, he asked what color you were wearing. Then he left. He brought you home asleep, carried you in from the stables so no one would see. That's all I know."

Anne shuddered to think of herself in the power of Lord Crilley, or indeed any man. She realized she had been a fool to go alone with a party of people she barely knew. Tenbury obviously realized it, too. Otherwise he would not have followed her there. Why, of all men, must she find herself indebted to him?

Anne felt she could not trust Tenbury's motives. She had learned that lesson well and would not forget it. But she also knew that regardless of what his motives had been on the previous evening, he had rendered her an invaluable service.

She dressed carefully in the primrose morning dress and called upon Lady Tenbury as planned. The earl was not present when she arrived, and Lady Tenbury did not mention him. As Anne rose to leave, however, she found the courage to ask if he was home.

"I believe he is," her ladyship answered. "Shall I have Kimble send for him?" She rang the bell before Anne had time to object to this summons and, when Kimble appeared, dispatched him with a message for Lord Tenbury to attend her in the morning room.

"I had hoped to speak with his lordship privately, ma'am," Anne offered.

"And so you shall, my dear. I have a luncheon engagement and must hurry to be ready in time. I hope to see you again soon."

When Lady Tenbury was gone, Anne had only a few moments to wait before the earl appeared. He hesitated a moment in the doorway when he saw her, then came into the room and securely closed the door.

"Miss Waverly. I am surprised to see you here."

"Did you think I would not appreciate your assistance last evening?"

"To be honest, I wasn't certain how you would feel. I thought you might have the headache today and prefer to keep to your bed."

"I have come to thank you, Lord Tenbury, though words alone seem inadequate. Why did you come after me?"

"Arelia heard at the Margate's ball that you had gone with Crilley, and she shared the information with me. All of London knows Crilley hasn't a feather to fly with, and the anonymity offered by masquerades provides an atmosphere for treachery."

She dropped her eyes to the reticule she clutched in her lap. "I didn't realize."

"Of course not. How could you?"

"I could have asked."

"True. And in future perhaps you will."

"Cassie said you followed us to the gardens. How did you find me?"

"I recognized you in the booth at dinner and followed when you walked with Crilley. When he took you off alone, I became uneasy and listened to your conversation. Had he acted the part of a gentleman, I would not have interfered. But when you complained of feeling ill, and he as much as admitted drugging you, I knew I must confront him. I wanted him to realize he had made a mistake in thinking you unprotected. Since I was masked, I doubt he knew who I was. I don't believe he will approach you again."

"Why did he do it?"

"I can't say, precisely."

"As nearly as you can say, then."

"He may have felt the drug would render you more compliant to his lovemaking. If Lord and Lady Summer were to return and find you locked in a compromising embrace, it would then behoove Crilley to make you an offer, which you, to protect your reputation, would accept. In the event you refused the offer, I have no doubt the Summers would have seen to it that the story was quickly spread all over town. If there was a flaw in Crilley's plan, it was that he overdrugged you and very nearly rendered you unconscious."

Her eyes, which had been fixed painfully on his throughout this conversation, widened with horror at this plainspeaking, then suddenly filled with tears.

He stepped quickly to her, taking her shoulders in his hands. "I am not speaking so to frighten you, Anne, but it would serve no purpose to protect you from the truth. You were in grave danger last night. You must guard continuously against similar situations. You must be very, very careful. London can be an exhilarating place, but for a single, wealthy woman, a woman with no family to protect her, it can be fraught with peril. I am not suggesting you retreat to the country, but I do suggest you carefully consider every move you make. Try to discover if there are ulterior motives behind the things people say and do."

His hands dropped as she turned away and sat on a nearby chair, staring at nothing in particular. "As there were ulterior motives behind all you said and did last summer," she said. Since she was not looking at him, she did not see the expression of pain and regret that passed over his face. "How horrible it is to be unable to take people at their word," she continued, "to be unable to trust anyone."

"I know, but I am afraid it is necessary."

"This is what the duke meant when he said great wealth can be a curse."

"I'm sure that is what he meant, and I am even more certain that he was correct."

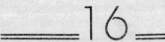

Anne's near disaster with Lord Crilley had one good consequence. She believed now that besides those merely curious about her wealth, there could be others who meant to do her harm.

She took Lord Tenbury's warning to heart and moved about the city with greater care than she had shown in the past. When she needed to go out alone, she took the coach and two or three strong, young footmen with her. At all other times she insisted Sophy Boone join her. In the evenings she attended parties only with people she knew and trusted: Arelia, Lady Tenbury, Jack Saunders, and several of their closest friends.

Anne was discovering, as she had at Tenton Castle, that all she had read and learned over the years had a much larger application than she had been afforded in debate and discussion with her father.

The provocative, stimulating conversations she had shared with Arelia and Dennis were only the beginning. London, the world for that matter, offered hundreds of new thoughts and experiences only waiting for her to take part.

After the night at Vauxhall Gardens, she took care to avoid Lord Crilley, while he made no attempt to approach her. If he had shared the details of his unpleasant encounter with her "protector" with lords

Blake and Farringdon, they seemed undaunted by it. They were still to be found among Anne's followers, usually claiming a dance when they were present at the same function.

Anne found Lord Blake too obvious in his attentions. When he discovered she liked poetry, she suspected he dashed home to memorize a piece to share with her at their next meeting. When she mentioned once in passing that she admired yellow roses, a huge bouquet was delivered to her house the following morning. She thought he might be—as the Duke of Chadwicke had warned her—the man who would ultimately pay compliments to the color of her eyes.

Lord Farringdon she found fascinating, despite Arelia's warning that he was a dissolute gambler. He never paid her outrageous compliments, but engaged her instead in lively and intriguing conversation. He had a singular sense of humor and was a remarkably fluid dancer. She found as the days passed that she looked forward to meeting him.

Tenbury viewed Anne's cautious behavior with approval and was able to relax his vigilance somewhat. If there were those few mercenaries who could not see past her wealth, there were a great many others who were slowly coming to know the real Anne Waverly. Her freshness and innocence colored every word she spoke. This was no jaded heiress, but a simple woman from the country with honest values, an optimistic outlook, and a superior understanding. Her unusual education made her conversant with so many topics that she could speak interestingly and knowledgeably on nearly any subject her varied companions raised.

After their discussion on the morning following the masquerade, Tenbury hoped he would see some softening in Anne's position toward him. He was to be disappointed, for although she was unfailingly polite whenever they met, she gave no sign that she had forgotten his behavior of the summer, or that she wanted to pursue a relationship with him.

With Jack, however, she showed no similar reserve. She met him at a ball several days after his return to town. Tenbury witnessed the warm smile she generously bestowed on his younger brother and had to admit to a pang of jealousy.

"Have you saved a dance for me?" Jack asked Anne.

"I didn't know you would be here," she complained, "but as it happens I am free for the next."

He offered his arm and they walked off together. "It seems ages since I last saw you," she said. "Tell me about the horse races. I have never been, but I think I should enjoy it above all things."

They were soon beyond Tenbury's hearing, but he continued to watch them as they joined the other dancers in a waltz.

Two weeks later, while Lord Tenbury stood in conversation with Arelia at the edge of another crowded ball room, she pointed out that Jack and Anne were dancing for the second time that evening.

"I have never known Jack to take such interest in a woman," she said. "He shows a decided preference for Anne's company, and he has grown very particular in his attentions. She is older than he, of course, but I can't think it would matter if she returned his regard. Do you think he has formed a serious attachment, Nate?"

When Tenbury realized she was waiting for an answer, he replied offhandedly, "I'm sorry, Arelia, but I really haven't thought much about it. If you will excuse me, I see someone I must speak with." He left her and made his way across the room. He did not stop to speak with anyone but called for his coach and left the ball. Within fifteen minutes he was home, seated before the fire in the library with a large brandy in his hand.

He had lied outright to his sister-in-law. Lately it seemed that the relationship between his brother and Anne was never far from his mind. They rode together, they drove together, they danced and talked and laughed together. And while their relationship continued to bloom, Tenbury's efforts to reinstate himself in Anne's good graces had failed utterly. Once when he asked her to drive with him, she excused herself, claiming another engagement; the one time he asked her to dance, she pled fatigue.

Always he clung to the memory of her kiss at the pool that moonlit night. She had kissed him; she had returned his embrace. And yet, no sooner did that incident comfort him than he remembered the evening he interrupted Jack and Anne kissing in the library. They had offered excuses he had never truly believed. No doubt they had been strongly attracted to each other even then.

Arelia's mother lived in Bedfont. Confined to a wheeled chair by a severe bone disorder, she had invited her daughter and Miss Waverly for tea. On Monday, just two days prior to the planned expedition to Bedfont, Anne shared luncheon with Lady Tenbury at Tenbury House, then stayed afterward talking with Jack in the library.

Just after one-thirty, Arelia joined them, an open letter in her hand. "I have just received this message from Tenton," she said. "It seems there has been some new problem with Tom. Mr. Pearce thinks I should come immediately to the Castle."

"What does he say?" Anne asked.

Arelia read: " 'I fear Tom has discovered some new mischief. I am uncertain how you would have me deal with it. I would not ask you to undertake the journey from London if I did not consider the matter grave. . . . ' Do you think I should ask Tenbury to go?"

"He's *your* son, Arelia," Jack responded. Then, feeling he had been too harsh, offered, "Shall I go? I will, if you like."

"No. You're right, Jack. He is my son, and Mr. Pearce has asked for me, after all. But I must leave immediately, or else wait until tomorrow morning. I will need to send a note to my mother, telling her we cannot come on Wednesday."

"Don't do that," Jack said. "There's no need to disappoint her. If the weather is fine I will borrow Tenbury's curricle, and Anne and I will drive down to visit with her."

"You wouldn't mind?"

"Not at all. Your mother's cook makes the best macaroons this side of the Channel."

"Glutton," Arelia accused, but she smiled all the same as she planted a kiss on his cheek. "Another thing. There's a trunk I planned to take along. It holds the fabric I bought Mother for new drawing room draperies. I promised I would bring it Wednesday, she'll be disappointed—"

"We'll take the trunk along. Where is it?" Jack asked.

"In my bedchamber; Barrett will show you. You're a sweet brother, Jack. I am indebted to you."

"I'm keeping score," he answered as Arelia bid Anne farewell and rushed off to supervise the packing for her journey.

Since Lady Tenbury had some affairs of her own to attend to in the country and didn't care for the idea of her daughter-in-law traveling alone, she decided to accompany Arelia to Tenton. They arrived at the Castle on Wednesday in the late afternoon. Cold nights had already begun to turn the edges of the leaves yellow and scarlet, giving the forests a permanent frosted appearance. Along the hedgerows, tangled masses of bittersweet, blackberries, and elderberries offered a banquet to a great number of finches. Soon they would gather in flocks to journey to a warmer clime for the winter months. The last of the crops had been gathered, the soil turned by the plow to rest until spring.

Arelia had been gone only five weeks, yet she was pleased to be back again. She knew she delighted in Dennis's company; she hadn't suspected how much she would miss him. When Lady Tenbury retired to her apartments to rest before dinner, Arelia hurried to her own room to wash and change her dress before descending to the salon and summoning Mr. Pearce.

He came immediately. His smile of greeting was thin.

"I am sorry to have disrupted your stay in London, Mrs. Saunders," he said, quite formally, "but as I mentioned in my letter, I felt I needed to speak with you personally."

"I almost asked Tenbury to come in my stead," Arelia confessed. "But Jack pointed out that Tom's problems are more mine than Tenbury's. What has he done now? You might as well tell me with no roundaboutation. I doubt there is much that would shock me anymore."

"Late one night, several days ago," he said, "he and Will rowed across the lake, then hiked to Winthrop. There is a comely kitchen maid who works at the Duck 'N' Drake. As I understand it, when her chores are finished belowstairs, she earns additional money working upstairs. Tom and Will were caught climbing the trees behind the inn, trying to see through the cracks in the curtains."

Arelia sat down heavily on the couch behind her, as if her legs could no longer support her. She had been wrong: there was still something Tom could do to shock her. Assailed by a horrifying thought, she asked, "Was there a man?"

"No. The landlord assured me that on this particular evening the young lady had no ... customer."

"But what about other evenings, Mr. Pearce? How can we know there weren't other times, times when the boys weren't caught?"

"I asked Tom specifically about that. He swore to me—and I believe him—that this was the first time he had ever done anything like this."

"What did you do?"

"I took Will home and turned him over to his father. I intended to have a serious discussion with Tom, but knowing you hired me only to teach academics, I didn't feel I had any right to speak until I had conferred with you."

"He promised he would do nothing disgraceful," she said. "Tenbury will be furious."

"I was myself at first. But even the most solemn promises can at times be hard to keep, especially when the temptation is great."

"There is that word temptation again. For a man of the cloth, you seem very understanding of people who give in to it. I am more accustomed to the sentiments your brother espouses: flee temptation, repent, reform, adhere to the straight and narrow."

"Anyone with a particle of sense knows it is difficult for boys to avoid mischief."

"That may well be, Mr. Pearce. Unfortunately, recognizing that fact does little to ease the present situation. Tom made a promise to Tenbury and Tenbury is miles away. How do I confront Tom with this? How can I tell him not to spy on naked women?"

"If you wish, I will speak with him," he offered. "I believe I know why he did it, and I know what to say. But he must understand, and I will tell him at the beginning, that I am speaking for you."

"Please, do what you will, say what you will to him. I trust you to handle it in the best way possible.

But tell me this, Mr. Pearce. What will I do when the day comes when Tenbury is not here, when you are not here, and Tom needs you? What then?"

"You could marry again. If Tom had a father, a worthy man to emulate, things might improve."

"He has Tenbury. One would be hard pressed to find a better example for any boy."

"Perhaps," he conceded, "but he is Tom's uncle, not his father. There is a bond between a father and son that is unique. Any other relationship is an imperfect substitute."

Arelia rose and walked toward the fire, her back to Dennis. "I have considered remarrying. But since Henry died there has been only one man I have loved."

"If you were to marry him," Pearce suggested, "you would be able to share responsibility for Tom."

"It isn't so simple," she said, turning to face him. "First of all, I'm not certain he knows how I feel, and secondly, he has not asked me to marry him."

"What manner of man is he?"

"He is a man of high principle. He lives his life without pretense. He is a trusting and unselfish friend, who puts the needs of others before his own."

"Have you any hint as to why he has not spoken?"

She turned away again, unable to keep up the charade with his eyes so steadily upon her. "There could be several reasons," she said. "He may simply not admire me, or he may prefer his life as it is. But I think it most likely that he disapproves of me and believes I would make a poor job of being a clergyman's wife."

An intense silence followed Arelia's words. She waited in something approaching pain for him to speak. But he said nothing, nor did he move. Still with her back to him, she closed her eyes and concentrated on breathing evenly.

She had spoken too soon; she had been wrong about him; she had made a fool of herself. Well, it wasn't the first time. He couldn't forgive her dalliance with Wilmington. She couldn't blame him.

These thoughts lurched to a halt as she heard him move. Coming close behind her, he reached both arms around her shoulders and pulled her back against him. When she dropped her chin to brush his hand, the scent of his warm skin sent a frisson of desire racing through her. He rested his face against her hair as he whispered, "I have loved you for months, but you seemed unattainable. I am nothing like the men you appear to admire. When you sought my company, I thought you were merely being kind."

She turned within his arms, her doubts vanishing. All that showed in her face and her eyes was a love she had never expected to find again. "Dennis," she whispered provocatively, "I have imagined a thousand times what it would be like to kiss you. How much longer do you intend to make me wait?"

After several minutes of satisfying her curiosity on that point, Dennis finally put her away from him. A moment later the door opened to admit Belinda who, hearing of her mother's arrival, had hurried downstairs to greet her. Emerging from Belinda's hug, Arelia met Dennis's gaze.

"I will go now and speak with Tom," he said. "Later we must find an opportunity to speak privately, for we have much to discuss."

At six o'clock Anne and Jack left the home of Arelia's mother and made their way back to the Great West Road. The sun was already sinking, but the fair evening promised a pleasant trip back to the city. Not more than twenty minutes into their drive they came upon a carriage that had broken down at the side of the road. As Jack slowed the grays from a trot to a walk, he could see a lady standing in the road while two men stood near one of the carriage wheels.

"Should we stop to help?" Anne asked. "If the problem is serious, perhaps we could convey the lady to the next inn and send help back for the coach."

"I can't imagine what could be wrong," Jack said. "The wheel isn't off, as you can see, nor has the axle broken."

As Jack pulled his team to a stop he glanced again at the lady and realized his mistake. Her cloak hung a few inches short of the road and on her feet were—boots—men's boots. When the "lady" turned round and took hold of his leaders, Jack reached instinctively for the pistol he knew Tenbury kept beneath the seat, but even as he leveled it, one of the other masked men fired first.

Startled by the deafening shot, it took Anne longer than Jack to realize what was happening. When Jack lurched against her and the pistol spun from his hand, she bent to retrieve it, but the second man was too quick for her. She had the pistol in her hand, but he had her wrist gripped tightly. He increased the pressure until she cried out in pain, dropping the weapon to the floorboards. As he passed it to his companion, she turned to Jack. He had moved his left hand to clutch his right wrist, over which a red stain was rapidly spreading. Anne momentarily ignored the strange men, ceased to wonder why they had stopped the curricle, and why they should wish to shoot Jack. All she could deal with was the knowledge that he was injured.

"Jack," she cried in despair, "What can I do?" She looked down helplessly at the tiny reticule hanging from her wrist. She had a flimsy handkerchief, nothing more.

"My neckcloth," he said, "Help me get it off." Anne was only dimly aware that the curricle was being led off the road into the shelter of the woods as she stripped the large rectangle of white from Jack's neck and wrapped it tightly around his wrist.

He placed his own hand over it. "Good, that's good," he said. "Thank you."

"Good? What's good? You have been shot!"

"I'm sorry I wasn't quicker," he apologized.

Before Anne could reply, rough hands seized her, dragging her over the side of the curricle. She cried out in dismay. Jack shouted an objection, but was silenced as he was yanked down from the opposite side and thrown to the ground.

At this cruel treatment, Anne finally turned her anger and confusion upon the three strangers. "What is the meaning of this outrage?"

"We 'ad not intended bloodshed," one man, obviously the leader, offered. "The young fool should 'ave known better than to loose a barker." Then turning his back on her, he ordered, "Collect their baubles; we cannot afford to dally 'ere."

The men took Anne's reticule and the cash from Jack's coat pockets. They stripped Jack's watch and rings, as well as Anne's rings, her gloves, and the silver clasp from her cloak.

"I'll have them pins from your 'air, missy, if'n you don't mind. My woman'll fancy 'em."

"But I do mind, sir," Anne objected. "I mind a great deal."

"Give him the hairpins, Anne," Jack said, his voice quiet and more serious than she had ever heard it.

She said nothing more, but pulled the pins out quickly and laid them into the man's grimy outstretched hand.

"Could be the lady 'as a necklace," one robber told the other, "or mayhap a brooch." He snatched the fur-lined cloak from Anne's shoulders before she could object. Her gown was modestly cut, but the round neckline nevertheless revealed the gentle swell of her breasts and the soft whiteness of her shoulders. She felt Jack stiffen beside her as the second man swore, —" 'sblood, but ain't she a pritty thing?" A gold necklace gleamed against Anne's pale skin. Jack forestalled the thief by reaching for the necklace himself and detaching it from Anne's neck. He also took the pearl brooch from her bodice and proffered both to the men.

"I hope you are content now, we have nothing else," Jack said.

"Wouldn't be to sure o' that my fine sir," the leader replied. "I'll have those fancy boots you're sportin', and I believe the lady's cloak might fetch a coin or two."

While Jack sat to remove the boots, the man dressed as a woman spoke. "Ought I to unharness these 'orses?"

"We'll take 'em back to the road and turn 'em loose," the leader replied. "They are no use to us. Anyone o' us seen with a blooded prad would find ourselves swingin' from the nubbin'-cheat in a fortnight."

Within a few moments the 'woman' entered the coach and the second man climbed onto the driver's box. The leader collected his horse and mounted, then paused beside Jack and Anne. "Without your boots or your carriage I can't see you'll be reportin' this little mishap right soon. 'Twas a pleasure, sir, madam." Catching one of the curricle leaders by the bridle he trotted off toward the road while Anne and Jack stood in silence, watching him go.

Neither of them spoke until the highwaymen disappeared from view, though Jack immediately removed his cloak and placed it around Anne's bare shoulders.

"Let's go," he said quietly. "I don't want to be here if they decide to come back."

"Why would they come back? They have taken everything we have."

Jack didn't answer. He considered their plight to be serious enough without enlightening her about something a young woman had that three rough men would want.

——17——

The landlord of the Blue Swan, a large and prosperous posting inn on the edge of Hounslow, was called to the door by one of his ostlers. The man had managed to stop an empty curricle as the horses trotted down the road past the inn.

As some people pride themselves on never forgetting a face, Jerry Weaks prided himself on never forgetting a horse.

"I know this team, Harry," he said to the young man. "Give me but a moment and I'll remember. . . . The Earl of Tenbury . . . they're his grays, I'd wager a shillin' on it. Take a horse back along the way they come. See if you find any stranded travelers or any sign o' foul play. Ben, help me stable these beasts."

As Weaks began unbuckling harness he noticed sticky blood on the edge of the carriage. "Harry!" he exclaimed, "There's blood on the seat here. Best take Ben along wi' you and a cart as well, just in case you find the poor soul whose blood this here is. I think I had best drive this team on into London and test my theory about their owner."

"They look more than tired, sir," Ben offered.

"And a good thing. I doubt I could handle 'em if they was feeling prime." Weaks checked the traces to be certain they were clear, then climbed into the driver's seat.

Arriving in Mayfair, Mr. Weaks spoke to several pedestrians before one was able to direct him to Lord Tenbury's residence. It was nearly dark by the time he turned into Grosvenor Square. He tossed a penny to a boy in the street to hold the team and knocked loudly on the door of Tenbury House.

Already concerned that Mr. Saunders and Miss Waverly had not returned when expected, Kimble did not slam the door in the face of this man, nor direct him to the servants' entrance. Instead, he asked him to state his business.

Mr. Weaks gave his name and his occupation before he revealed his reason for being there. "I have a team in the street that I believe to be his lordship's. Would you have someone about who might know 'em?"

Kimble directed the man to the stables, then hurried in search of Lord Tenbury.

"Excuse me, my lord," he said, finding Tenbury in his bedchamber and interrupting him in the delicate process of tying his neckcloth.

"Yes, Kimble, what is it?" Tenbury asked irritably.

"The landlord of the Blue Swan at Hounslow has brought a gray team to the stables, sir. He found them running loose. He believes they may be yours."

"Did Jack take the team today?"

"He drove Miss Waverly to Bedfont. They were due back more than an hour ago."

Tenbury was instantly on his feet and out of the room, leaving his valet holding the coat he had been about to put on.

He ran through the house, down the service stairway, and out the back door to the stables, heedless of the stares of his servants. The team would not be his. Jack and Anne would arrive at any moment; they had merely stayed longer than they intended. He stopped at the stable door as the gray horses stood before him. He didn't want them to be his, but they were.

"Your name?" he demanded of the strange man who stood there.

"Jerry Weaks, m'lord, of the Blue Swan, Hounslow."

"How came you by this team?"

"One of my lads caught 'em as they trotted past on their way toward town. They are yours, then? I thought as much. I seldom forget a team as impressive as this. There is blood here on the seat, sir, as you'll notice. I sent two of my men back along the road to see what they could find. I assumed you'd been drivin', and I thought you would want your people here to know of the loose team right off."

Tenbury had not seen the blood. He stared at it now, barely hearing what Weaks was saying. It must belong to Jack or Anne; neither possibility was acceptable to him.

"Could there have been an accident?" he asked Weaks. "Are the horses injured? Were the traces tangled?"

"No, sir. Not a bit. Looks to me as if the travelers might have been set upon by highwaymen. If they were asked to step down, and the horses not held . . . well, a high-spirited team like this un could have up and walked away. Perchance your friends have been simply left afoot."

"That wouldn't explain the blood."

Weaks's brow clouded. "No. I s'pose not. I can't think what else to tell you, sir. I'd be willin' to drive back wi' you and help you look, assumin' my men haven't already found some'at by the time we get back."

Find them, Tenbury thought. How? As two bodies lying alongside the road?

His first thought after Kimble's announcement was that Anne had been abducted, and as horrible as the prospect was, he hoped now that it was true. At least, then, she would be alive. If she and Jack had been stopped by highwaymen, they could both be dead. Suddenly remembering the pistol kept beneath the seat, he reached for it, only to discover it gone.

His mind raced on, considering possibilities. If Anne had been abducted, who was responsible? It could have been Blake, or Farringdon, or even Crilley. It could also have been one of half a dozen other desperate fortune hunters, not foolish enough to advertise their intentions by placing a wager in a public betting book.

Weaks broke in on these thoughts to ask, "Who was it, drivin' in this vehicle, m'lord?"

"My younger brother, and a young woman."

"A woman, you say. Well, now, that's an unfortunate thing. Mayhap we should go back to the Blue Swan, sir. Who knows but what my lads may have found 'em by now."

"Murdock, saddle Orion," Tenbury ordered, "and a strong horse for Mr. Weaks, and one for yourself. We leave in ten minutes."

Hurrying back to the house, Tenbury found Kimble hovering just inside the area door, the obvious question on his face.

"Yes, Kimble, it is my team. I'm going to Hounslow with this innkeeper. Stay by the front door, and keep a man posted at the back as well. If any news or message should come from Miss Waverly or my brother, send a rider immediately to the Blue Swan. If a written message should come, read it before you send it on, in the event it should go astray and not find me. I will check back with you as soon as possible."

"What do you think happened to them, my lord?"

"I don't know. The innkeeper thinks they may have been stopped by highwaymen."

"I don't know if you'll consider this important, my lord," Kimble offered. "I thought nothing of it at the time, but when Mr. Jack was late returning, I did wonder."

"Wonder about what?"

"Mr. Jack and Miss Waverly took a trunk with them. Two footmen carried it down from upstairs, and Mr. Jack had it carried out and strapped to the curricle."

"What was in it?"

"I have no idea, my lord, and it wasn't my place to ask. But Mr. Jack is usually punctual, especially when he is escorting a lady."

"What are you suggesting, Kimble? A flight to Gretna Green? What possible reason could Jack have to elope?"

"I am suggesting nothing, my lord. I am only considering possibilities based on the information we have. What of Miss Waverly's household?" Kimble asked sensibly. "They will be concerned before long."

"We must invent some story to take her out of town. Send a note to Mrs. Boone. Say that Miss Waverly will be spending the night here and has decided to accompany Lady Tenbury and Mrs. Saunders to Tenton Castle in the morning. I doubt anyone in Charles Street knows they have already gone. Instruct Cassie to pack what her mistress will need for a two-week stay in Wiltshire. Have the coach collect her, then keep her here with the baggage until you receive word from me."

Tenbury quickly retraced his steps to his bedchamber. Once there he hurriedly changed into riding clothes. When his valet went to fetch a driving coat as protection against the cool of the evening, Tenbury placed a heavy purse of gold in his pocket then extracted the special marriage license from a shallow drawer in his desk and slipped it into an inside pocket of his coat.

Jack led the way east for some time, leaving the Bedfont road behind. The highwaymen had chosen their location well, for Jack and Anne found themselves in a vast heavily wooded area with few paths, no lanes, and no signs of habitation. Only after a goodly stretch of woodland lay behind them did Jack stop. "The sun will soon set. Once it's dark, we must wait till the moon comes up. It will light our way and keep us headed in the right direction."

"Which direction is that?"

"East. If I remember correctly there is a good-sized village somewhere east of here. If we keep walking east, we should cross the road. Only thing is, once we do, I'm not certain which direction we should go—north or south."

"Maybe we will meet someone we could ask," Anne suggested.

"Perhaps," Jack agreed. "We shall see." He didn't tell her that their close call with the three highwaymen had made him aware of just how vulnerable they were. He would not be eager to approach strangers.

Even in the fading light of evening, Anne thought that Jack appeared pale. "I want to look at your hand, Jack. It must hurt dreadfully."

They sat together on a fallen tree trunk while Anne carefully removed the heavily starched neckcloth from the wounded wrist and began to replace it with soft strips from her petticoat. "These will make a better dressing." She wound the strips gently about his wrist, which had nearly stopped bleeding, then tied a secure knot. "We're fortunate this is only a flesh wound. It could have been much worse," she said. "If the bone had been hit or a large vessel—"

"I bungled it, Anne. I'm sorry."

"Don't be silly. How could we know they were anything other than they seemed: travelers in distress, possibly in need of help."

"But Tenbury warned me to be doubly cautious. I should have noticed the boots sooner."

"The boots? What boots?"

"The lady in that little group was wearing men's boots."

"I didn't see, but it can't matter now. I think we should move on, get as far as we can before dark. I feel guilty using your cloak."

"I'm not cold; I have my coat," he replied.

They walked on in silence and were soon descending a steep bank. At the bottom was a gently flowing stream, perhaps eight feet wide.

Eyeing it with some misgiving, Anne said, "Maybe we could find a place to step across on stones."

Jack glanced both upstream and down, and seeing no such natural bridge said, "Come, I'll carry you over."

"That you will not!" she objected. "You will soak your feet, and you are without your cloak."

"My feet are already wet from the ground and the wet leaves. Besides, we have no time to argue."

Then, ignoring her protests, he swept her from her feet and carried her across the icy water, setting her down on the opposite bank. He then took her hand and continued into the darkening woods. Soon the brambles thickened, and in places they had to force their way through.

"Take care to keep them from your face," he warned. Anne used her hands to ward off the thorns as they continued steadily eastward.

By the time Tenbury, Murdock, and Weaks arrived at the Blue Swan, the ostler and the stable boy had come back from their search of the road south toward Bedfont and were awaiting their employer in the tap room. When questioned, they revealed they had traveled the road and several of its major tributaries until sunset. They had found no pedestrians, nor anything else that might suggest why the team was running free.

All they had to offer was a tiny white purse they had found off to one side of the road. Seeing the delicate reticule in Ben's hand, Tenbury snatched it away, much like a thirsty man reaches for water. One reticule was much like another, yet they were not commonly found lying along the road. This one had a silk monogram, AW, embroidered on its side. When a knot in the thin draw-ribbon failed to yield immediately, Tenbury impatiently broke it and spread the top to look inside. It was empty.

"It's Miss Waverly's reticule," he said, "There can't be any question. The road where this bag was found must be searched again, Weaks," Tenbury said. "I'll need to have your men take me there, and I'll need to borrow whatever lanterns and men you can spare. They must understand they are looking for someone who might be wounded."

When Weaks nodded in assent, Tenbury once again regarded the delicate purse in his hands. "As I see it," he said, addressing his groom this time, "we have only this lead and must pursue it."

He extended a hand filled with gold coins to Mr. Weaks. "Thank you for your help, Weaks. Whatever the outcome of this, you did your best. If you hadn't sent your men out quickly, we may not have found this tiny bag until morning."

"Harry will go wi' you now," Weaks said, "and Ben and I will come along as soon as we've collected some help."

As Tenbury and Murdock remounted in the stable yard, Weaks handed them each a lantern. "I would be obliged if you would send word to my butler," Tenbury said. "Ask him to dispatch my coach here as soon as possible."

"I will do so, my lord."

Tenbury, Murdock, and their guide soon left the Blue Swan behind. The slice of moon, which had aided them on their way out of London, was increasingly obscured as heavier clouds moved in from the west.

* * *

Jack judged it to be well past midnight before he and Anne finally pushed their way through one last maze of underbrush and found themselves on a narrow country lane. The road was deserted in both directions; there was no light, nor any sign of habitation. He offered Anne his arm and turned to the north, hoping he was choosing correctly. His feet had been numb for hours and his wrist throbbed incessantly. He knew Anne must be cold as well, though she didn't complain.

Less than a mile down the lane they met a crossroad. At this junction, set back slightly from the road, was a small tavern. A sign bearing its name hung suspended over the door, though it was impossible to read in the darkness. A dim light glimmered through a crack in the shuttered downstairs windows. After Jack tried the handle and found the door locked, he plied the knocker heavily. His summons was answered almost immediately by a tall, spare man with a bushy beard who opened the door only a crack at first, then swung it wide to allow the interior candlelight to shine over the young man and woman.

"I know it's late," Jack said. "But the lady and I are seeking shelter for the night."

"Come in then," the man said, stepping aside to allow them to enter. As he looked beyond them for the carriage or horses that had conveyed them to his establishment, Jack said, "We have no horses. We came on foot."

As Jack and Anne came closer to the candles situated in a wall sconce of the common taproom, the proprietor stared in astonishment at the lady with her hair hanging loose and the gentleman without boots. Behind the counter, Anne noticed a young girl who stared just as boldly.

"I know we must appear odd," Jack offered. "The fact is we were robbed on the Bedfont road west of here. The brigands took all our valuables and left us afoot. We need shelter, and we need someone who can carry a letter to my brother in London to tell him where we are."

Jack paused, allowing the man to speak if he wished. When he said nothing but only continued to stare, Jack said, "We have no money and cannot pay you in advance, but I can guarantee payment when my brother arrives."

The landlord only nodded as he took in the fine cut of the gentleman's clothes and the quality of the lady's gown as she removed her cloak and walked toward the warmth of the fire in the hearth.

"I have just the one room, sir. It be small."

Anne, who had said nothing but was nearly holding her breath, praying the man wouldn't turn them away, turned to him and smiled graciously. "I'm sure it will suit us perfectly, sir. You are most kind."

"Can't hardly turn a lady out into the night now can I?" the man asked reasonably. "But I can't be sending no message 'fore mornin', for there's none here to carry it."

"I understand," Jack said.

"Mandy," the proprietor called to the young girl. "Show the lady and gent to number three."

Without a word, the diminutive maid took a candle and led the way up the dark creaking stairs to a room beneath the thatch. She preceded them into what was indeed a tiny room. The door swung into the only open space, while the bed pushed against the far wall covered more than half of the room's total area. A small washstand with a pitcher and bowl was the only other furnishing.

"This be it," the maid said, as she kindled a candle stub on the washstand.

When she turned to leave, Anne spoke quickly, "Mandy? That's such a lovely name. I was wondering if it would be possible for us to have something to eat. We have had nothing since noon, and we walked a long way." When the girl looked doubtful, Anne added. "We have no money, but I have a petticoat you might like. It has real lace." Anne noticed Jack's frown but ignored it. "Step into the hall with me, and I'll show you," she told the girl.

They went outside together, closing the door on Jack. Anne had torn one of her petticoats to make Jack's bandages but the other was still entire. Lifting her skirts she untied it at the waist and let it fall to the floor. Gathering it in her hands she held it up to the candlelight and watched Mandy's eyes widen in delight. "Take it, and if you could find us something in the pantry—anything—we would be grateful." Anne pressed the petticoat into the girl's hands, then turned and reentered the room.

"You'll never see that girl again," Jack prophesied.

"Cynic," Anne chided. "Well, isn't this wonderful," she added, gazing at their accommodation for the night.

"Forgive me I if don't share your ecstasy."

"Come now, Jack, this is surely better than spending the night in the woods, especially since it looks as if it might rain before morning. How long do you think that stub of candle will last?"

He eyed it measuringly and predicted, "An hour, perhaps less."

"Then we must not waste any time," she said. "The first thing you need to do is take off those wet socks."

"I really don't think—"

"Take them off, Jack, and I will rub your feet. I often did so for my father. He had poor circulation."

"I don't suppose it would do me any good to object?" he asked.

"Not the slightest," she confirmed.

Jack seated himself on the bed and stripped off the socks, while Anne knelt before him and took one foot in her lap. "Oh, Jack," she said, concern in her voice. "They are chilled to the bone." She began to chafe the cold foot in earnest, driven by her fears that such a chill might do him grave injury.

He wanted to object, but found the warmth of her hands too comforting to refuse. Almost twenty minutes later there came a gentle tapping at the door, and Anne opened it to find Mandy standing outside. She passed Anne a small bundle and an extra blanket, then hurried away down the hall without uttering a word.

Anne turned to Jack with a triumphant smile.

"Very well. You were right, and I was wrong," he admitted, "But don't get too pleased with yourself until you see what she has brought."

"The blanket alone is enough to be grateful for," Anne said.

When she opened the blanket a large pair of men's woolen socks, much darned but clean, fell to the floor. She handed them to Jack and hurried to unwrap a large cloth napkin, tied together at the corners. Inside was a small piece of cold mutton and a rather larger piece of goat's cheese.

"Dinner," she announced.

"I despise goat's cheese."

"I am not fond of it myself, but beggars can't—"

"I know, I know," he agreed. "Hand me a piece, then, and be done with your lectures. We had best eat quickly and settle ourselves for the night, for the candle is nearly spent."

When they had finished their meager meal, Anne walked to the nightstand and peered into the pitcher. "There is some water here. I want to wash your hand and do a decent job of bandaging it. Does it hurt still?"

He submitted to having the hand washed and redressed. By the time this was finished, the candle was nearly a puddle with a tiny scrap of wick remaining.

Anne eyed the bed suspiciously; it was covered with a homemade quilt that appeared none too clean. She reached to turn back the covers. "Do you think there might be . . . ?"

"More than likely," Jack said. "The sheets have probably served for the last twenty guests or so. If you take my advice, you will sleep on top of the quilt and cover yourself with my cloak."

"What about you?"

"This blanket doesn't look so bad. I'll settle myself against the door. That way we can be sure we won't be disturbed."

"Who would bother us?" Anne asked reasonably. "We have nothing left to steal."

So accordingly Anne lay down upon the bed, gathering Jack's warm cloak closely about her. Jack blew out what was left of the candle, then, taking the blanket, settled himself on the floor, leaned his back against the door, and stretched his legs out before him. They nearly touched the edge of the bed.

Anne thought she would be asleep in moments after the exertion of tramping for hours through the woods, but to her surprise she was very alert. She could hear any number of tiny scurrying feet, no doubt belonging to various rodents. Some seemed to be within the walls, while others were overhead in the thatch. She sincerely hoped that none would decide to fall upon her from above.

She soon realized the cloak was insufficient protection from the increasing cold of the night. The walls of the old tavern did little to keep out the damp, and now that she was no longer actively moving about, her discomfort steadily increased. Barely twenty minutes had passed before she whispered, "Jack?"

"Yes."

"I'm cold and wide awake."

"Me too."

"Which—cold or awake?"

"Both."

"I think you should come up here with me," she suggested. "If we share the blanket and the cloak we will both be warmer."

There was a pause before he replied, "I can't sleep in the same bed with you, Anne."

"Then we won't sleep. We'll sit up and talk. If we sit close, we will keep each other warm."

When she heard him rise from the floor, she pulled herself up to lean against the headboard and moved to the far side of the bed. Jack sat beside her and together they spread first the cloak and then the blanket over them both. The difference was immediately evident. Their combined body heat, held in by the thicker covering, soon began to warm them.

"You're right," he said. "We will definitely be warmer this way. Now what diverting subject shall we discuss to wile away the night?"

___18___

Tenbury wearily dismounted from Orion in the stable yard of the Blue Swan and walked inside. It was nearing two o'clock in the morning, yet the tap room was awash with light and a large fire burned on the hearth. As Tenbury placed his unlit lantern on one of the trestle tables, Weaks hurried in from the kitchen.

"Shall I refill it for you, my lord?"

"Fill it if you like, but we won't be going out again. We have searched the ditches where the reticule was found, even the nearby woods. We covered a goodly distance in both directions time and time again. There is no trace of them. I want you to draw me a map with all the public houses and as many of the farms and cottages as you can remember. At first light, we will start calling at them, starting with the ones closest to where we searched tonight."

"Perhaps you and your groom should eat something, my lord, and sleep, to be better prepared for the morrow."

Both Murdock and Lord Tenbury ingested some cold meat and sliced bread, but when Murdock accepted the offer of a pallet near the kitchen fire, Tenbury refused to retire. He spent what remained of the night in the taproom, pacing the worn oaken floor before the hearth, stopping only occasionally to add another log to the fire.

He had begun his search earlier with high hopes, convincing himself that Jack and Anne had simply been left afoot and that a diligent search would discover them. But after miles of searching and hours of calling, they had found nothing, no trace, nor had any sound answered them from the silence of the night woods.

Now his weary mind thought back to Kimble's information concerning the trunk the couple had taken with them. Tenbury supposed it could have contained the necessities for a journey. They could have departed in the curricle to allay suspicion, then switched to a post chaise once they had won free of the city. There could be no denying a strong attraction existed between his brother and Miss Waverly.

Yet despite the evidence in support of this theory, there was much about it that made no sense. Primarily, there was no need for this particular couple to even contemplate a run-away match. They were both of age; they could marry where and when they chose and needed no one's permission or blessing. Secondly, such unconventional behavior was not typical of Jack. Another fact, perhaps trivial, was Tenbury's feeling that even if Jack had eloped and switched at some point to a chaise, it was not his way to simply turn loose a team that his brother prized. Tenbury was certain that Jack would have arranged to have the horses properly returned to London. Finally, there was the blood on the curricle—a circumstance not easily explained.

As the first blackness of night lifted in the east, Tenbury was convinced that with the new day he would find the missing couple. They would be in a farmhouse, or in a forester's shed, somewhere . . .

When it came time to leave, Tenbury reviewed the map Weaks had drawn, then he and Murdock walked together to the inn yard where their horses waited.

Just before dawn a light mist began falling. By the time they called at the first three farms on their map both the rain and the wind had increased. Neither man seemed to notice. Despite the cold rain slicing against their faces, they trotted their horses steadily on.

They rode without speaking along a gently descending road. Trees crowded close on both sides. Such a wood normally reverberated with bird song at this time of day, but the chill rain had driven most of the birds to seek shelter beneath branches and bushes. The full-throated chorus of a normal morning was limited to an occasional isolated twitter. A pond soon appeared on their right, where frogs emitted their monotonous call, undaunted by the wet morning. A thin layer of fog hovered three feet over the water, while the pond's surface rippled with the impact of closely falling raindrops.

As they passed the pond and rounded a corner in the road, they approached a crossroad. Set off to one side was a public house, the Boar's Head. Leaving Murdock with the horses, Tenbury entered the small establishment and encountered a bearded landlord in the tap room. He immediately stated his business, as he had at his previous stops that morning.

"I am searching for a young man—fair, twenty-five, and a young woman—dark-haired, tall, and thin. Have you seen such a couple?"

"Well now, sir," the proprietor replied slowly, scanning his tall aristocratic visitor from top to bottom. "It's not my 'abit to be givin' information to any nob what 'appens through my door—" He broke off suddenly and his eyebrows raised with great interest as Tenbury tossed two golden guineas onto the counter between them. "Come in the middle of the night, they did, on foot," he promptly offered. "Bone tired they was. I 'ad number three empty, and like I told the lady, I could 'ardly turn 'er away."

Tenbury heard nothing beyond the room number. This had to be Jack and Anne. It would be too much of a coincidence otherwise. He climbed the narrow stairs two at a time, hope putting a tired smile on his face.

The numeral indicating room number three appeared to have been carved into the wood with a knife. The door was neither locked nor bolted. It opened noisily on rusty hinges to reveal a tiny room under the thatch. A not particularly large bed occupied a space less than four feet from where Tenbury stood, and on the bed, cuddled together like two newborn hares in a nest, were his brother and Miss Waverly.

Conscious of the landlord standing at the bottom of the stairs and gazing up at him, Tenbury stepped into the room and closed the door. His budding relief at having found Jack and Anne did not survive the condition in which he found them. He had been prepared to find them tired, perhaps hungry, cold, or without money. He even knew that one of them could be wounded, perhaps seriously. He was not prepared, however, to find them intimately asleep in the same bed.

The closing of the door, which Tenbury did with more force than was necessary, brought Jack instantly awake. He sat up suddenly, a movement that woke Anne as well.

"Tenbury!" he exclaimed. "I knew you would come."

Tenbury stood immobile, appearing huge in the small room, his wet cloak dripping onto the floor at his feet. He neither smiled nor moved, but said, "Very pretty Jack, very pretty indeed."

Acutely aware of their extremely compromising situation, Anne sat back in the corner of the bed, closely gathering Jack's cloak around her. Tenbury's face was more stern than she had ever seen it. She struggled to explain. "We hadn't intended . . . we were talking . . . we needed to keep warm—"

"I can explain everything, Nate," Jack offered.

"Later," the earl replied. "I have paid your shot here. The coach will collect you in half an hour and convey you to the Blue Swan. I believe you will find that Kimble has sent along anything you might need." He tossed a small pouch of coins onto the bed beside his brother then turned and left. They heard his booted feet descend the stairs and the soft thud of hooves as he rode away.

"Is he angry?" Anne asked.

"I think it's safe to say that, yes."

"But why? We didn't do anything wrong."

"You didn't, Anne. But I am very much at fault in this whole situation."

"You're not!" she insisted.

"I am. I should have been more careful on the road, and I should have slept in the taproom last night or, at the very least, on the floor in here."

"It was too cold to do that." Tears glazed her eyes and threatened to fall. "We were only being practical. Is that so wrong?"

"Don't cry," he said. "I'll make it all right with Tenbury; I promise. We can't undo what's done. We know what happened here last night—that's really all that matters. The coach will be here soon. Make yourself presentable while I go try to find myself some boots."

When Anne and Jack had been conveyed from the squalor of the Boar's Head to the relative luxury of the Blue Swan, Mr. Weak's short, spare wife stood just inside the door to receive them. If this good woman had any misgivings about the strange goings-on of the previous night, she had no intention of voicing them. When a customer was as free with his gold as Lord Tenbury was, she could show as little curiosity as an idiot and be quiet as a mute. Regardless of what she thought about the relationship between the lady and the two gentlemen, her natural sympathy was aroused by her first sight of Anne. With her hair loose and tangled and her dress crumpled and soiled, she was a sorry sight.

"The maids are already carryin' hot water for your bath, miss," Mrs. Weaks said. "And your own maid is abovestairs awaitin' you. I will show you up now, if'n you like." Then turning to Jack she added, "His lordship should like to speak wi' you in the private parlor, sir. It be that door to your right."

As Mrs. Weaks turned away, Anne hesitated. "Should I come with you, Jack? If he is angry—" She broke off, conscious of the landlady waiting, hearing every word.

"You go upstairs," he reassured her. "I'll talk to him alone."

She nodded and then smiled wearily as she turned away. The prospect of a hot bath was wonderful to contemplate, especially since she knew she was not prepared either physically or emotionally for a confrontation with Lord Tenbury.

Jack entered the private parlor to find his brother seated alone at a cloth covered table, eating.

Tenbury glanced up as the door opened and asked, "Are you hungry?"

"Ravenous."

"Sit then, and eat, and tell me what happened yesterday." As Jack pulled out a chair, Tenbury noticed the bandaged wrist for the first time. In his shock at finding his brother and Miss Waverly sleeping together, he had completely forgotten the blood on the curricle. He pointed at the wrist with his knife hand. "Is that serious?"

Jack shrugged. "It throbs. It hasn't been properly cleaned."

Tenbury rang the table bell and Weaks himself appeared in the doorway. "Can I get you somethin' more, my lord?"

"Have you a doctor nearby?"

"There's one in the next village, sir. Shall I send for him?"

"Please do. My brother's arm needs attention."

Weaks nodded and disappeared, while Jack took an empty plate and commenced piling it with sliced beef.

While he ate and related the events of the robbery and the subsequent trek through the forest, Tenbury said nothing. His lack of comment struck Jack as severe criticism of his actions, and he finally departed from his methodical telling of details to declare, "I'm sorry, Nate, but I did the best I could. Had I been alone, I would have simply followed the road to the nearest inn. But I couldn't hike down the road with a woman. I couldn't risk those fellows coming back. I had no way of knowing there would be miles of bloody thicket between us and the next road. Add to that the darkness and the cold—"

"Jack—enough! I haven't said I disapprove of your actions. I would have probably done the same thing under similar circumstances."

"What is it, then? You're sitting there like a statue, cold and distant. Is it how you found us? In the same room?"

"In the same bed," Tenbury corrected.

"I can explain."

"So you said earlier."

"It seemed such a little thing after the struggle of our walk. We had found shelter for the night, and we were both cold. Anne thought if we sat together and shared the blankets we would be warmer, and she was right—we were. We planned to talk but—we were both exhausted. . . . "

"And that's all there was to it?"

"What do you mean? You certainly don't think I would take advantage of a situation like that? Of course that's all there was to it. I respect Anne. I would never do anything to harm her."

"Yet your little adventure has compromised her."

"I am well aware of it, and I am prepared to make things right in that regard. I decided last night that I would ask Anne to marry me."

"Have you already done so?"

"No. There was no appropriate moment."

"Would you ask her to marry you if the past twenty-four hours could be erased?"

"If you are asking—are we in love and was I contemplating marriage?—the answer is no. We are close friends, no more than that."

"In that case, Jack, I am afraid I must take exception to this match. I cannot permit it, even assuming Miss Waverly would accept your proposal, which is not at all certain."

"You cannot interfere, Nate. It is a question of honor."

"I understand that. But I think you must also see that I am not willing to stand by idly while you offer for the woman I love."

"You? In love with Anne? I would never have guessed it! The two of you are always so formal, so . . . Does she love you?"

"There was a time when I believed she did, but we had a disagreement. Lately, as you remark, she has kept her distance."

"If you are in love with her, then you must have been ready to strangle me this morning when you walked in on us."

"Very nearly. I applaud myself for showing admirable restraint."

"I can see that this complicates matters," Jack said.

"Rather," Tenbury agreed. "I had hoped that in time, Anne and I could come to an understanding, but now my hand is forced. I must make an offer today."

"Will you tell her how I feel? What I offered?"

"I believe I must, yes. Though somehow I am hoping that I will ask, and she will accept, and there will be an end to it."

Some minutes later, a knock on the door heralded the arrival of the doctor. While the physician attended to Jack's wrist, Tenbury observed his efforts with a critical eye.

Cleansed by a hot bath and draped in a warm dressing gown, Anne felt much restored. Restless and overtired, she ate sparingly, then lay down at Cassie's insistence and was soon lulled to sleep by the steady rhythm of raindrops on the roof overhead, a sound that from her earliest memories had soothed her. When she awoke nearly an hour later, she found Cassie bent over a trunk, extracting a gown of moss green muslin.

"Cassie. Did I sleep?"

"A bit, miss," the girl replied, curtsying. "I was just about to wake you. His lordship means to travel today and wants us belowstairs in thirty minutes."

Anne threw back the covers and rose immediately, her relief at being safe again causing her to make light of the previous day's exertions and the shortness of her rest. She dressed quickly, then allowed Cassie to arrange her hair. When she descended the steep stairs, Mrs. Weaks scarcely recognized her as the same wretched woman of a few hours earlier.

"His lordship wants a word with you, miss. This way, if'n you please."

As they moved down the corridor Anne said, "I should like to thank you for your kindness."

" 'Twas nothing, miss, I'm sure."

The landlady opened the door to the private parlor and Anne stepped inside. Tenbury stood before the fireplace, where several large logs crackled and hissed, driving away the dampness.

Anne realized that Kimble had overlooked no detail when he dispatched the coach to Hounslow, for Lord Tenbury had also been transformed since the early morning. He wore a dark gray cutaway coat and a waistcoat buttoned over a crisp white shirt and snowy cravat. Pristine breeches disappeared into top boots shiny enough to be used as a looking glass. He turned his head when she entered and smiled at her.

"Your appearance is much improved since last I saw you," he said as he indicated a bench near the fire. She walked to it, the smell of freshly baked bread making her realize she was still hungry.

"I think the landlady barely knew me," she remarked.

"Quite likely," he agreed. "Earlier you looked more like a ragged beggar than a lady of quality."

She feigned a look of outrage. "Perhaps I did. But how ungallant of you to say so, sir."

"Are you not the one who insists upon honesty in all things?" he challenged. "No half truths—no deceit?"

His voice had gone in a moment from lightly teasing to deadly serious. She looked up to see him regarding her, his blue eyes penetrating.

"Yes, certainly," she replied. "Honesty in all things."

He sat beside her near the warmth of the fire. "Jack explained what happened. He regrets that you had to endure such hardship," Tenbury said.

"Mine was not nearly so difficult as his. I had shoes, and my feet for the most part stayed dry. Did he tell you that he carried me across a stream, walked through freezing water in stocking feet, just to secure for me some degree of comfort?"

"No, he didn't tell me. But I'm not surprised."

"Did he explain that our being on the bed together was my idea? He was on the floor to begin with, but if you had felt his feet, they were like ice, and his wrist I know must have pained him dreadfully, though he never complained. I insisted it was the only prudent thing to do."

Tenbury turned slightly and took her hands in his. "Your concern is touching, and I'm sure there is no one who could find fault with your motives. Believe me, I understand."

"You looked very angry when you first found us."

"I was up all night. I was anxious for your safety. I apologize if my reaction overset you."

He raised one of her hands to his lips, and pressed a gentle kiss on it. "What happened to your wrist and your hands?" he asked as he took them and held them palms up before him. The right wrist was discolored and swollen, while both hands were crisscrossed with long reddened scratches, some of which had raised welts.

"When Jack dropped the pistol, I picked it up. The highwayman twisted my wrist until I dropped it. The scratches are from the brambles in the woods. In some places they were very thick, and even though Jack broke a path, I still had to fend them off."

He lowered his head and kissed each of the scratched hands, while his lips lingered even longer on the bruised wrist. It was an action so unexpected, Anne knew not how to react.

Even as she struggled for words, he saved her from having to respond by rising to his feet in a sudden change of attitude. "I will ask the landlord's wife to put some ointment on the scratches. Then we must be on our way. We should easily reach Tenton tonight."

"Tenton? Are we not going back to London?"

"When you disappeared," he replied, "I had no idea what had happened to you, or how long it might be before I could return you to Charles Street. I sent for Cassie, informing Mrs. Boone and your household that you were accompanying my mother and Arelia to the country. It was the best I could do to allay suspicion. I doubt they believed the half of it, but they have no evidence to support any other theory."

He strolled into the hall calling for Mrs. Weaks while Anne looked after him with a troubled frown.

213

═══19═══

A short time later, Tenbury's coach set off toward Wiltshire. While Jack occupied one seat and Cassie and Anne shared the other, Tenbury and Murdock accompanied the coach on horseback. When Murdock suggested that his lordship travel inside the coach, seeing as he had not slept the night before, Tenbury replied that if he had been interested in his groom's opinion, he would have asked for it. Murdock thereafter lapsed into silence, speaking only when spoken to. The trip passed uneventfully, the coach arriving at Tenton Castle after dark.

Arelia and Lady Tenbury made a great fuss over Anne and Jack, hovering like mother hens and directing servants to prepare their rooms. They all settled in the salon, where Arelia demanded to be told all the details of the robbery.

"I need to speak with Miss Waverly," Tenbury said. "If you will excuse us, perhaps Jack can answer your questions."

Anne accompanied Tenbury across the hall to the library. When they were inside and the door firmly closed, she took a seat while he stooped to stir the fire to life and add a few logs. Next he kindled a taper and began lighting candles.

Anne sat regarding him expectantly. He had asked

for the interview but now seemed reluctant to begin.

"What was it you wished to say to me, Lord Tenbury?" she asked.

Tenbury extinguished the taper and replaced it on the mantel before coming to sit near her. "You asked me earlier today if we were returning to London. You do understand why we cannot?"

"Because you think people will discover what happened last night."

"I can't say, and it doesn't matter what story the gossips ultimately spread. What matters is that you were seen leaving town in an open carriage with my brother. You did not return at the time you were expected; in fact, you did not return to your home at all. Even in my household, where the servants are loyal to the family, such a tale would leak out. In your house, with servants newly hired, there is no question the story will be all over town in a matter of days."

"I was considering this on the drive down here," she offered, "and I have decided that perhaps it would be best if I returned to Pentworth House."

"The scandal will eventually follow you there. There can be no escape from it."

"You draw a grim picture, my lord."

"Perhaps I do, but I assure you it's a realistic one. It is vital that you understand the seriousness of the situation."

Feeling the pressure of tears mounting behind her eyes, and unwilling for him to see her cry, Anne rose and walked to the fire, pretending to warm herself. His words had, in fact, chilled her to the quick. Her future, which only a few days ago had appeared so rosy, now loomed before her as a fearful, bottomless chasm.

"You may, of course, go to your home if that is what you truly wish," he said. "There are, however, several other options you should consider."

She turned, forgetting her tears, eager to hear of

this ray of hope in a seemingly hopeless situation. "And what are they, my lord?"

"You could marry—as soon as possible. The gossiping tongues would not be stilled, but they would speak of elopement, not ostracism. Is there anyone to whom you have formed an attachment—someone in London perhaps?"

"There is no one," she said, almost imperceptibly.

"I must tell you that Jack is most willing to offer. He is very conscious of his obligation—"

"I could not accept him," she interrupted, "for I do not consider any of what happened to be his fault. He was wonderful—brave and caring. I would not reward him by binding him in a marriage he did not seek."

"Do you love him?" Tenbury asked, holding his breath while he waited for her answer.

"I love him as a dear friend."

"There is one final option you must consider. I would be honored if you would agree to become *my* wife. I have a special license. With your consent, I will go and speak with Dennis Pearce immediately; he could marry us tonight."

Dozens of questions leaped to her mind together, all struggling for the uppermost place. Why was he offering this? Did he feel responsible because Jack was involved? Or was there more to it? Then there were the questions on her side. How did she feel about Tenbury now? Could she trust him, or was there still, as there had been when they met, a motivation she knew nothing of?

With all this turmoil in her mind, her voice was still. He seemed to take this lack of objection as a form of consent. "I will go and speak with Pearce," he said and turned to leave the room.

In desperation, she found her voice. "Please wait, my lord. You must give me time to think."

"I am afraid there is little time, and even less to

216

think about. You may return to Pentworth, a social outcast who will be the butt of jokes and crude speculation, or you may choose to be my wife."

She lowered her eyes to the floor, once again blinking away tears.

Her total dejection, her grim, hopeless attitude was too much for Tenbury. He had decided during his long ride home that he would not complicate the necessities of the evening with protestations of love. He suspected she was a long way from trusting him, but he found now that his resolution would not hold. Whether she believed him or not, he must at least say he wanted her for herself, not for any other reason. Walking to her, he took her hands and led her to the sofa, then sat beside her.

"You haven't asked how I come to have a special license in my pocket," he said.

She said nothing, but the question was in her eyes.

"That night at the pool," he said, "I would not have behaved so, had my intentions not been honorable. I nearly asked you then to marry me, but I didn't like having secrets between us. So I went to find Chadwicke. On my way through London, I picked up the license on a whim, hoping I could convince you to marry me at once. The memory of that night made me impatient to have you in my arms again."

His voice had trailed nearly to a whisper. What he saw in her face did not encourage him. She looked troubled, confused. She was so close, her lips so inviting, her expressive eyes swimming with tears. Would action serve him where words had not?

He linked his hands behind her neck and brought her mouth to meet his. As she closed her eyes a tear slipped away and coursed a path down her cheek, yet when he felt her respond, his hopes soared. He ended the kiss before he wished to, even though she had made no attempt to stop him. He held her face in his hands as he whispered, "Anne, I love you. Forget the

217

rest; forget the questions and the doubts and think only of that." He pushed himself up from the sofa and rang the bell. "I'm going to find Pearce. When the footman comes, have him bring you something to eat."

A moment later she was alone, but those three magic words he had said echoed again and again through her ears. "I love you." Her father was the only other person who had ever said them to her. Did Tenbury mean them? Or were they uttered from obligation? from guilt? from expediency? He had never wanted any of the women society had to offer—why should he want her?

There was only one answer. She was wealthy, naive, and amenable. She was quiet and unassuming; she would never put herself forward. Tenbury could have her wealth yet continue to live his life much as he always had. She would be there, stuck away in a corner. She would never challenge him; he would go his own way.

As unappealing as this was to her, it had two strong elements in its favor. First, as he had pointed out, she had little choice. It was either marriage or social ruin. Secondly, she felt that being a part of his life, even a minor part, would be better than being no part at all. If she ran away to Pentworth and resumed her reclusive life there, she would probably never see any member of the Saunders family again.

The servants brought her a tempting dinner tray but she had no appetite. She had made her decision: she would marry Lord Tenbury.

When Arelia entered the room a few minutes later, Anne was able to greet her with an outward appearance of calm. Arelia came to sit close beside her, her concern for Anne's recent ordeal plain.

"Jack has been telling us what happened. You must have been terrified."

"The highwaymen were rather frightening, but

Jack knew just how to handle them. Then he led us safely through the forest."

Arelia reached to take Anne's hands, her countenance grave. "Jack says that you are fine. Is it true? Or is there something you couldn't tell the men?"

Anne shook her head. "I told them the truth. My legs are sore, and my feet blistered, and I have these scratches on my hands; that's all."

"If I had ever suspected that road would be so dangerous—"

Arelia paused as the door opened and Tenbury entered. He glanced first at Anne, then spoke to his sister-in-law. "Have you been sharing your news with Miss Waverly?"

"No," Arelia answered. "We have been discussing the events of this past night."

"It seems congratulations are in order," he continued, as he drew Arelia to her feet and planted a kiss upon her cheek. Turning to Anne's inquiring gaze he added, "Mr. Pearce has just informed me that he and Arelia became engaged yesterday. My felicitations, Arelia. I think you have chosen wisely, and I wish you well."

Rising herself, Anne added her good wishes to his. She embraced her friend warmly as she exclaimed, "Oh, Arelia, I am so pleased for you—and for Dennis, too! I'm convinced you belong together, and I wish you happy."

Anne's worries, momentarily forgotten in the face of Arelia's news, came crashing back upon her at Tenbury's next words. "I hadn't intended to upstage you, Arelia," he said, "but I fear we will be before you to the altar. Anne is about to become my wife."

He took Anne's hand possessively in his as Arelia regarded them suspiciously. Tenbury looked cool and confident, while Anne's eyes dropped to the floor.

"Has she agreed to become your wife, or is she being bullied into accepting?" Arelia demanded, her voice disapproving.

Tenbury's eyes hardened as he met Arelia's challenge unblinking. "She will make a free choice." Then turning his gaze to Anne, he added, "And she can certainly speak for herself."

Arelia directed her next question to Anne. "Is this truly what you want?"

Forced to meet Arelia's penetrating gaze, Anne answered, "If his lordship wishes it, I agree to wed him."

"If you have any doubts," Arelia pursued, "we will seek another solution."

"If you intend to offer alternative options, Arelia," Tenbury said, "I suggest you enumerate them. What specific solutions do you have in mind?"

"Well, I don't know," she answered. "There must be something. We must think."

"I did just that all day. If the solution Miss Waverly and I have chosen is agreeable to us, I fail to see what right you have to object."

Arelia looked at Anne again, hoping to see in her eyes what she seemed unable to say. "If this is what you want, I certainly won't object. But I don't wish to see you made unhappy."

"If you believe I would make her so, Arelia," Tenbury said, "you have missed the mark."

"I do not think you would intentionally do so, Tenbury, but marriage is—"

"Different things to different people," he interrupted. "I suggest you confine your thoughts to your own upcoming nuptials and leave the concerns of ours to us."

Arelia easily detected the edge to his words, a tone she recognized as one meant to silence her on the subject. She bit back her next response.

Tenbury turned to Anne, collecting her other hand. "I think we could both benefit from a few hours' sleep. Pearce said he would meet us in the chapel at ten o'clock. Is that acceptable?"

She smiled tentatively and nodded.

"The chapel, then, at ten o'clock," he said.

"I will be there."

Anne and Arelia left the room together. Within a few minutes, Tenbury also went abovestairs to bathe and rest. He had been in the saddle for the best part of twenty-four hours. Warmed and refreshed by a hot bath, he stretched out upon his bed and was sound asleep within seconds.

Arriving at her room, Anne declined to rest. She had slept at the tavern and in the coach. She insisted she was not tired and knew she would never sleep with her wedding only a few hours away. When Arelia, despite Tenbury's warning, tried to question Anne further on the subject of her marriage, Anne burst into tears and was unable to answer.

Having shattered what little control Anne had left, Arelia was instantly remorseful. "I'm so sorry, love. Tenbury warned me to say no more, and I should have heeded him. You have been through much more than anyone should have to bear—I promise I will not add to your distress. Come, we need to choose a gown for your wedding. What shall it be?"

Since Cassie had been unpacking for an hour, the two trunks were nearly empty. Anne's gowns hung in a row in the wardrobe. Arelia drew forth an evening gown of ivory silk, decorated with row upon row of French lace.

Anne seemed not to care what she wore. When it came time to dress for her wedding, she stepped without comment into the underclothes Cassie set out for her, then allowed herself to be buttoned into the gown. With her hair dressed to Arelia's satisfaction, she accompanied Arelia and Cassie to the drafty chapel in the oldest part of the Castle. It lacked two minutes before the hour of ten.

There had been insufficient time to properly warm

the apartment, therefore the damp stone walls of the small chapel emanated cold air. Slivers of moonlight penetrating the high, narrow windows did little to dispel the gloom. On the altar, however, many candles had been set. Their flickering light bounced off the uneven stone walls, casting eerie shadows. In the circle of light Dennis waited, dressed in his robes of office. Lady Tenbury sat with Jack in the first pew while Tenbury stood nearby, partially facing the door at the back.

He saw Anne the moment she entered and came immediately to meet her, taking her hand and threading it through his arm. "You look lovely," he said as he smiled at her and led her down the aisle to where the others waited. "Mr. Pearce requested Cassie and Murdock as witnesses," Tenbury explained.

When Dennis glanced at his betrothed and saw the concern in her face, he suddenly wondered if all was as Lord Tenbury had explained to him. He shifted his gaze to Anne. She was returning Lady Tenbury's smile. The smile seemed genuine enough, yet there appeared to be a great deal of sadness behind it. Despite Lord Tenbury's assurances of Anne's compliance in the ceremony, Dennis felt constrained to speak. He stepped nearer to Anne. "Is it your wish, Anne, to wed Lord Tenbury?"

Looking him straight in the eye, without blinking, and with only the slightest tremor in her voice she said, "Yes, Dennis, it is."

"Very well," he said, addressing the group altogether, "Shall we begin?"

═══20═══

The small group gathered before the altar, and Dennis began the familiar marriage ceremony. As he spoke each portion of the service, Tenbury and Anne made the appropriate responses—promises to love, honor and obey, forsaking all others, for better, for worse, for richer, for poorer. . . .

When Tenbury took her hand to place the ring on her finger, he found that her hand was shaking. The ring was a family heirloom, one of many gold rings in the Tenbury collection. He slipped it over her knuckle, solemnly repeating the final words he needed to speak: "With this ring I thee wed, with my body I thee worship, with all my worldly goods I thee endow."

In a moment she would be his wife. It was what he wanted. Anne looked up to meet his eyes, and what he saw in them shook his resolution to its foundation. He knew that a bride should have joy and love shining in her eyes. As he looked at Anne he saw only strife, fear, and sadness. He was getting what he wanted, but she—she had been given no choice.

Through this maze of thought Dennis's voice penetrated. "By the authority—"

"Wait," Tenbury interrupted, halting Dennis in mid sentence. Ignoring the others, looking only at Anne, holding her hands in a viselike grip, he said,

"I can't do it. I thought I could . . . but I can't be sure . . . and I won't force you." Then he spoke to the others. "I must apologize for calling you here unnecessarily. Forgive me."

Without another word to anyone he walked down the aisle and left the chapel. The door slammed shut behind him, echoing hollowly through the room.

None of those left behind spoke, none moved. They all stood as if turned to stone, all trying to understand what had happened. Tenbury had been the impelling force behind this ceremony: he had suggested it, ordered it, arranged it, taken control. Then, at the climactic moment he had called a halt.

The minutes dragged by. Anne stood with her head bowed, turning the ring on her finger. She had his ring but was no bride, no wife.

She looked up to find Dennis watching her, then turned quickly to Arelia, Lady Tenbury, and Jack. Anne was first to break the silence. "What did he mean? I don't understand. He was the one who insisted. . . . " When no one answered she asked, "Did any of you have his confidence? Do you know what he meant? What couldn't he be sure of?"

Murdock nodded silently to Cassie and they withdrew to the back of the chapel, out of earshot, affording the others privacy.

It was Jack who finally answered Anne. "He told me earlier that he has been in love with you for some time, but he has never been certain of your feelings for him."

"My feelings for him?" Anne echoed. "I have no idea what they are."

"Then it is easy to understand why Tenbury is confused," Lady Tenbury said gently. "Is it true, Anne? Is he in love with you?"

"He has said he is, ma'am," Anne replied. "I cannot be certain if it is true."

Here Arelia joined the conversation. "If Nate said he loved you, then he does. You must know him well enough to know he would never lie—especially about that."

Perhaps he wouldn't lie, Anne thought, but isn't deceit the same thing? He did deceive me, for months. Then suddenly she realized she had forgiven him long ago. "He said he wanted to marry me even before the events of last night. I know I'm not beautiful or accomplished like the women he admires—"

"My dear, dear child," Lady Tenbury interrupted, "You underrate yourself. Had Tenbury been seeking only superficial qualities in a wife, he would have married long since. He found in you something we have all seen, something rare. How willing were you to marry him tonight?"

"I agreed, but not willingly," Anne admitted.

Her ladyship nodded knowingly.

"Then we have answers to the questions you asked," Dennis offered. "At the last moment Lord Tenbury found himself unable to turn the unfortunate happenings of yesterday to his gain. Not certain of your feelings, he feared forcing you into a marriage you might find repugnant."

"It seems to me," Arelia said gently, "that the next move is yours, Anne. What do you intend to do?"

"I don't know."

Dennis, who had recognized her regard for Tenbury months ago, decided to give providence a shove. "I think we should finish the ceremony," he said unexpectedly. Raising his voice he called Murdock and Cassie back to the front of the chapel.

"Can you finish without Tenbury?" Arelia asked, amazed that he should even suggest it.

"I certainly intend to," he replied. "Tomorrow, when his lordship is more amenable, we shall do this last bit once again, just to be sure we get it right."

Then, with all the pomp and ceremony he could muster in the absence of the groom, Mr. Pearce declared Lord Tenbury and Miss Waverly husband and wife.

Amid kisses and congratulations, done as if the groom were indeed present, Dennis placed a gentle kiss on Anne's cheek and whispered in her ear. "I have given you some ammunition, Anne. Go to him and use it, and remember in all things to let your heart lead you."

When Anne scratched at Tenbury's door and he snapped, "Go away!" she knew he thought her his valet, so she ignored the command. She opened the door instead and slipped inside, closing it quickly and leaning against it in trepidation. Tenbury was seated in a deep armchair near the fire. From where she stood, all she could see was his forearm and hand extended to hover over a glass of brandy on the table beside him.

Her slippered feet made no sound as she padded across the soft carpet toward him. Her gown, however, rustled quietly, and he turned his head in annoyance to see who dared disobey him. When he saw her, he rose quickly from the chair and turned to face her. He had removed his coat and waistcoat, and discarded his cravat. He stood now in his shirt sleeves, with several buttons undone at the throat.

"You should not be here," was all he said.

"No? I thought a wife was always welcome in her husband's room."

"You are not my wife, nor I your husband. Pearce never declared us so."

"Oh, but he did," Anne insisted. "Had you stayed to the end of the service, you would have heard it."

His eyes narrowed, and she could see he was wondering what game she was playing at. "He could not finish the ceremony once I had gone," he said unequivocally.

"But I have just told you that he did. And they all heard him—your mother, Arelia, Jack, Murdock, and Cassie."

"It matters not what they heard. There was no

valid marriage." Walking to the brandy decanter, he refilled his glass.

"Then you did not mean the vows you swore tonight before God?" she challenged.

His eyes glinted angrily as he replied briefly, "Take care what you say, madam."

"It is a simple enough question, sir. Either you meant what you swore, or you lied before God. Which was it?"

"I meant what I swore."

"So I thought. Therefore it makes no difference to me whether the service finished or not. I heard your vows, and I wear your ring. In God's eyes I am your wife."

"Enough of this foolishness," he said impatiently, "Why have you come?"

"I believe it is customary for a wife to spend her wedding night with her husband."

"That may well be, but it is also customary for the husband to come to her, not vice versa."

"I would not presume to argue with you, for you must understand these things better than I," she replied. "But I happen to believe that were I to go to my room as you suggest, you would not come to me. Therefore, I hold my plan to be the better one."

Walking to him, she deliberately turned her back. "You must help me out of this gown. As you can see, the buttons are at the back."

Despite himself, Tenbury found his melancholy mood dissipating in the face of Anne's uncharacteristic behavior. "You will catch cold at this game, my dear," he warned. "You have not enough experience to play the part of bold fancy."

She said nothing, but stood still before him, presenting her buttons. He half smiled as he reached to undo them, willing to take part, to a point, in her little charade. Yet as he slowly undid the gown, the soft scent of her hair rose to greet him. The slippery silk yielded beneath his fingers to expose a soft cotton chemise beneath. Then he was remembering the night at the pool, her vibrant body molded closely to his. The last button opened, he slipped his hands under the gown and eased it off her shoulders, allowing his fingers to gently caress her skin. She shivered involuntarily as the gown slithered over her hips and into a heap around her feet.

Probing gently in her hair, Tenbury removed the pins one by one, casting each in turn upon the table until her hair cascaded in heavy waves down her back. He then crossed to his chair by the fire and reseated himself, took a swallow from his brandy, then set the glass aside and folded his arms across his chest, regarding her in the candlelight.

"You may proceed, now, madam. I have conquered the difficult buttons for you."

Anne sat on the small couch opposite his chair and removed her delicate slippers. Next, she began to roll down her stockings, baring her shapely legs. When she finished she stood and laid the stockings neatly aside, then stooped to collect her gown from the floor.

He had known from the beginning that her role of seductress would carry her only to the point where her natural modesty would intrude. He suspected she had nearly reached that point. She no doubt expected him to be involved by now, taking the initiative. Standing in her chemise, with her hair tumbled about her shoulders, she looked ridiculously young. Her inexperience and insecurity showed in every aspect of her bearing, from the worried look in her eyes to the nervous clenching and unclenching of her laced fingers.

"Proceed, madam wife," Tenbury taunted again. "You have my complete attention."

Anne stood dejectedly before him for as he suspected, she had come to a point she had no courage to pass. Why can't I ever do anything right? she asked herself. She had thought this through carefully before she came to his room. She needed to show him that she cared. She thought if she could reestablish the closeness they had shared that night at the pool . . . then perhaps the barriers between them would crumble. But nothing had gone as she planned. She had tried, as Dennis suggested, to follow her heart. It had brought her to this.

As she looked at Tenbury, sitting very much at his ease, swilling brandy as if he had not a care in the world, she realized there could be only one explanation for his behavior.

"You never wanted me, did you?" she challenged. "It was a lie, after all."

"I do want you—very much."

"But you walked out on our wedding."

"Because I wanted you to have a choice! I wanted a willing bride, not one forced to wed me through circumstance."

"Did my wealth play any part in your wish to marry me?"

"No."

"I thought it did. The Duke of Chadwicke said many men would overlook my shortcomings because of my fortune."

"You have no shortcomings, my love."

"He also said men would pay me effusive compliments."

He rose finally from his chair and came to her, pulling her down to sit beside him. He collected his brocade dressing gown from the back of the couch and draped it round her, partly because he felt she must be cold, and partly because he found her low-cut chemise and bare shoulders distracting. "I'm sorry if you thought the inheritance influenced me. Unfortunately, there is no way I can prove that it did not, since I knew of it before we met."

"You proved it to me in the chapel, beyond any doubt."

"And how, pray, did I do that?" he asked.

"By leaving me at the altar. If my money had been

your motive, you would have finished the ceremony."

"Are you saying that my outrageous and dishonorable behavior tonight has convinced you that my love is sincere?"

"In a way, yes. That, and several things your mother and Arelia said."

"You haven't explained why you permitted the marriage ceremony to continue after I left."

"It was Dennis's idea," she said, "but I could see it was a good one. As you know, yesterday and this morning were not particularly pleasant for me, what with the robbery, and Jack being shot, then our cold walk and unpleasant accommodations at the Boar's Head. After all that, I didn't much care for being left at the altar. It didn't seem quite fair, for I don't feel any of it was precisely my fault, and I would rather not retire to Pentworth House and live in obscurity. If I did so, I doubt I would ever see you again."

"I wasn't sure you would forgive me for conspiring with Chadwicke," he said.

"I realized soon after I left Tenton that you had little choice. You were doing the best you could, within the limits of my grandfather's directives."

"I know I have botched this whole affair from the beginning," he said, "but you must understand something: I have never been in love before. I never knew how strong a force it could be, or how firmly it could take control of one's thoughts and actions. The day I saw you and Jack kissing, I reacted with scorn and disapproval. I didn't realize until much later that my response was rooted in jealousy. Only that night at the pool did I finally understand how much I loved you."

He paused a moment to take her hand and hold it gently between his. "Anne. That night . . . when you were in my arms . . . I believed you wanted to be there. You responded so naturally; you felt so wonderful. Was I wrong to think you enjoyed the moment as much as I?"

"No. I did enjoy it. But later, when I took time to consider, I decided my response was one of passion, and therefore not to be trusted."

His features had passed from faint hope to dejection during her short speech, and she would alter them once more as she continued. "But I was wrong, because I see now that I must have loved you even then, though I—"

What more she had to say would have to wait, for when those words he had hoped so long to hear greeted his ears, he swept her into his arms and silenced her with kisses.

When they emerged from the embrace some minutes later, Anne could see in his eyes that he did not intend to desist for long.

"Perhaps I should mention," she said, "while I have the chance, that Dennis should like us all to gather again in the morning to complete the wedding service properly."

"Jade," he accused, rising to his feet. "You insisted he finished without me."

"He did. But he also said we should do it again with you there, to be sure all would be right and tight."

Bending over, Tenbury collected Anne in his arms, then walked with her to his bed and unceremoniously dropped her onto it. "By all that's wonderful!" he exclaimed. "I have a lady in my bed who is not my wife."

"We swore our vows before God," she insisted, "and to each other."

"So we did," he agreed. "And I will do so again tomorrow if Pearce wishes it, and the day after, and every day if need be, so long as I live."

"I could dress again, and we could collect Dennis and Jack and Arelia and your mother—"

"I have no patience for that," Tenbury interrupted. "Tonight you will in truth be my wife. Tomorrow will be time enough to worry about legalities."

Regency...

HISTORICAL
ROMANCE
AT ITS FINEST

VG